FLOR DE MUERTOS BOOK 1

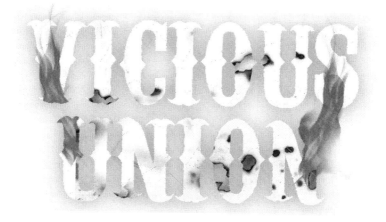

JOCELYNE SOTO

VICIOUS UNION

FLOR DE MUERTOS
BOOK 1

JOCELYNE SOTO

The son of the most dangerous kingpin in Mexico.
The heir to the throne.
The man that individuals fear the most, next to my father.
According to my father, those are things that I should be proud of. I should be proud of my heritage and wear it on my back with honor.
I'll honor my heritage, but I will not honor the path that is set out for me. The life that my father lives is not for me. I will do anything in my power to walk away from that life, and that apparently includes getting married in Vegas after a night of drinking.
She's beautiful, everything that I have ever wanted, but I can't have her. Not with the life that I live, not with the blood I have on my hands.

CONTENTS

Write the story that speaks to you in the moment. Maybe it will be a great one.

AUTHOR'S NOTE

This story contains on page violence, gun violence and death by gun. If this is something that you are not comfortable reading, please do not continue.
If you would like more information about the content warnings related to this book, please visit my website for more information.
Thank you.

PROLOGUE

LEO

A KILLER.

A drug dealer.

Above the law.

All things that have been used to describe the type of person that I am.

Is there truth to them? I want to say no, there isn't, but then I would be adding liar to the list.

I've moved more drugs than any pharmacy.

On top of everything else, there has been more blood on my hands than any normal person could comprehend.

I look at the body in front of me, being drained of all the blood that flows in its veins and try to find something within me to feel remorse.

There isn't any, or even guilt for what I did or what I've done in the past or what I will continue to do for as long as I live.

All there is, is anger. Anger at the man that was once a

friend but turned into a narc. Anger at myself for not seeing the signs sooner.

Anger at my father for turning me into this kind of man. A man that will kill one of his soldiers because he was communicating with the DEA. A man that hates the life that he was born into.

A man that just wants some sense of normalcy. That wants to build a life outside of the cartel, outside of the drugs, the guns and the blood. A life away from it all.

Even with a body in front of me, I can't help but laugh at the thoughts running through my head.

I will never live a normal life, never be a normal human being with a normal occupation.

I will never be able to walk away from him.

I'm Leonardo Morales and my life belongs to the Muertos Cartel.

To my father.

This will forever be my reign.

SERENA

BORING.

Bad in bed.

Way too stubborn.

You're probably wondering, Serena, why are you listing these things?

Well, those are the things that my now ex-boyfriend used to describe me as he was breaking up with me.

He didn't think I was bad in bed whenever I took his pencil of a cock in my mouth and let him come on my chest.

Stupid ass bastard.

Maybe if he knew how to pleasure a woman, he wouldn't have to come up with lies when ending a relationship.

Oh, and boring? How am I boring? I'm the life of the freaking party. I'm not boring.

Says the girl that is currently snuggled up on the couch watching Ginny and Georgia on Netflix.

Shut it, mind. I wasn't talking to you.

Oh. My. God.

I'm yelling at myself in my own head. I'm officially going crazy.

I grab the nearest decorative pillow that's on the couch and scream into it.

"Whoa, who pissed in your Cheerios?" my roommate, Aria, asks as she walks into our tiny apartment. If I didn't love her so much, I would tell her to fuck off, and to let me scream in peace, but I do, so I answer.

"The douchebag of a donkey's ass," I mutter out.

"What?" she says, coming to stand in front of the TV and look at me head on.

"Jeremy! He broke up with me and called me boring and bad in bed," I wave my arms around to get my point across.

What kind of man even says that? If you want to break up with someone just do it, don't make up stupid lies and insult them. That speaks more about you than it does about them.

"Seriously?" Her eyebrows raise, along with her voice.

"Yes! Oh, and he also said that I'm way too stubborn. Who says that?"

"Well, you can be stubborn at times," she shrugs, her blonde ponytail swaying with the motion.

"Hey! You're supposed to be on my side. Not agree with the bastard." So much for being my best friend.

"I am on your side," she holds up her hands in defense. "I'm just saying that he might be right about that one thing." I give her a death glare as she comes to sit on the couch with me, putting the TV on mute in the process. "Can I just say that I'm so damn happy that you are done with that bastard? He never treated you right and every time he slept over, he gave me the creeps."

"Yeah, he gave me the creeps too," I sigh, leaning my head against her shoulder.

"Then why did you stay with him for so long?" I can hear the judgment in her voice.

Why indeed.

How do I tell Aria that even at twenty-seven years old, I stay in relationships because I don't want to feel alone? Pretty sure it stemmed from my childhood when my parents thought it would be better to leave me with the neighbor to go out or on one of their vacations, than spend time with their kid.

It's not all my parents' fault, my relationship issues have a lot to do with the fact that I feel like I'm not worthy enough to be loved.

God, I sound pathetic.

"Because sometimes it's better to feel wanted than completely lonely," I mumble out, hoping she doesn't understand the gibberish, but she does. She's Aria of course, she's been at my side since junior year at San Francisco State.

"You will never be completely lonely. You have me. We can be completely lonely together," she jokes, and I can't help but laugh at her comment. She is just as afraid of being alone as I am.

"Thanks, I really appreciate that. Maybe we will get a thousand cats to keep us company. Or we should buy stock in a sex toy company because we both know we are going to need something to get through life," I joke, but seriously, I'm going to need something to get me through life without sex.

"You know what you need?" She pushes off the couch and stands up, looking at me with excitement in her eyes.

"What do I need?" I'll humor her. Maybe she will suggest sushi or maybe some ice cream to go with this Netflix binge.

"A girls' trip." She gives me jazz hands, excited about her idea.

"A girls' trip?" I feel my eyebrows hit my hairline. A trip wouldn't be a bad idea, but I much rather take a trip from the couch to my bed, to the kitchen and repeat the cycle at least ten times.

"Yeah, just you and me and a bunch of dresses that show off our bodies." She shimmies to show off her excitement.

"And where exactly are we going to wear these dresses that show off our bodies?"

"Vegas, baby!"

No lie, my idea sounds way better.

I let out a groan. "Why Vegas? Why can't we go to Aspen or somewhere that's not so loud?"

"No, if we go to a place without any noise, you will wallow all weekend and will want to come home to get back together with Jeremy. Vegas is a perfect distraction." Her eyebrows wiggle and I can tell that she is super excited about heading to Vegas.

Given that Aria is a nurse, she must also be excited for the possibility of getting a few days off.

Going to Vegas, wouldn't be the *worst* idea. I would be able to day drink without being judged and I would also be able to indulge in good food.

Plus, there are shows, you can't forget the shows and the possibility to people watch.

Maybe Aria does have a good idea brewing. Maybe she's right and the distraction of all the lights and noise will be good for me.

Thinking about it more and more, Vegas sounds way more appealing than my bed at the moment. Even more if I could drink all freaking day.

"Okay, then, let's go," I tell her.

"Wait, really?" I think she was expecting me to tell her no.

"Yeah, really. You're right, it would be a good distraction. Maybe by the time we get home I won't want to kill pencil dick." I shrug.

"Yay!" Aria jumps up and down, even clapping at just how excited she is about this. She is so excited that she runs out of the living room and goes straight down the hall, to her room I'm guessing.

She's back a few seconds later with her laptop in her hands and a huge smile on her face. I think she's more excited about going on this girls' trip than I am.

She can be excited for both of us.

"Can we stay at the Aria or at the Cosmo? I want to be at the center of it all."

As she sits back down on the couch with her laptop

opened on her lap, I lean my head back on her shoulder and give her a smirk.

"Sure, you plan everything out and I will go along for the ride."

"You know what? Just for that, not only am I going to book this trip, but you will also have no say in what you pack. I will be doing that too."

She gives me a devilish smirk and starts booking our hotel and flights.

I'm not going to tell her this, because it might go to her head, but I'm happy this girls' trip is happening.

The break-up with Jeremy really messed with my mind. I need a distraction

And Vegas will be the perfect one.

2

IF YOU EVER WANT TO DIE A SLOW painful death, cross a Mexican cartel and they will make sure that your wish is granted.

It's as simple as lying to them or not giving them their money and you will see your painful untimely death.

Sometimes, you won't see it coming, other times you will get the kingpin himself standing before you, ready to pull the trigger. And if the kingpin isn't available, he will send his second in command to get the job done.

And in that case, that would be me.

My whole life, I have been trained, educated and beaten for this position. It was ingrained in my brain from the day I was born that one day I was going to be the head of this family.

Whatever that meant to a child.

I knew early on that I would never live a normal life, no matter how much I wanted one. Everything from the day I was born was planned out. There are days that I wonder what my father would have done if one of my sisters had been born first.

Something that I'm very much grateful for.

You may be wondering who I am. Wondering why I am talking like this. Talking about being trained and working for a kingpin, dealing drugs and all that jazz.

You see, my name is Leonardo Morales. I'm second-in-command of the Muertos Cartel, the largest cartel in Mexico.

We run the biggest drug trade this side of Arizona has ever seen. So big that the cartels in Colombia and Brazil can't touch us. Even they started to work for us.

You want to get the best cocaine that the Colombians have to offer? You come to us.

You want to get your hands on state-of-the-art weaponry? We will take care of you.

All of it coming at a price.

It's your choice on how you pay us. Hard cold cash or your dead body, we'll take either one, we aren't picky.

My father, Ronaldo Morales, started his operation when he was barely nineteen years old, smuggling marijuana through Texas. He worked for a lesser-known cartel and because border operations were not as strict as they are today, he was able to get away with it.

Ronaldo was able to expand his smuggling ring and as the years went on, it became an empire that instilled fear in people. Fear that grew as quickly as the body count.

The number of dead bodies grew more and more each year, and the citizens of San Pedro, the small border town that my father made the cartel's home base, dubbed my father and his crew, *Los Muertos*. The Dead.

Ronaldo ran with the name, even incorporating the marigold flower, which in Mexico is *la flor de Muertos*, the flower of the dead, into the cartel insignia.

The people of San Pedro even started to honor every single individual that was killed by my father or his men during the *Dia de los Muerto*s traditional celebration every November.

As the years went on, the body count continued to rise and more drugs started to move to different countries, *Los Muertos* became the Muertos Cartel. The deadliest cartel in the world.

My father's power kept growing until he sat at the top. Now he has the most rich and powerful individuals in his pocket, waiting to use up every favor he can. Legal or not.

He built a life around this world, brought a family into this life and we will all die before we are able to leave it.

If my two younger sisters and I leave tonight, by sunrise our blood would be on our father's hands. Our bodies rotting within a week.

A part of me wants to say that I'm exaggerating but when it comes to my father, it can be a deadly game.

Just as it's a deadly game for the gentleman that is currently sitting in the chair in front of me.

Face is swollen beyond recognition, blood covering ninety percent of his clothes, and arms limp at his side.

He's nearly gone, only a few more hours before he is dead.

The sight of this man in front of me is everything that I

despise, that I wish a thousand times over that I wouldn't have to witness ever again. A traitorous soldier.

But he betrayed me, and he needs to pay.

About two weeks ago, I found out that one of my main soldiers, Adolfo, was speaking to the DEA. Giving them intel on our inner workings. Deals that were about to happen and maps of routes that were being used.

I was only able to find out because the fucker got sloppy and talked about it to my right hand, Santos, one night after one too many bottles of tequila.

Santos came to me that night and we started planning ways to get rid of Adolfo. We played it as if nothing was wrong for the next week, finally pulling the rug from under him before he was supposed to go on a run. A run that the DEA knew about and were waiting for Adolfo's orders to seize the merchandise.

All that went to shit.

We went after of the men under him first, drained their bodies of blood. That didn't send the message, so we went after Adolfo himself.

After a few pulled nails and a repeated broken nose, Santos and I were able to get somewhat of a confession out of him. Nothing that told us exactly what the DEA offered or why he talked but he admitted that he did.

So, for the past week, we have been doing to him what we have done to countless others that have betrayed us.

Tortured him.

Now the fucker is hanging onto the last inches of his life, waiting for us to put him out of his misery.

"Let's light him up." Santos voices from his position

against the wall.

Santiago Reyes, or Santos as everyone calls him, has been my best friend since I was born. He's been by my side through everything and knows this life just as well as I do.

He's just as much a part of this life as I am.

"*Esperate.*" I circle the chair, taking in every single detail. This is just a big waiting game. "I think that that tongue of his needs to suffer a little, don't you?"

Adolfo lets out a whimper, and Santos gives me a smirk, one that I know all too well.

Santos leans away from his position against the wall slightly to reach into his waistband and produces a karambit knife. He hands it to me, and I toy with the blade, feeling a sadistic grin forming on my face as I feel the sharpness of it.

My right hand lands on Adolfo's chin and I lift it up until he is making eye contact with me. Well, as much eye contact that he can give me, what with his eyes almost completely swollen shut.

"Tell me, *pendejo*, did you think that you were going to get away with it? That you can narc to the feds and that I would never find out?"

This was a power move on Adolfo's part. In his mind, if he spoke to the DEA without anyone finding out, then my father and all the lieutenants under him will be no more and he will take over the throne.

He would be in power, be the most feared man in Mexico and in some parts of the United States. All the money, the drugs, the weapons, the women, would be all his.

Now because *el pendejo* doesn't know how to hold his liquor and keep his mouth shut, he will have all of that taken away.

Just a distant dream now.

I run the blade along the edge of his mouth, digging it deeper into his skin as I go along.

Adolfo whimpers as he feels the blade, his teeth chattering in fear. The tip of the blade slides to the edge of his lip and he yells out, giving me enough chance to press my thumb down into his tongue.

"I treated you like a brother, my father treated you like a son, and this is how you repay us?" I slide the blade into his mouth, the tip digging into the flesh of his tongue.

Adolfo screams and all it does is make me press the sharp end down harder.

I slice the flesh; blood covers the blade and my fingers.

Adolfo screams his way through the detachment, tears running down his swollen face.

My hand is covered in blood when I stand up straight. Looking down at the piece of flesh I hold reminds me that I should have worn gloves.

Too late now.

I throw the piece of flesh on the ground and just watch as Adolfo continues to scream out in pain.

Time to let him out of his misery.

With a nod to Santos, I take a step back and let him finish our former friend and brother off. A shot straight to the head and within seconds he is gone.

There is a silence that rings through the dark room after the shot is fired. It's eerie and does something to me that makes me wish for a different life, one where I'm not the sadistic fuck that I am.

"Burn it all down." The order leaves my mouth as I turn and walk out of the dark room. Santos will take care of it and make sure there is no trace of blood or Adolfo left.

I make my way through the dark hall that is the basement of my father's estate here in San Pedro, a small little town across the border that lays only miles away from the state of Texas, and head to my wing on the estate.

There is blood all over my arms and on my shirt, something that isn't out of the ordinary here, but it's something I don't want my younger sisters to see.

I'm able to make it to my quarters and into the shower without any fanfare.

The water is scorching hot around me, and I watch as it turns red, washing my sins down the drain.

Every single time that I do something like this, it gets easier, and it shouldn't. It should be getting harder, it should be making me sick to my stomach, but it's not.

I'm turning into my father and there is nothing I can do about it.

For the remainder of the shower, I try to not think about who I'm becoming and whose blood my hands were covered in.

About an hour later, once all the blood is gone, and I'm in clean clothes, I head to the patio where all the wings of the estate meet.

My father's home would make the Queen of England jealous. It's over fifty thousand square feet and can house over one hundred individuals comfortably.

The north wing is housed by my father and his staff. The south, west and east wings are all dedicated to myself and my sisters, even though at times I call Austin, Texas, my home base. It's like having our own places, all under the watchful eye of Ronaldo.

As I walk outside, I see that at the patio table sits Santos, who has cleaned up as well from our extracurricular activities earlier. With him is my father and Emilio, my sister Isabella's future husband.

Emilio is the son of the head of another cartel. It's a lesser-known cartel that doesn't have a whole lot of power. The marriage between Emilio and Isabella is meant to be an arrangement to merge the two cartels. Dividing territories up in a way and ultimately giving more power to the Muertos. This arrangement is not something that my sister is very happy about.

Bella hates Emilio and hates the fact that she is being forced into this marriage, but with my father's thirst for power, she has no say.

The only reason that Emilio is here is because my father wants to show a sign of respect, even if he is hated by everyone within a hundred feet.

All three men go silent as I approach and pull out a chair.

"Is it taken care of?" My father's voice, laced with a thick Mexican accent makes me stop in my place.

I give him a curt nod, "It's done."

"*Bien*, now onto the next thing."

The next thing? What is he talking about?

"What's the next thing?" It's as if my best friend read

my mind.

"Emilio and Isabella's engagement, of course." My father voices.

I swear I could hear Santos' molars grind at the mention of my sister's impending engagement.

For as long as I have known him, Santos has loved Isabella. He never saw her as a little sister as he saw my other sister, Camila. No, Bella to him was the queen of the castle that was untouchable. He loved her from afar for years but has never voiced it. It's one of his many secrets.

But I know, because I'm not fucking stupid. I'm also not blind to the fact that Bella looks at Santos the same way.

Both of them are stubborn as fuck and will never voice their feelings for one another. It makes me wonder if Santos will stop the wedding by finally speaking up.

"What about it?" I ask.

Is there a reason why my father is bringing this up now? We just dealt with a mole, now he wants to plan a wedding?

"In a few weeks' time, Emilio will be proposing to Isabella, but you two have yet to treat him like he is a member of the family." That's because we both hate the prick.

Santos lets out a growl that sounds more like a groan, and I just leave my sight on the douchebag that is going to marry my sister.

"I want him to go with you to Las Vegas this weekend. So he can earn your trust, and at the same time prove himself to me."

There it is. Ronaldo has a job for his future son-in-law

and if he succeeds, he gets to marry Isabella. If he doesn't the deal between the two cartels, is off.

Santos and I had planned to go to Vegas to meet with casino owner Sterling Chambers, who is looking to partner with us by moving a few ounces of coke here and there.

But that is a deal my father isn't involved in. So, what is he trying to do?

I know how my father plays these types of games. Always have. And he is trying to play one now.

At the mention of proving himself, Emilio gives my father a cocky grin. Well, this should be fun.

"And how would I prove myself to you, Don Ronaldo?" The asshole asks. This cocky motherfucker thinks that it will be easy.

Not a chance in hell.

"By running the meeting with the individual that Leonardo and Santos have set with. You get him to agree to my terms, you get to propose to my daughter."

That is all the Don says before he pushes his chair back and walks away from the table.

Fuck.

Santos and I had a plan for this deal, and Ronaldo just threw all that out the window.

He just ripped a deal out of my hands, and I will try my damn hardest to make sure Emilio doesn't succeed.

"Looks like we're going to Vegas." Emilio smirks before pushing back and following my father out of the patio.

"Hip, hip fucking-hooray."

We're going to fucking Vegas.

3

SERENA

NOTHING like the hot desert heat to beat down on you and make it acceptable to drink a bunch of liquor before three in the afternoon.

"I'm so freaking happy that we decided to come this weekend." Aria sits next to me sipping on her margarita, a large sun hat covering most of her face.

"You know, we could have stayed home and done this exact thing." I'm playing with her. I'm happy that we decided to leave Austin, otherwise I would be cyber-stalking Jeremy and fighting the urge to contact him.

Not to get back together with him, but to find him and kick him in the balls for calling me things.

All in all, though, I needed to get out. I needed a place that would help me forget and Vegas was the right place to come.

"Oh, shut it. You're having fun, you can admit it." She throws her little umbrella at me and I can't help but laugh.

"Okay, okay. I'm having fun. Thank you for making me

come. I didn't realize just how much I needed it." I give her a big smile, one that I actually mean.

"Now we just have to find you a sexy man to bang, and everything will be all better." I groan when she does the shimmy.

"Can we not? I literally just got out of a relationship. I don't want to jump into another."

Aria feigns shock and places a hand on her chest, "I would never suggest you jump into a relationship so soon." She takes a drink of her margarita. "But I would suggest you jump some hotties bones, even if it's only once."

I'm already shaking my head. "Not going to happen."

Don't get me wrong, I have nothing against one-night stands, but like I told Aria, I just got out of something.

Yes, Jeremy was a prick, but I was still with him for a long time, I need time to adjust to the change.

"Fine, we'll do it your way, but you bet your sweet little ass that we are going to dress slutty tonight and go clubbing." You would never guess that a nurse in a children's hospital would have this side to her.

I give her a bright smile and nod. "Okay, that I can do." We clink drinks.

For the rest of our Friday afternoon, we continue to sit by the pool and drink our body weight in alcohol. It's around five when we decide to head back to our room, and if I'm being frank, I have no idea how to get there. Not with the amount of alcohol flowing through my body.

"Are you sure we are on the right floor?" Are we even in the right tower, should be my next question.

I lean myself against the wall of the hallway to steady my drunk ass as I watch Aria walk to another door.

"I think so," She swipes the key card against the pad on the door and the light turns red. "Okay, next."

We've been doing this for what feels like forever, I don't know just how much more trying doors I can take. My eyes already feel droopy.

We continue to check door after door, even when they become more sporadic. This is definitely not our floor. All the doors are doubled and they look like they lead to penthouses or something.

We sure as hell can't afford a penthouse.

"Aria," I whine as she tries one almost at the end of the hall.

The alcohol has finally started to take a toll on me because I feel my body sway and then all the sudden, it feels like I'm falling back.

I don't do anything, just let my body fall, and I end up hitting the hard ground, but it doesn't feel like the ground.

The ground shouldn't feel like it has a tight grip around my body, should it?

Somehow, I'm able to turn without loosening the tight grip on me. That's when I see that it's not, in fact, the ground holding me, but a set of arms that are bulging against the fabric surrounding them.

My eyes travel higher and even through the haziness of the alcohol, I'm able to see a pair of brown eyes that look like they can suck your soul right out.

They are beautiful and are framed with long thick

eyelashes. It's like if I'm not careful, that set of eyes could possibly ruin me.

I move my gaze from the gorgeous set of eyes looking down at me, to the rest of the face of their holder.

A chiseled jawline that is covered in a thin beard that frames his face, a straight nose that would make any supermodel jealous and dark ink like hair that looks long enough to get a good grip on. Skin that is bronzed and looks like it can be warmed by the sun instead of getting burned.

I'm in the arms of a gorgeous, perfect male stranger.

A giggle escapes my mouth. "My prince finally has come to rescue me."

Oh my god, did I really just say that?

I'm way more drunk than I thought I was if I'm reliving my precious princess days.

"Your prince, huh? Well, it looks like the princess is too drunk to distinguish a prince from a villain."

Oh that voice, it just makes me want to melt even more into his arms.

"Has anyone ever told you that sometimes the princess prefers the villain?" I need to shut up. I'm in a stranger's arms and I'm making a fool of myself, talking about princes.

"And why is that?" A smirk forms on his plump lips that I just want to kiss off.

"Because the villain would destroy everything in his way to get to the princess and keep her safe." My hand, having a mind of its own, travels up this man's bicep, savoring every moment before it lands on his cheek.

The perfect stranger doesn't shake off my touch, he lets it sit against his face, giving me another smirk and a look that looks like it's filled with lust.

"What's your name, *princesa*?" He speaks Spanish, I like him even more now.

"Serena." It's not even funny how fast I said my name.

"I'm going to take a wild guess that you two ladies drank too much by the pool and now can't find your room."

I nod, feeling my head getting heavier.

"It's all her fault." I point at Aria, at least I think I'm pointing at her.

A chuckle leaves the perfect stranger's mouth.

"I think we need to find your room." All I do is nod at the perfect stranger's statement, finally dropping my hand from his face when he takes a step back.

Who's we?

Out of nowhere another guy comes up next to the perfect stranger and walks past us to where Aria must have been. Seconds later, the guy comes back with Aria in his arms, almost asleep.

"Do you remember your room number?" the other guy asks, and I nod and tell them. Before I know it, I'm in the perfect stranger's arms, just like Aria is in his friends.

A giggle escapes my lips when I get situated in this gorgeous man's hold

I shouldn't be this carefree with a stranger, I should be demanding that he put me down right this second. For all I know, these two gentlemen aren't even guests of the hotel and are hitmen or something.

Oh my god, maybe they are going to kill us.

Bound us to chairs and torture us.

I need to get away from them, I need to get Aria away from them.

How can I be so stupid? No way would sober Serena would have let this happen.

I'm about to push myself off the perfect stranger when I feel my body being put down.

Wait, what?

Sometime around when he put me in his arms, I must have closed my eyes because when I open them, I'm staring up at the stranger while I lay on my bed.

We're already in our room?

I look around and sure enough, I see my stuff on the couch by the window.

How did we get here so fast?

"Sleep, *princesa*." The perfect stranger says to me as he brushes his fingertips along the edge of my face, like I did to him earlier.

I'm about to answer him, thank him and his friend for bringing Aria and me back to our room, safely, but I finally lose the battle with my eyes.

The drowsiness from the day drinking has finally caught up to me and the last thing I see is the face of the perfect man smiling down at me.

Hopefully when I wake up, I remember that this wasn't a dream.

There is a guy out there that is absolutely perfect, and I want him and all that he can offer.

4

SERENA

"FUCK." I feel like I was hit by a garbage truck. How much did I have to drink?

"Time to get up, sleepyhead. We need to get all slutty to head to the club." Aria's voice sounds so fucking cheery that it makes me want to get up and strangle her.

I feel around for my phone, finding it on the night-stand next to me and check the time. It's nine twenty-two. Last time I checked it was around five.

How did we get back to the room?

Brown eyes that you would get on your knees for. A chiseled jawline, and hair that you wanted to run your fingers through.

So it wasn't a dream.

He was real and I will most likely never see him again.

Great.

I get dumped and drunkenly meet the man of my dreams without getting a name, all in a matter of days.

Sitting up, I try to get my bearings all in order, noticing a bottle of water and some Advil on the nightstand.

Oh, sweet baby Jesus, thank you Aria. Sorry for the strangling comment.

The water is a glorious feeling and I swallow the pills down so fast, hoping the relief quickly approaches. Because my head is pounding.

"How are you up and getting ready?" I push myself off the bed and head straight to the bathroom, finding Aria already in a party dress and a curling iron in her hand.

"Honey, day drinking has nothing on dealing with a whole pediatric floor five days a week." She waves the wand at me. I roll my eyes and head straight to the little room where the toilet is.

After my business is done, I go to the sink and wash my face. Once my face is feeling all refreshed, I look up and make eye contact with Aria through the mirror.

"Are we really going to go out to drink when we had two literal strangers bring us back to our room earlier?" Can't we just stay in and get some pizza from the Secret Pizza place?

Aria gives me her puppy dog eyes, the same ones that I'm sure she gave me to convince me to come to Vegas.

"How about no drinking but we still go clubbing?" she offers like she knew where my mind was at.

No drinking.

In Las Vegas.

Is that even possible?

"Maybe we will even run into our mystery strangers." Her eyebrows wiggle, trying to convince me even more.

Trying to find the perfect stranger is very enticing,

especially because I want to know if he really is perfect or if it was just the alcohol playing tricks on my mind.

The more I think about it, the more I want to go along with Aria's plan.

Besides if we do go out tonight, I can recuperate tomorrow and be good as new by dinner.

I give Aria a smile. "Okay, let's see what slutty dress you packed for me."

"Yay!"

———

It never surprises me to see how many people are out partying on a Friday night in Vegas. The club at the Cosmopolitan is packed to the brim, and it's just ten thirty. The club just opened half an hour ago.

You can barely move an inch without touching someone else. It's fucking crazy.

Somehow Aria knows where she's going because after standing in line for twenty minutes and finally making our way into the club, she drags me along like she has a destination in mind.

I try to ask her where she is taking me but there is no point since she can't hear me over the music. It's best to just let her drag me along.

The club is dark but filled with colorful lights. There are reds, pinks, and oranges everywhere. I bet if there weren't a whole lot of people all crammed in here, I would find it pretty.

Aria continues to trot us along until she reaches a sitting area that surprisingly isn't overflowing with people.

She must see my questioning look because she leans into my ear to explain. "I may have paid to reserve a table."

My eyes go wide.

Holy. Crap. That had to have cost her a least a grand to do that.

"Aria," I start to reprimand her, but she holds up a hand to stop me.

"Jeremy dumped you. I wanted to make you feel better. Let me do this for you, because I know you would do the same for me."

She's right. I would do this for her.

Without a word, I break the distance between us and wrap my arms around her, giving her a tight hug.

"Thank you for being my best friend." I say into her ear.

"Thank you for being mine." She gives me one more tight squeeze before she lets go. "Okay, should we order a bunch of vodka sodas, hold the vodka?"

I can't hold in my laugh at her statement. "How about one actual vodka soda and then a bunch of vodka sodas, hold the vodka?" I can compromise.

"Done."

We get situated at our table and the second the waitress comes by to get our order, Aria spits it out and soon we are swaying to the music, vodka sodas in hand.

As Aria dances by herself at the edge of the table, my eyes wander around the club to people watch.

The ratio between men and women is drastic. Makes you think about just how many women go clubbing in the hopes that they will meet a man to take back to their rooms.

I keep looking around until I meet the gaze of a pair of eyes that I know that I've seen before. They are dark, enticing, and are sucking me in.

The most beautiful eyes that I have ever seen.

It's him.

The perfect stranger.

He's here.

I take my eyes off his and move them down to the rest of his face. There is a smirk playing at his lips, telling me that I was caught staring.

My eyes travel away from his face to the rest of him. He's sitting back, relaxed in a lounger much like the one I'm currently sitting on, his arms and chest covered in a black button-up that accentuates everything about him. Every muscle, and every bulge pops out in that shirt.

God, this man is sexy.

And no, my imagination wasn't playing tricks on me. He is the same man that I remember from earlier.

I give him a tentative smile and in return he raises the glass he has in his hand to me.

A blush slowly creeping up my neck at his attention.

"Who are you looking at?" Aria's question pierces my concentration that I have on the perfect stranger.

"What?" I turn to her, trying to play it off as much as I can.

Of course, that doesn't happen. She narrows her eyes at

me and turns to look at where I was staring at a few seconds ago.

"Who is that and why in the world is he giving you sex eyes?" Aria grabs me by the arms and starts to dig her nails into my skin.

"That's one of the guys that helped us back to the room."

"How out of it was I? Because I sure as hell don't remember that fine specimen bringing us back to the room." I'm pretty sure she's drooling just looking at him.

I shrug, "I think you were already half asleep when his friend picked you up."

"Well, I'm not half asleep now." Before I know it, Aria leaves our area and heads over to where the stranger is sitting.

What the actual fuck does she think she's doing?

She's too far gone for me to stop her.

Oh my god, I'm going to die from embarrassment. I watch as she approaches the lounger and I just sit here, hoping for a hole to open up so it could swallow me completely.

Aria has his full attention when she reaches him, she is all head nods and hand gestures. I don't know what she is telling him, but soon he's nodding and standing up and waving at someone else.

What is *happening*?

Another guy comes over to where Aria is standing, and I'm sure that if she were right next to me, I would be feeling her swoon. This guy is just as gorgeous as the perfect stranger.

Oh wait, he's the stranger's friend. The one that carried Aria back to the room.

She talks to them, making the two of them nod and soon after that, the three of them are walking over to me.

There is a sly grin covering her face, giving me a wink as she walks.

Oh, I'm going to kill her.

Why? Why would she ask them to come over here?

I keep my eyes on the three of them, my eyes going straight to the two men that are walking a few steps behind my best friend.

Both men are gorgeous and have something about them that screams bad boys. They are both the equivalent of broody, dark and handsome, but it's my perfect stranger that has me wishing for his hands on my body.

Oh my god, when did my mind get so slutty?

I don't have time to answer myself because at my next blink, Aria and the two men are only about five feet away from me.

"Have you lost your mind?" I whisper yell to her when she is only a few inches away from me.

"Just getting you laid," She gives me a bright smile and a wink before turning back to the men, "Gentlemen, this is my friend Serena, my other half. Serena, this is, um, I'm sorry, I didn't get your names."

The men smirk at her statement. The man, the one that has hair the color of milk chocolate and carried Aria back to the room, answers.

"Santos." His voice is growly, sounding like something that would make people shake in their boots.

Who are these guys?

"It's nice to meet you, Santos," Aria purrs and I don't have to look at her to know she is giving him sex eyes.

"I'm Leo." My stranger voices.

Leo.

The perfect stranger's name is Leo. It suits him, he looks very much like a Leo. The only other Leo that I have ever found attractive is Leonardo DiCaprio, but that Leo has nothing on the one standing in front of me.

This Leo is the type to make your panties wet instantly and he *is* making my panties wet and all he has said is his name.

I blush at the thought, and I think he notices because his smirk grows even more as he walks closer to me.

"It's nice to meet you, Leo," I'm able to say, with him only about a foot from me.

"The pleasure is all mine, *princesa*."

Fuck, I think I need to change my panties now.

5

LEO

THE BEAUTY SITTING NEXT to me is like a puzzle that I can't crack.

There is something about her that has me wanting to touch her, to see how her skin would feel against mine.

Is she soft as silk?

If she were to moan my name, would there be a rasp to her voice?

So many questions that I have, and I want to find out, but I'm treading cautiously.

No need to scare this beautiful girl, especially not only a few hours after meeting her.

After the meeting with my father a few days ago, Santos and I started planning our trip to Vegas, and of course, we had to account for our new addition.

Our plan was to be in and out, do what we had to do to meet with this owner, get him to agree to our terms and get out. All that went to shit when Emilio got involved. He started talking about having one last hurrah before he gets engaged.

Not something you should be telling the brother of your would-be future bride, but to each his own.

Our plans went in the wrong direction during the meeting, when the fucker started speaking with the casino owner. The meeting that Santos had set up was the only thing that had gone to plan. Emilio turned it to shit by giving him the option to back down from our deal. Emilio told him he had until Monday morning to decide if he wanted to take our product at a higher cost.

Fucking Monday morning.

The meeting happened this morning and it's fucking Friday.

I wanted to beat him to death when we walked out of that conference room, but I held back because all I could hear was my father's voice telling me that I better not ruin the deal that he has with Emilio's father.

The fucking deal.

So, I conceded, and let it be. I was going to give Emilio until Monday morning, not a second longer, otherwise I was going to step in and unleash the monster that everyone is afraid of.

So, I was going to let it be. By letting it be, I mean that I kneed Emilio in the balls before storming off and heading back to the fucking suite at the hotel we were staying at.

Santos was able to calm me down somewhat and convinced me that we should head to the tables after freshening up a bit.

We were almost to the room, and I was about fifty percent calm when I saw her standing a few feet away.

There were two women in front of us, exploring the halls and clearly drunk, and my eyes went straight to her. The beauty that was swaying slightly, trying to keep her balance.

Hair that went down her whole back, and it made me want to reach out to see if it was as soft as it looked. Would it still feel that way if I wrapped my fist around it?

The next thing that caught my attention was her tight little body. From what I could see through her cover-up, this woman had curves in all the right places and an ass that could surely fill my hands.

I was concentrating too much on how her body would feel in my hands that I wasn't paying attention when she stepped in front of me, almost falling. My hands went straight to her waist to steady her.

Her eyes were this hazel color that had more gold than blue. A plump, luscious pout that I wanted to sink my teeth into.

Her voice had a raspiness to it, that it felt like I was feeling the vibration of it in my bones.

Then her hand traveled to my cheek and I did everything that I could, not to lean into her touch. She was a strange woman in a vulnerable position and I in no way was going to take advantage of that.

Here was a beautiful woman with eyes that were mesmerizing and her body fitting perfectly against mine and I had the urge to protect her.

So, I did.

I asked her for her room number, nodded at Santos to grab the other woman and we headed to their room.

The woman named Serena had called me a prince and I was acting it out as I carried her back to her room. If only for a small amount of time if someone wanted me to be a prince instead of the villain, then I would do it. For this woman, I would do it.

We took them back to the room, and I took one last look at the sleeping beauty lying in front of me. I thought that would be the last time I saw her, but boy, I was wrong.

We had come to the club at the Cosmo to get away from Emilio and his string of pussy that was currently taking over the penthouse.

After our meeting with the casino owner, he decided to celebrate his fucking misfortune and fuck prostitute after prostitute.

I thought that the vein in Santos' neck was going to pop out when the fucker came to the room with three women on his arm. He may not be engaged to Isabella just yet, but he was still disrespecting her.

Disrespecting our family.

So, we came to the club.

Santos and I started drinking, the occasional girl coming up to us and grinding their asses against us. I was about to call it a night when I felt the energy in the room change. When I looked up, that's when I saw her.

Serena was all done up and wearing a tight little dress that accentuated her curves. Her hair was in curls and she looked fucking mouthwatering.

My eyes followed her every step and when she was

finally at her table and our eyes met. It took everything in me to not get up and go over to her.

To take her in my arms just to see what it would feel like to have that little body of hers grind against mine. To see if it would feel as good as it did earlier.

After I saw her arrive, I pushed all the other women aside and just sat there, looking at her.

Then her little friend came over to our table and asked Santos and me if we would be interested in joining them for the night

As a thank you for taking them back to their room in one piece.

Normally if something like that happened, getting asked back to a woman's table, we would decline. Yet, the second that she gave us her invitation, I wanted to voice my answer.

Yes.

Anything to sit closer to her friend.

So we said yes and I got my wish, because I'm currently only inches away from the brunette beauty, fighting not to touch her.

"I'm a little surprised that you are drinking. Especially after the way we left you earlier today," I give her a smirk when she stops mid drink, with eyes wide in surprise.

Serena lowers her drink, turning to face me before she answers. "It's club soda with lime, actually. No way would my stomach be able to handle anything other than that. I passed my one vodka soda over to Aria."

She nods over to her friend, that is currently eye-fucking Santos. He won't fuck her, not in the way that Aria hopes for. The most he will do is let her grind her body against his and steal a kiss or two, but nothing else.

Even with the arranged marriage on the horizon, Santos will forever be loyal to Isabella. No matter how hard he tries to deny it.

"Smart move. Yet, I wouldn't mind carrying you back to your room again." A slight blush creeps up her cheeks, giving her a perfect glow.

"Is that a normal thing for you?" She asks, a smirk on her lips.

I place my right arm on the back of the couch, leaning closer to her, my fingers inches away from her bare shoulder.

"What is?" My eyes travel from her eyes to her lips, where her tongue sticks out, sliding across her bottom lip.

If only I can trade her tongue with mine.

"You finding drunk women roaming the halls and then being their prince and taking them back to their rooms?" She raises an eyebrow, challenging me, calling me out.

I let out a chuckle. "Am I a gentleman? Yes, because I am the man that my mother raised after all. Have I run into drunk women and then taken them back to their rooms, no questions asked? No, you would be the first. And I'm no prince."

"You said that earlier, and I don't believe you."

I lean closer to her, my lips brushing against her ear. "And why is that?"

"Because you haven't shown me anything that tells me that I should be afraid of you."

I can show her everything that would tell her exactly why she should fear me.

Bodies. Blood. Everything.

Leaning in even closer to her, I nip her earlobe, marveling at the little yelp she lets out. "It's not my actions with you that you should be fearful of, it's my actions with others that should have you running for the hills."

The words are meant to come off as a warning. As something that should instill fear in her and make her run away. Run as far away from me as she possibly can.

Pulling back, I see that Serena's eyes are slightly wide. "What does that even mean?"

I give her a smirk. "It means if you really knew the kind of person that I was, you wouldn't be sitting next to me right now. You'd be running away."

There is something in her eyes as I say the words, that I cannot decipher.

Is it fear? Curiosity? Confusion?

I can't really pinpoint.

Serena stays silent for a few minutes, her gaze never wavering from mine. I fight the urge to brush her hair back and push the fallen pieces behind her ear. I already nipped her; I don't need for her to think I'm an absolute lunatic.

"I'm not running away." She finally breaks the silence, making me lean in closer to her until my lips are barely touching the flesh of her jaw.

"You should, and if you did, I wouldn't judge you for it."

My words are like a whisper against her skin, a slight breeze that she feels as I say the words.

"Let me show you." Her voice sounds breathless, needy. Seems she is as affected by me as much as I'm affected by her.

I pull back, putting a few inches between us. "Show me what?"

She gives me a smirk and stands up with a purpose. "That I'm not going to run away from you."

I quirk a brow. "And how will you do that?"

Her smirk grows into a full-blown grin. She holds out a hand to me, offering me to take it.

"Do you like pizza?"

SERENA

YOU'D BE RUNNING AWAY.

Those are the type of words that I should be listening to. If a guy tells you to run away, then there has to be a good reason behind it, right?

I should heed the warning and walk away. That's what I should be doing. I shouldn't be holding the guy's hand, walking out of the club, leaving my friend behind with his and walking him through the casino to take him to a secret pizza place.

Those are things that I shouldn't be doing, but I'm doing it anyway.

Why?

Because a part of me really wants to show this strange man that he's not as scary as he thinks he is.

Maybe he is and you are about to put yourself in the devil's den.

I think I will take my chances. Especially if it means

that I could forget about my unfortunate relationship with pencil dick.

"Are you going to tell me where you are taking me?" His voice is like a vibration that I'm able to feel all over my body. It's like a whisper prickling my skin that I want to feel every single time I breathe.

With my hand flexing in his, I turn slightly to give him a smirk. "It's a secret."

It really is.

If you ever want to have good pizza in Vegas, look no farther than the Secret Pizza place at the Cosmopolitan. Its location? It's a secret of course.

Someone that doesn't know about this place will never know it exists. Tucked away in the back dark corner of the third floor, you'd never guess that a small pizza parlor was there. The pizza is delicious and greasy and freaking mouthwatering, and what I need after a day of drinking in the hot Vegas sun.

When I held my hand out to him earlier, I didn't think that he would take it and follow me out of the club. I thought that he would just brush me off and tell me to sit down.

But his hand landed on mine, and I tried my hardest to control the butterflies I felt fluttering the second I felt his rough palm touch mine.

His hand tightens in mine, and I continue my mission through the hotel until we reach the dark corner of the third floor and enter the small hallway to the pizza parlor.

"This is it?" Leo looks at the pictures on the wall and

then at the long line of people in front of us before looking down at me.

I nod. "It's takeout pizza, and you can get slices or the whole pie. It's delicious and helps soak up all the alcohol."

Leo lets out a small chuckle. "I bet that's exactly what you need after the way we found you two ladies in the hall."

"Oh god." My hands go straight to cover my face and I bow my head, cowering into his chest. "I'm never going to live that down, am I?"

A hand lands on my hip and brings me closer to his body.

Oh my god, did I just step into a stranger's arms without even thinking?

Yes, yes, I did.

Why the hell are all my defenses down when it comes to this guy? What is it about him that has me throwing all caution out the window?

His hands are sturdy on my hips, holding me to him and if I was a stronger woman, I would pull back. Yet I don't. I burrow deeper into his arms, his scent forming a cloud around me, making my mind swim, wanting more.

Leo lets out a small laugh, one that I feel vibrate through his chest. His well-defined, very hard chest.

"I'm sure that, that topic of conversation will make its way out again sometime throughout the rest of the weekend."

Rest of the weekend?

He sure didn't mean to say that, right?

No way he would want to hang out with me for the rest

of the weekend. I'm probably a nuisance and he is taking pity on me.

I pull back slightly and look straight into those dark orbs. I'm sure if I stare into them long enough, a black hole would appear.

The question about the meaning behind his weekend comment is on the tip of my tongue, but his stare has me captivated.

Not only are his eyes enchanting, but everything about him is also. His eyes, the way he holds me, the way he holds himself, his mouth.

All those things are making me not want to step away. Making me want to stay here wrapped in his arms for as long as I can.

It's as if there is a spark happening between us and the way that his fingers are flexing against the material of my dress, I'm not the only one to feel it.

Much like earlier, my hand travels from where it lays on his chest up to his face, cupping his cheek. I rub my thumb along his jawline, bringing my face closer to his.

Our mouths are mere inches apart when someone clears their throat, forcing us to step back.

I look up, finally breaking from Leo's stare that was holding me, and see that the line is way ahead of us.

"Sorry," I mutter to the people behind us, my cheeks heating up from embarrassment as I catch up with the line.

"No need to be embarrassed, *princesa*." Leo's voice comes up behind me as I approach the edge of the counter where all the pizzas are displayed.

I blush even more. "I almost kissed you," I whisper, not even turning back to look at him.

God, I'm freaking mortified. This is definitely not the way I should be getting over a breakup.

"A kiss that I would have reciprocated." This time I turn back to look at him.

Did he just say that? That if I had kissed him, he would have kissed me back?

Now I mentally sound like a teenager. Great.

"You don't even know me." We've spent maybe an hour and a half together. No way that was enough to know you wanted to kiss someone.

It was enough for you and let's not forget that you wanted to kiss him five seconds into meeting him.

Fuck.

Mind me is right. I did want to kiss him at first sight.

But I'm going to blame the alcohol for that.

"And yet, I still find myself fantasizing how that sweet mouth of yours would taste." There is a sultriness to his voice, one that I'm able to feel all the way to my core.

I don't respond to his words since the guy behind the counter calls for the next customer. We place our orders, two slices for me and four for Leo and soon we are walking out of the pizzeria with our slices and back down the long hallway.

Where do we go from here?

Do we find an empty table somewhere in the hotel to have our pizza? Or do I invite him back to my room?

"Do you want to head up to my room?" I should really

think more before I throw things out there like inviting a stranger back to my room.

I want Jeremy to call me boring now.

Leo gives me a nod. "Lead the way."

With a simple nod and without another glance to my companion, I make my way to the elevators, heading up to the forty-fifth floor.

The elevator ride is silent, and I try my hardest to not look up and make eye contact with Leo through the doors' reflection.

I can feel his intense stare on me, and I don't know why I find it embarrassing all of the sudden. I almost kissed the man earlier, for crying out loud.

One question keeps circling in my brain.

Does inviting him back make me a hussy?

Yes, yes it does.

Do I care?

Fuck no. If all I get out of this invitation is a kiss on the cheek, I will be golden.

The elevator dings indicating that we have arrived at my floor. As the doors open, Leo hangs back waiting for me to walk through them first.

This time I turn to look at him, giving him a small smile before I step off the elevator and head down the hall to mine and Aria's room.

"Do you think that Aria and Santos will be alright?" I should have asked this question when we left them at the club earlier tonight.

Leo gives me a curt nod. "They will be fine. Santos won't let your friend get too drunk. He'll bring her back to your room or take her up to ours in an hour or so."

When we had left the club, I checked my phone and it was past midnight. It should be closer to two right now, so an hour isn't that crazy.

I nod at his statement and continue to lead him to my room. Within seconds, we are in the room getting situated on my bed. Me leaning against the headboard and Leo sitting on the corner edge.

"Do you want to watch something?" I offer him and he just shakes his head.

"I would rather learn about you." I swear his voice is like butter. Smooth and rough, I fucking love it.

"What do you want to know?" I open my pizza box and lift one of my slices bringing it up to my mouth. I can feel the grease all over my mouth and chin.

That has to be the least sexy thing that I have done in front of a man.

"What are two beautiful girls like you and your friend doing all by yourselves in Vegas?"

I can go with the honest answer and tell him that I'm here trying to get over my small dick ex-boyfriend or I can make something up and have him question me.

Honesty is the best policy, right?

"I got dumped two weeks ago, so Aria thought that it would be good to escape and forget about the asshole." Clearly, I'm not bitter at all.

"Well, he must be stupid on top of being an asshole." I look up, his comment catching me by surprise.

"And why is that?"

"Because only a stupid fool would walk away from a beautiful woman like you, *princesa*."

Princesa.

Why does the Spanish word for princess make me want to fan myself?

"Maybe I'm the stupid one in this scenario, for staying with him for as long as I did." I should have broken it off with Jeremy a long time ago, he wasn't worth my time.

Leo shrugs, taking a bite of one of his slices. Who knew that watching a man eat pizza could be so sexy?

"Anyway, that's why I'm in Vegas." I'm done talking about my ex, so I need to divert the conversation. "Why are you in good ol' Las Vegas?"

If I wasn't watching him, I wouldn't have noticed the way that his body tensed up when I asked my question. It was as if that was the one question that he didn't want me to ask. He's tense for only a few seconds and then he relaxes a bit as if the moment didn't happen.

"I'm here to do some business." His words are strained, even with the forced smile he's currently wearing.

Why do I get the feeling that this business that he is speaking of is the bad kind?

I brush it off and decide that it's best to not ask any more questions. I don't want to make him even more uncomfortable than what he already appears to be.

We eat our pizza in silence for a good five minutes before he breaks it.

"Did your ex tell you why he ended it?"

I thought we were going to abandon this topic.

I chew for longer than needed, thinking of a way of how to answer the question without looking pathetic.

"I think he might have met someone at work that was younger than I was, but that's just a theory. All he told me was that I was too stubborn, boring and um, bad in bed."

The last three words come out as a mumble but with the snort that Leo lets out, I know he heard it.

"I really doubt that." He gives me a smirk and a look that is asking me to challenge him on it.

"Maybe you should see if he was telling the truth. You won't know otherwise." Crap. This was supposed to be a challenge that stayed inside my head, not one that I voiced.

Yet, the look in Leo's eyes is making me glad that the statement was voiced. His eyes look as if they are filled with lust, maybe with some wonder thrown in there? The one thing that I for sure see, is a hint of darkness. Darkness that I should be afraid of but feel the need to run towards.

"*Princesa*, you shouldn't challenge a man if you don't want him to comply. Especially a man like me." He tells me with a smirk and all it does is make me want to hold my legs tighter.

"Maybe I challenged you to see if you *would* follow through." What am I saying? Did I just tell a stranger I met a few hours ago that I wanted him to fuck me?

Yes, you hussy. You did.

Keeping his gaze on me, Leo puts down his slice of pizza, getting up from his spot on the bed, and giving me a smirk before heading to the bathroom.

I sit on the bed, hearing the sink faucet run for a little

bit before it gets shut off and Leo is walking out seconds later.

He has this swagger to his walk that not a whole lot of guys have, one that makes his sex appeal go through the roof.

I watch as he approaches the bed, coming closer, as he picks up the pizza boxes and places them by the TV and then as he comes back to where I'm sitting.

The closer he gets, the more I try to move back, as if I'm afraid of his prowl.

"What are you doing?" I ask when he climbs onto the bed and crawls closer to me, his hands barely skimming my body.

"Accepting the challenge. I want to see just how *boring* you really are for myself." He growls out, his face inching closer to mine.

I let out an audible gulp as his lips ghost over my skin.

"Will you let me accept the challenge, *princesa*?" His lips are only an inch away from mine. I feel like I'm panting with how close he is.

I don't have to think, because I'm answering him right away.

"Yes."

His lips instantly land on mine.

#

7

I TRIED to hold off on tasting her for as long as I possibly could. I knew that the second my mouth got even a minuscule of her, I would want more.

She looked sweet and delicious, and I wanted every inch of her that I could get.

So I held off even touching her because I learned earlier tonight that when I was around her, my self-control was weak.

Then I held her hand, after that, I held her in my arms feeling her warmth all throughout my body. When she invited me back to her room, I wanted to turn her down, go my own way, but I couldn't make myself do so.

All because I wanted to be another person just for one night, not the kingpin's son as people know me as.

Even if it was for a little while, I wanted to act like someone who wasn't labeled as a killer or a drug lord. So I gave in and accepted her offer.

When I accepted the offer did the thought that maybe I

would see this woman completely nude cross my mind? Absolutely, but I wasn't going to force it. Maybe the woman only wanted to talk, if that were the case then I would be a good ear.

Definitely did not think that it would progress the way that it's currently going. With me between her legs, my cock pressing against her pussy and her tongue in my mouth.

She challenged me and I was more than happy to prove to the fucker that broke up with her, that Serena was indeed not bad in bed.

And by the way her greedy little cunt is grinding against my clothed cock, this girl is anything but bad. She's a fiery little vixen.

Serena tastes as sweet as I thought that she would and the more I taste, the higher the possibility of being addicted to this woman becomes.

"Wait." Serena pulls back, putting a few inches between us. My lips fall from hers down to her neck.

"What's the matter, *princesa*? Do you want to stop?" I would if she told me to. I may be many things but I'm not one to pressure a woman. Certainly not like Emilio is known for.

The fact that the bastard is set to become a member of my family makes my blood boil.

"No, but what if Santos brings Aria back? You said that they wouldn't be long."

She doesn't want to get caught.

I smirk against the delicateness of her neck. "I texted

Santos when I went to the restroom. He's going to take Aria to sleep in our suite."

All I had to do was text him a simple word and he knew not to come to this room, something that we came up with when we were teenagers.

Serena lets out a sweet moan as I graze my teeth against her skin.

"So, no one is going to walk in?" Her legs open up a little wider, letting me settle more at her core.

"No one is going to walk in." I run my tongue along her most prominent vein, making her squirm beneath me.

"Good."

I let out a small chuckle at her response and before I can say anything else, she is pulling me by the hair bringing my lips back to hers and devouring my mouth with her tongue.

The sweetness of her mouth has me thinking about how she will taste when I have another set of lips against mine.

Her legs wrap around my waist bringing her body closer to mine. The heels she never took off are like little daggers pressing into my ass.

I have a feeling that this girl likes to play, and I am about to give her everything and anything that she asks for. What she begs me for.

My hands make their way to where her dress meets her thigh, bringing the fabric up until it's bunched up at her waist. Her legs are wrapped around me tightly, but I'm still able to get my hand between us, instantly feeling her heat.

I run a finger along the fabric that is covering her pussy, finding her wet.

"Already wet. I wonder if your stupid ex was able to get you this turned on with just a kiss." I say the words before taking her bottom lip between my teeth.

It's when I finally let it go that she finally responded. "He wasn't. That should have been my first sign to call it off."

"It should have, but his stupidity is my reward." I slide the fabric of her panties to the side and run my finger along her slit. "So wet."

She squirms looking for more friction, I just smirk not giving her what she is silently asking for, not yet at least.

Separating our lips, I let my mouth travel down her jaw then to her neck until I meet the swell of breasts that are barely covered in the scrap of material that she calls a dress.

Her tits have been taunting me since I laid eyes on her at the club. I wanted my hands on the luscious globes, then my mouth and then maybe my cock between them. I wanted to fucking devour them.

"How attached are you to this dress?" My finger continues to run through her slit as my mouth marks her chest with open-mouth kisses.

"I like it enough," she pants out, clearly enjoying what I'm doing to her body.

"I'll buy you a new one," I say before I pull away from her, my finger leaving her pussy and my mouth leaving her chest. I lean back enough to place my hands on her ribs, my fingers landing on the edge of the dress that lines her chest.

Her face is filled with confusion, but I just give her a smirk before pulling at the fabric, ripping the dress to shreds.

Serena lets out a gasp at my actions, which just makes me smirk even more. I continue to rip the dress off her body until she is just lying there bare-chested, panties to the side, pools of material around her.

I stand up from the bed and just marvel at the sight before me.

Glistening bare pussy, nipples that are the perfect peaks standing up looking for attention. This woman is fucking perfection and I'm about to have my way with her glorious body. About to find out just how tight she really is.

"Such a glorious sight. Wet and needy. Makes me wonder what you would look like on your knees with my cock in that pretty mouth."

Standing at the edge of the bed looking down at this beautiful woman makes it difficult to not grab my hard cock and give it a few strokes. The way that she is looking at me though, has me giving in and giving myself a few tight grips through my slacks.

Serena's eyes instantly fill with lust, her chest rising more rapidly as if it just became heavy. She wants what I just suggested.

"Get on your knees," I growl at her, her eyes glowing at my command. Abandoning the ripped dress, she crawls over to me, settling on the edge of the bed, her hazel-colored eyes looking up at me. She gives me a smirk before she reaches for me, replacing my hand with hers.

"May I?" Her facial expression looks so innocent, that look alone has me almost breaking.

"Take me out." Another command that she takes with ease and does exactly what I asked.

With a hand wrapped around my cock, she takes me out, her eyes getting wider when she sees my size. There is nothing small about me.

And I'm a cocky motherfucker that has no qualms with saying that.

"No pencil dick." Did she just say pencil dick? Did I hear that right?

"I'm sorry?"

Her eyes move from my dick in her hand to my face. From the look of embarrassment, I don't think she wanted to say what she did.

"Sorry." With a shake of her head, she goes back to stroking me. "The ex, he had a pencil dick. You certainly do not."

"And is that a bad thing?" A man's got to ask.

"Absolutely not," Serena affirms her statement by taking me in her mouth, her lips wrapping around my girth.

This wasn't how I was expecting my night to go, but fucking hell this is much better. My hand travels to Serena's hair, driving my cock deeper into her mouth.

"Fuck, baby. You definitely know how to use this mouth of yours." I grab a handful of her hair, holding her in place.

This woman knows how to drive a man crazy with her

tongue and mouth. So crazy, that I'm trying my hardest not to explode into it.

It takes a lot of willpower, but I'm able to loosen my grip on her hair and pull my cock out of her mouth with a pop.

"Why did you stop me?" She looks hurt, but she won't have that look in a few seconds.

"Because I would rather come while wrapped tightly by your pussy than down your throat right now." I was right. Her eyes get masked with excitement at my words. "Stand up."

She does as I say and stands at the foot of the bed. I step closer to her, placing my hands on her hips and pull her to me. I take her mouth again and as my tongue fucks her mouth, I rip her panties off her body just like I did with her dress.

Serena gasps and I let out a chuckle. "I'll buy you panties too."

The ripped panties fall to the floor and then I follow suit, getting on my knees, Serena's pussy looking back at me asking to be licked.

Without warning, my lips land on her and she lets out a moan, loud enough that I'm sure the whole floor hears her.

"Such a sweet pussy," I say against her, her hand landing on my hair like mine was on hers, holding me in place.

She's as sweet as I thought she would be. I could eat her for hours and never get tired.

I place my hands on her ass, spreading her, bringing

her closer to my mouth. As my tongue is circling her clit, I move a hand to her front, sliding a finger along her folds before inserting it into her. Serena lets out yet another moan, encouraging me even more. Nibbling on her bundle of nerves, I bring my finger out before inserting two fingers into her this time.

She's close and it doesn't take much before she is tightening around my fingers, panting out my name as she explodes and coats my hand.

"That's it, baby. Say my name." I lick her as she continues to come down and once, I think she won't fall over, I stand up and place my lips on hers once again. Letting her taste herself.

Her arms wrap around my neck. "Fuck," she pants out, giving me a sex-filled smile.

"I'm not done with you." I kiss her one more time before pulling away from her and undressing completely. Her eyes stay on me, following the movements of the discarded clothing, licking her lips when I'm completely naked in front of her.

Keeping her gaze, I reach for my discarded slacks pulling my wallet out and getting out the condom that I have stashed. I put it on and hold out a hand for her, which she instantly takes.

"We're just getting started, Serena." That's the first time I've said her name. The whole night all I've called her was *princesa* but saying her name sounds a lot more intimate and I like the way her name falls from my tongue.

"Have your way with me." Her words are like a light whisper against my chest.

"I plan to." Placing a finger under her chin, I bring her mouth to mine and show her just how I plan to have my way with her.

Without taking my mouth off her, I walk us through the room until we reach the window. This room has a perfect view of the strip below us.

I press her body against the glass and she lets out a whimper at the coldness. "Have you ever been fucked against a window? For all the world to see?"

"No," Serena says against my lips and I can't help but grin. I move my hand from her waist back to her pussy, finding her even wetter and needier than before.

"It turns you on, doesn't it? The thought of people being able to see you all the way from the street?" I know it does. I can feel it in how her body is responding to all of this.

"Yes," she pants out when I move my lips down to her neck.

"Good," I bring my hands to her ass, lifting her up so she can wrap her legs around me. "Because I'm going to fuck you for the whole Las Vegas Strip to see. They will get to see exactly what I do to this little body of yours."

I pull back slightly, only to position myself at her entrance and slide into her.

"Your ex was wrong. Not boring at all."

I start slow but then I'm moving fast and hard, doing what I promised.

Fucking her for the whole Vegas Strip to see.

Fucking her so the world could see she is mine, even if it's just for one night.

8

SERENA

THERE IS a soreness to my body that typically isn't there on a normal Saturday morning. Even as I stretch, I can hear my body groan with discomfort.

Sex would do that.

Sex.

I had sex last night. Hot, sweaty, glorious sex. With Leo, the perfect stranger that brought me back to my room after a day of day drinking. The perfect sex god of a stranger.

I shift on the bed, when I hit something hard. Prying my eyes open, one by one, I see that the hard something is in fact Leo, sleeping next to me on his stomach, one arm stretched out toward me.

Memories from last night start filling my mind and I can't help but smile at each and every one of them. The hair pulling, the licking, the fucking against the window that overlooks the Strip, then the fucking out on the balcony. Leo fucked me hard and fast, and I fucking loved every single second of it.

He's a commanding man that sure as hell knows what he wants, and I found myself wanting to fulfill each of his orders. I'm not usually the submissive type but for some reason with this man, I want to be.

As I watch him sleep, I check out his body. A body that I was drooling over as he was standing naked in front of me.

Leo is a beautiful man, one with a stature that is well over six foot three, abs that would make any professional athlete jealous, and tattoos everywhere. I didn't get a chance to look last night at the intricate artwork adorning his body. Now that I look at all the different pieces that cover his back, I see that this man is indeed a piece of art.

There are black and gray roses that decorate his shoulders. All the while in the middle of his shoulder blades lies a skull. It's menacing and dark and beautiful with all the intricate line work. This piece must have taken hours to complete.

My eyes travel from his back to the arm that is closest to me and study that artwork. There is a very detailed Virgin Mary surrounded by more flowers on his forearm. His bicep and upper arm have intricate tribal work that looks like it's of Aztec descent.

Each of his pieces complements each other and fits well perfectly together. I've never been overly attracted to men with this many tattoos on their bodies, I've always seen them as the bad boys, the untouchable, but a night with Leo has definitely changed that.

The person lying next to me is all man and his art just adds to his appeal. He's hot as sin and even in a sleeping state, he has me squirming, making me want to relieve some of the pressure that is building up between my legs.

Involuntarily, my hand slides up his arm, and my finger traces all the delicate lines that I can see. He must feel my movements on his skin, because he starts to shift, soon turning his head in my direction.

I don't meet his gaze, not yet at least. I just keep my eyes on my finger as it tries to memorize all the fine details. When I finally make it to the edge of his shoulder, where it meets his back piece, I look up.

Leo's dark eyes are on me, hooded from the sleep he just woke up from, looking down at me with wonder and curiosity.

"Would it be weird for me to say that I didn't think you would be here in the morning?" I don't stop my finger motions as I whisper the words or take my eyes off his.

He continues to look at me for a few seconds longer before he shifts his body so that his chest is facing me and his hand lands on my hip.

"Do you think I'm the type of man that would walk out on a woman without saying a word?" He asks, a dark eyebrow rising in question and a smirk playing on his lips.

I get lost in the small circles his fingers are drawing on my hip for a few seconds while I think about how to answer.

"I think that you're the type of man that knows when not to cross a line. Maybe even the type of man that doesn't view sex as more than just a one-time thing." I voice.

"Maybe you're right, maybe I am that man. Or maybe I stayed because I met a beautiful woman. One that I wanted to spend more time with and reap the benefits of waking up next to her."

The smile he gives me makes me melt. If I wasn't already lying down, I would for sure need to be, because this man's swoon level is off the charts.

"And what benefits would you be reaping?" I ask as I scoot closer to him, my bare chest meeting his, continuing to run my fingernail along his skin.

Without warning, his calloused hand moves from my hip to my pussy, making me yelp in surprise.

"Fucking this sweet cunt with my cock until you are begging me to stop." His words vibrate in me as he strums his finger on my clit. "Maybe even fuck this ass of yours so that I can claim every inch of you."

With a nudge of his hand, my legs open up just wide enough for his hand to move down to my entrance and for him to rapidly slide two fingers into me.

"Fuck," I pant out, grabbing on to his hand keeping him right where I need him.

"Such a greedy little thing. Your pussy is so fucking wet, I'm sure it could take my cock and milk me dry," Leo says the words before he attaches his lips to my neck.

There are so many sensations happening all at once. His fingers, his mouth, his tongue, his words, everything is becoming too much.

He must feel just how close I already am to exploding around his hand because when I'm only seconds away he pulls his hand away.

"What are you doing?" There is so much need in my voice.

I almost beg him to make me come, but I don't. I just keep my eyes on him as he gives me one last kiss, gets out of bed to grab his slacks from the floor and watch as he grabs a condom from his wallet.

Leo swiftly covers himself before climbing on the bed again and leans down to kiss me just as swiftly. The kiss only lasts a few seconds before he pulls back, grabs me by the hips and flips me over on my stomach.

"Such a delectable ass," he says right before he gives my left cheek a hard slap. A moan instead of a yelp leaves my mouth, enjoying every single second of pleasure he is giving me.

On my stomach, Leo straddles my thighs positioning himself so that he is lying almost completely on top of me, his arms holding most of his weight.

He places kisses on my shoulder, moves my hair out of the way to place some more along my neck. The whole time he is grinding his cock along my ass and then spreading my cheeks to inch into my entrance.

As he slides into me, I try my hardest not to scream at just how amazing he feels as he fills me up. No man has ever made it feel this good.

"Leo," I pant against the bedding, taking a tight hold of the sheets so I can hold myself from exploding.

"So fucking good, *princesa*."

It doesn't take much after he calls me *princesa* that I'm milking him for all that he's got. All the while, I'm surrounded by a million little stars trying to find where I start and he begins.

———

"Bitch! Tell me everything!" Aria screams out as soon as I approach the table she is sitting at, still wearing the same dress from last night.

After an amazing morning with Leo with so many orgasms I lost count, I finally checked my phone. I don't know how, but I missed like fifty messages from Aria. Everything from telling me that she wanted details as soon as we left the club, to telling me that she made it back to Santos and Leo's room in one piece, to even telling me that she did not, in fact 'fuck' Santos. The last couple of ones were from around seven o'clock this morning telling me to meet her for breakfast.

I very much didn't want to leave my bed or Leo but when he said he had to head to a business meeting for a few hours, I decided to appease Aria and meet up with her.

"Well, good morning to you too." I give her a smile before pulling out my chair and sitting across from her.

"You look well fucked." Her smile is bright just like her eyes, and definitely does not look like she spent all day drinking yesterday. From the looks of the champagne glasses on the table, I bet we're drinking today too.

When in Vegas, right?

"Well, I definitely feel well fucked, that's for sure." Aria shrieks at my statement.

She's so excited that she calls over the waitress and orders bottomless mimosas, because according to my best friend, we are celebrating the fact that I got good dick.

I would say spectacular dick, but I will keep that to myself.

"Cheers to getting over that douchebag of a donkey's ass as you so pleasantly called him." Aria holds up her champagne glass filled to the brim, and I can't help but cheers with her.

"You're ridiculous." I let out a laugh after taking a drink from my flute.

"Says the woman that abandoned me at the club with a complete stranger to go get her puddy cat slapped by another complete stranger."

I snort up the champagne. "You did not call" —I look around to make sure there are no kids around— "my vagina, a 'puddy cat'," I whisper-yell across the table.

Aria shrugs. "I can't very much say the other word, we're in public."

I let out a laugh and thankfully the waitress comes over to take our food orders. Once she leaves, Aria asks me every single question from the moon and back. When she said earlier that she wanted to know everything, she wasn't kidding, she wants to know everything.

Is Leo as hot naked as he is in a suit?

Yes.

Does he have tattoos?

Gorgeous ones.

Is he a dirty talker?

The dirtiest and I lived for every second of it.

"I'm so jealous. Only half a day and you were able to find someone to fuck your brains out and make you forget about your ex." I have known this girl long enough to know she's not jealous.

"Wasn't that the reason you made me come to Vegas in the first place? To forget about Jeremy?"

"Well yeah, I just thought it would take longer than a few hours for you to find a good dick to ride. Nonetheless, I'm glad that you did and were able to move past Jeremy, the donkey ass." She gives me an affirmative nod before chugging down her mimosa and pouring herself another.

"Me too, but enough about me. Tell me about your night. What happened between you and Santos? Or a better question, what didn't happen?"

I may have been a little surprised when I read her message about not sleeping with him. The way she was looking at him at the club, told me she was attracted to him and wanted to jump his bones.

"Well for one, I drank way too much at the club to be able to make any kind of decision about having sex with anyone, so there's that. And two, we got to talking, things got a little personal, and I didn't want to ruin that moment with jumping his bones."

Wow, not what I thought that she would say.

"What did you two talk about?" I ask as soon as the waitress comes over with our food.

"Just stuff. I told him about work and how we met in school. I asked him about his life and all I can get out of him was that he and Leo have been friends since they were kids." Aria takes a bite from her crepes before she continues. "Oh, I was also able to get out the fact that he is pining over a girl that is getting married soon. Isn't that crazy?"

"How did you get him to tell you that?"

"I was talking about a romance book I had just picked up, he made a comment about how sometimes romance and love are better left to the book and movies. He said because in real life it's a whole different ball game."

Never would've thought that someone like Leo would have a friend that knows how to pull at a woman's heart-strings like that.

"Wow, that's not something I would have expected the man from the club last night to say." Sometimes it's always the silent types that surprise you.

"Right? I said the same thing."

We continue our conversation for the rest of brunch and finish off the mimosa pitcher without ordering another one. Both Aria and I agree to not drink another drop of alcohol until at least tomorrow.

After brunch, we head back to our room to get ready to do some retail therapy. When we are standing outside of our hotel room door, Aria asks me the one question that has been preoccupying the back of my mind since this morning.

"Are you going to see Leo again?"

Am I?

When we went our separate ways this morning, we didn't really talk about what would happen after our glorious night together. We just kissed and said that we would see each other later.

Did that mean we were going to meet up somewhere?

We didn't even exchange numbers. How will I know that's what we will be doing?

I don't, so I just have to live with the fact I may never see Leo again.

I shrug, "We didn't talk about it, so I would say I don't think so."

That thought shouldn't make me sad, but it does.

"That's too bad." Aria gives me a sad smile before heading to the restroom.

I make my way to my bed, thankfully the room was cleaned while we were at brunch, and I lie down.

It's when my head hits the pillow that I hear a crinkling sound. Sitting up, I see that there is a piece of paper on the pillow with my name on it.

Opening it, I see who it's from.

Serena,
Meet me for dinner.
9 pm.
In the lobby of the ARIA.
~Leonardo.

I FEEL A SMILE CREEP UP.

It looks like I'll be seeing my perfect stranger again after all.

"IF YOU WERE ANYONE ELSE, I would be beating the shit out of you for making me wait." Santos is leaning against the wall that is adjacent to a suite door we are about to enter.

I check the time on my watch before responding to him. "I'm two minutes early."

"I've been waiting for twenty." Punctual bastard.

"Yeah, well I had other pressing matters." Like pounding into Serena in the shower before finally leaving her room.

After a fucking amazing night together, I couldn't find it in me to leave her warm body. It was five in the morning, and I was contemplating on whether to walk out of that hotel room and never see the woman again or to stay. My decision was made when she rolled over and she molded into my side.

Serena looked innocent and content and I couldn't pull myself from her, no matter how hard I tried. Like hours before, I chose to be someone that I wasn't and stayed with a woman until she woke up.

Everything was fucking amazing until I got out of the shower and saw a text from Santos telling me that he had arranged a meeting.

With one simple text, my pretending to be a normal man was thrown out the window and I was reminded of exactly who I was.

The heir to the cartel throne. The devil's spawn as some would say.

Serena shouldn't be associated with someone like me, so I left. I left her with a simple 'I'll see you later' and a kiss, one that would most likely be the last, and went back to my own room to get dressed.

It didn't take long for me to get dressed, but the whole time my mind was preoccupied with a brunette vixen. I had a feeling that she was going to be on my mind until I had her again.

So I did one thing that I have never done with a woman. I went back to her room and left a note for her to meet me. The housekeeper was just finishing up the cleaning, so I was able to get in and place a note on her pillow.

I invited her to dinner. Now it's just a waiting game to see if she actually shows up.

"You want to tell me who this meeting is with?" I straighten my suit jacket as I approach the door.

"Elliot Lane."

This fucker.

"You're serious?" I look at my friend incredulously.

Santos shrugs. "Heard he was in town, thought I would

set up a meeting just in case your future *cuñado* messes things up with our other deal."

If I had my way, Emilio would never be my brother-in-law.

Shaking my head, I get back to the task at hand. Meeting with a nephew of one of the most prominent and powerful businessmen in the whole United States.

I give the door a hard knock and only seconds later the door opens with Elliot Lane himself standing there.

Stupid smile on his face and all.

"Leo."

"Eli."

Did I mention that I have known Elliot Lane since we were teenagers when his uncle shipped him off to a boarding school in Texas?

"Still traveling with your right-hand man, I see."

"Still have no concept of what it means to have security, I see." You would think that a man that comes from a family like his, he would have at least one bodyguard standing at the door.

If I were in Mexico, I would.

"Our security team has more pressing matters." Eli opens the door wider, waving Santos and me in. Closing the door, he leads us over to the couches in the middle of the penthouse that are facing the TV on the wall.

He offers us a drink, which we accept and get to business.

"Not that I didn't jump for joy when I saw Santos' name pop up on my screen, but what is this meeting about?" No bullshit, all business.

I let Santos lead since this is his master plan.

"How do you feel about doing business with the Muertos Cartel?" Santos leans forward, standing his ground.

The room is silent. Everyone is processing where this conversation is going to go.

Eli takes a drink of his scotch before he nods. "I'm listening."

———

TWO MINUTES AFTER NINE.

The meeting with Eli ran a little longer than necessary, but it's a done deal.

Santos called the meeting with Elliot Lane to propose a plan. If things were to go south with Chambers on Monday morning and he rejects our offer, Eli will step in by helping us move merchandise through the Canadian border and Chicago.

A deal with the Lane family would be a lot more beneficial to us than anything a hotel owner could offer.

Now it's just a waiting game from now until Monday.

In the meantime, I'm going to preoccupy my mind with the beautiful woman that is currently standing in the middle of the lobby of the Aria hotel.

She is looking up at the glass chandeliers that are hanging from the ceiling, so she doesn't see me approaching.

I take a second to look at her and take in her presence. She's wearing a mini black dress that goes mid-thigh, stiletto heels that shine with the light and her hair is in waves again, flowing down her back.

This woman is absolutely gorgeous, and I have no right to take any of her time.

Yet, I'm doing it anyway. There is something about her that makes me want to throw everything I am away, and that alone is a dangerous thought. I just met her and have only spent a handful of hours with her.

What will happen if I spend days, months, or years with her?

It could be a very dangerous path, more for her than it would be for me.

Tonight, I will not think about that. I will not think about what me being the person that I am, could do to a woman like Serena. For the rest of the weekend, I will be just Leo.

Not the drug lord.

Not the killer.

Just Leo. Whoever the fuck that is.

I approach her and the closer I get to her the more I want to touch her. The more I want to have her in my arms.

When I'm mere inches from her, I can't hold off any longer. I come to a stop, leaving only an inch or two between us, and wrap an arm around her waist before pulling her closer to me.

Serena lets out a little gasp when she feels my presence, getting ready to fight but melts into my arms when she turns her face slightly and sees that it's me.

"You look beautiful, *princesa*." I press my face into her hair, taking in her scent.

"I thought I wasn't going to see you again," She whispers, her breath is like a kiss against my ear.

I press her tighter to my body, not wanting to let her go. "There was a possibility that would've happened, but it looks like I can't get enough of you."

Serena turns in my hold, wrapping her arms around my neck. "Is that a good thing or a bad thing?"

"I haven't decided yet." I lean in, placing a chaste kiss on her lips, and giving her a small smile when I pull back. "How do you feel about Mexican food?"

"Are you cooking it?"

I can't help but let out a booming laugh at her comment.

"Unfortunately, no, but I know a place that makes a mean dish. If you're up for it, of course."

"I guess that will have to do. I have been in the mood for some Mexican a lot this weekend." She gives me a smirk and then a wink telling me exactly what she was insinuating.

"Who said I was Mexican?"

Her eyes go wide. "Oh my god. I'm sorry, I just assumed." I let out a laugh.

"Well, you assumed correctly. I am Mexican, through and through."

I smile when she relaxes in my arms. "I seriously thought I had offended you and that you were going to go off on me."

"Never." I give her one last kiss before taking her hand

and guiding her through the casino until we reach a black hole in the wall that is actually a restaurant.

The hostess smiles and when I tell her the name on the reservation. She nods and directs us to our table right away, which happens to be in the private room in the back. Away from all the noise and the other guests.

"The private room? How much is this going to cost?" Serena almost yells out when the hostess leaves after telling us our waiter would be right in.

"I don't know, I guess I'll see when I get my credit card statement," I tell her, making my way to the table to pull out a chair for her.

Vegas is expensive, getting a private anything in this town is a few grand. Serena knows that. I know that. No need to tell her just exactly how much this dinner is going to cost.

"Leo, we can just get a burger or something. We don't have to have such an expensive dinner." I think I might like this girl.

I walk over to her, putting my hands on her hips. "Don't worry about it. Money is not a big deal in my life. Let me spoil you while I can."

Before the weekend is over and we go our separate ways and never see each other again.

She looks up at me like she is wondering what to do, capturing her bottom lip between her teeth. I brush my thumb along her mouth releasing the hold that she has on it.

Serena keeps her eyes on me before she finally nods,

accepting the expensive dinner and letting me walk her over to her chair.

For the next three hours or so, we eat, talk and drink and just enjoy each other's company. She tells me about her life in California and growing up with two not so loving parents and no siblings. I tell her that she didn't miss anything given that I have two sisters myself and they aren't anything special.

She laughed and then asked about my childhood. For a quick second I contemplated telling her the truth, telling her that I'm the son of a kingpin, the most notorious kingpin in the world, just to see if she would run away. Just to see if her eyes would go wide with fear and if she would jump out of her seat for being so close to me.

But I don't.

Instead, I tell her some bold-face lie, one that isn't anywhere near the truth. The only truth that she was able to get was the fact that my mother was dead and that I missed her. That was it.

A part of me felt terrible for doing it in the first place, but if I'm not going to see this woman after this weekend, why does it matter?

"Okay, I think I want to marry this ice cream." I watch as Serena licks the spoon clean of the horchata ice cream she ordered.

"I told you they know how to make some mean Mexican food," I tell her with a smile.

"They sure do. Do you know how to cook this good?" She holds out a spoonful of ice cream for me to take.

I shrug. "I have my moments."

I'm not the best cook, that task is to be left to my sister Isabella, but I do know how to cook a good steak.

Forgetting about cooking, I lean forward and take the spoonful of ice cream that she is offering. Not moving my eyes away from hers. It's good, but I bet it would taste even better if I licked it off her body. Better yet, if I licked it off her pussy.

Okay, we need to leave.

"Ready to go?" I say, licking my lips in the process, a move that she certainly doesn't miss.

"What about the check?" she asks when I lick off the last of the ice cream.

"It's taken care of." I stand up and hold out my hand for her to take. She places her hand in mine and gives me a weird look.

"Who are you?" Any other time I would find it funny how she is currently looking at me. I know it's curiosity, and she has every right to be curious, but given the severity of that question, I'm stumped with an answer.

I think about the question.

The easy way to get out of it is to make it a joke and play it off. I can also lie to her like I have been for the better part of the night, but I don't know if I can handle throwing another lie at her tonight.

Placing my hands on her cheeks, I place a chaste kiss on her lips. "I'm Leo, your night and shining prince."

"You said you were the villain, not the prince." Her hands come to lay on mine, holding me in place.

I lean my forehead against hers. "I'm not, but if you let me, I want to be yours even if it's just for one more day."

I watch as Serena processes my words, how her eyes dart from mine to my lips and then back. After what feels like more than a few minutes, she gives me a nod.

"I will take you as my prince for as much time as I can get." There is no waiting period before her lips land on mine and she kisses me fiercely. I take whatever she is giving me and give it right back.

We kiss until we are both panting and trying to pull at each other's clothes. I finally get my senses right and pull away from her, grab her hand and walk her out of the restaurant.

I knew this would happen, so I planned ahead and got us a room in this hotel, because no way in hell was I going to be able to walk to the hotel over to have her.

We are barely able to make it to the room before we are completely nude.

I spend the rest of the night showing Serena how much of a prince I can actually be.

10

SERENA

"That's really pretty," I tell Aria about the Louis Vuitton bag she is currently holding.

"It's two months' worth of rent, of course it's pretty." She pouts, putting the bag down. "Sometimes it really sucks being an adult with responsibilities and bills."

Ain't that the truth.

At least Aria has the benefit of being a registered nurse and is able to make a little more money than needed. Me on the other hand, living on a teacher's salary can get tough. The only way I was able to afford this Vegas trip is because I've been saving money since my college days. So when I want to travel, the money is there.

"You should get that bag though," Aria says, getting me out of my little mind hole.

I look down at the leather clutch that the associate placed in my hands a little bit ago.

"You just said how it sucks to have responsibilities and

bills." I stroke the leather with my fingers. It's soft, and like I told Aria about the bag she was holding earlier, really pretty.

"Yeah, but you never buy anything for yourself. Apart from this Vegas trip," she adds on when she sees I'm about to rebut her. "You deserve to buy yourself nice things." She raises an eyebrow as to prove her point.

I purse my lips and think about what my best friend just said. She has a point; I don't buy myself extravagant things. The most that I have spent on a bag was fifty-eight dollars and that was a bag for school. Take last night for example, I about had a stroke when the hostess of the restaurant led Leo and me to the private room for dinner. It was an expensive dinner and I have no idea how he was able to afford it. I think the last big-ticket item I bought myself was my phone and laptop and that's because I really needed them.

I continue to stare at the clutch. It doesn't cost the same as Aria's, but it's still a hefty price. One I can't justify right now.

"No, I think I will wait on getting it. It's pretty, I just can't justify spending that amount of money." I hand the clutch back to the associate, giving him a sad smile. I feel bad that he wasn't able to make a sale today with us.

"No, she'll take it."

That voice.

I may have only known it for two days, but I know exactly who that voice belongs to.

Turning, I find Leo standing at the edge of the counter,

dressed in a black button-down with his sleeves rolled up and slacks. His dark hair looks like he just got out of bed when I know he didn't. Given that I woke up tangled around him this morning.

What is he doing here?

He is supposed to be in a meeting again today.

Also how did he know where I was? All I told him when he left this morning was that I was going to do more retail therapy with Aria.

"What are you doing here?" I try to control my voice but it's a little hard with having him only a few feet away.

"Buying you the bag." God that smirk.

"Um no, you're not."

Leo comes to stand next to me, placing a hand on my hip before leaning and I feel his breath on my ear.

"Let me do this for you, *princesa*." Why do I feel like melting every time he calls me that?

It doesn't matter what the nickname does to your panties, stand your ground.

Mind me is right.

"It's too much." The words come out as a whisper. They hold no power at all.

Goddammit, I'm supposed to be a strong independent woman, not give in when a stranger calls me princess.

"It's not enough," Leo whispers before placing a kiss on my cheek and pulling back to talk to the associate. "She'll take the one that she just had and if you have another one, we'll take that one too. For her friend."

I hear Aria gasp, but I don't turn to see her surprised expression. I'm sure it looks almost identical to mine.

"Leo."

"It's fine, Serena. Really. Let me buy you this." He leans down to give me another kiss on the cheek.

"But you already spent so much money at dinner last night." I don't even want to know how much that cost, and then there's the extra room on top of that. It's too much.

"I already told you it's not enough." One more kiss before he steps back and heads over to the associate to pay for the bags.

What the hell just happened?

I turn to finally look at my best friend. Her mouth is opened wide and so are her eyes. She can't believe what happened either.

"Did that just really happen? Like did your weekend fudge buddy just come in here and buy two LV bags? For us?"

I nod. That's the only response I can muster at the moment.

"If you don't want him, can I have him?"

No bitch, he's mine.

Whoa. Where in the hell did that come from?

Why in the world am I getting territorial over a man I just met two days ago?

I give my head a small shake to get my mind in order. It's still not in order by the time that the sales associate hands Leo two orange bags and tells him to have a great day.

Yeah, a great day.

He just spent over three grand on two clutches for two women he doesn't even know.

He knows your nether regions pretty well.

Shut it mind. I don't need judgment right now.

With two bags in hand, Leo walks over to Aria and me and waves for us to follow him out of the store.

I stare up at the man dumbfounded when we walk out the store and he hands each of us a bag.

"I don't know if I can accept this. It's way too much and we don't even know each other," Aria says, holding out the bag for him to take back.

Now she says something. She must have been just as shocked as I was, to utter a word about it in the store.

"We don't, but you're important to Serena. So you can accept it. Think of it as a token to remember this trip by." This man sure knows how to sweet talk people, doesn't he?

Aria thinks about it for a few seconds before she gives him a nod. "Thank you. I really appreciate it, you totally didn't have to do this."

"I wanted to, so it's my pleasure."

He gives her a smile and she gets a little blush creeping up her cheeks before turning to me with a smile.

Yeah, girl, same.

"I'm going to go get a pretzel. I'll be right back." She scurries off without another word, leaving me to face Leo alone.

I turn to him and see that he is giving me a lazy grin, one that I've come to enjoy seeing these last couple of days. Instead of reprimanding him even more for buying me the clutch, I stand on my tippy toes and place a chaste kiss on his lips.

There is no point in fighting this.

"Thank you. Even if you didn't have to. You really didn't have to. Thank you. It means a lot to me."

"You're very welcome. Let it serve as a reminder of our weekend together." He kisses me again and I can't help but feel a little ping of sadness when he pulls away.

A reminder of our weekend together, because we won't see each other after tomorrow.

I try to push that feeling down and enjoy the rest of the day. Leo said that he was done with his meeting and decided to join Aria and me as we continued our shopping.

It was nice and refreshing to spend the day with him and not have it be all about sex.

He even held my hand the whole time.

As Aria and I walk from store-to-store, Leo stays at my side, giving his opinion on a few pieces of clothing and shoes. He even tries to pull out his wallet a few times but those times I refuse to let him spend any more money on me. He didn't like it but when he saw how I stood my ground, he decided not to fight me on it.

He did treat us to lunch at a burger place, I'm a girl who will never say no to a good burger.

After shopping we end up heading to the pool for a little bit, where we meet Santos and have a few drinks poolside.

Around seven, which is when the pool closes, Aria and I decide to head up to our room to nap for a few hours before we meet the men again for dinner later.

"Are you okay?" Aria asks as soon as we get inside our room. Since the guys walked us to the door, she probably held that question in until we were alone.

I shrug. "I don't know, I've been feeling off since this afternoon. I think because I know this is the last night I will see Leo. It makes me sad just thinking about it."

"Maybe you guys will figure something out and see each other again after this weekend." She leans her head on my shoulder as we take a seat on one of the beds, comforting me.

"I don't want to get my hopes up. I don't even have his phone number or know his last name, or where he lives, for that matter."

Did I really spend a bunch of hours with someone and not learn any of the crucial details?

Who doesn't ask for a number in this day and age?

"I've seen the way you two look at each other, Ser. You will figure something out, of that I'm sure." If only it were that easy.

Aria gives me a hug and drops herself onto her bed when she lets me go. A few minutes after, she is snoring from our tiring day.

I follow suit, my mind filling with dreams of Leo and me in a different situation.

One where we wouldn't have to think about what to do after this weekend, where we just continue with what we have been doing.

Sex.

Getting to know each other.

Maybe even dating.

I don't know how long I sleep for but soon I'm being woken up by a loud knock at the door.

"Who is that and why are they so loud?" Aria groans into her pillow, which means I have to be the one to answer the door.

I look through the peephole and see a man in a nice suit standing on the other side, holding a white box.

"Can I help you?" I ask as I open the door.

"Miss Serena Davidson?" How does this strange man know my name? Maybe he got it from the hotel reservation?

"Yes?"

"Special delivery for you, ma'am." He holds out the white box for me to take.

"I didn't order anything."

"No ma'am, but Mr. Morales told me to bring this up to you."

"Morales?" My mind is not clear enough to figure out who that is.

"Yes ma'am, here you go." He hands the box to me, and I take it without asking any more questions. He's already down the hall before I can comprehend what just happened.

"What is that?" Aria asks as I head back to my bed with the box.

"No idea. Apparently, a Mr. Morales sent it up."

"Who's that?" I shrug. I have a theory, but I want to be sure.

I open the box and unwrap the white tissue paper. Underneath all the tissue, is a white silk dress. The fabric is soft to the touch and would no doubt feel like butter against my skin.

I pick up the dress by its thin straps and marvel at how beautiful it is. It's simple but beautiful, more beautiful than anything I have ever owned.

"Oh my god! That's gorgeous," Aria exclaims and I nod.

"It really is," I check the tag and see that it's exactly my size. "And in my size too."

"There's a note."

I look to see where she is pointing and sure enough there is a white piece of paper that must have gotten lost with all the other white.

I pull it out and see exactly who Mr. Morales is.

Princesa,

I know what you're going to say. It's too much. Maybe it is. But when it comes to you it will never be enough. Only a few more hours left of us being together before we go our separate ways.
Let's dress for the occasion.
Wear the dress for dinner.
I know I can't wait to see it on the floor later.

Leonardo

THIS MAN.

God. He sure knows how to make a girl fall for him.

"Leo?" Aria asks, taking me out of my stupor.

I nod. "Leo."

"You should marry that man. He sounds like a keeper."

I laugh at her statement. Imagine getting married to a stranger in Vegas. How cliché is that?

I drop the dress and we start getting ready for dinner. Aria does my makeup and I do my hair and before I know it, I'm putting on my shoes, which match perfectly with the dress and we are on our way to meet Leo and Santos.

We are smiling the whole way down to the lobby where we are meeting, and mine grows when I see Leo leaning against the wall.

There is no chance to marvel at how good he looks in his well-tailored suit because he looks up right away and meets my gaze. Like he knew I was approaching.

He walks over to me and places a kiss on my lips.

"*Hola, princesa.*" Two words and my panties are wet.

"Hi, handsome. Thank you for the dress. I love it." And I do. I have no idea how he knew my size, but it fits like a glove."

"It looks beautiful on you." He gives me another kiss before he takes my hand. "Ready to go?"

I nod and we follow Aria and Santos through the hotel and then follow them as they walk into one of the many bars the hotel has to offer.

I look at Leo.

"A drink to start off the night."

I smile.

Not even five minutes later, all four of us have a drink in our hands, ready to toast.

"To one last night together." Leo raises his glass of scotch and the three of us follow suit.

To one last night with Leo.

One last night won't be enough.

11

LEO

THERE IS A BLARING sound coming from somewhere.

It's loud and annoying and if my gun was anywhere near my hand, that sound would be demolished in seconds.

My head is fucking pounding and I don't want to deal with this bullshit right now.

"I think your phone is ringing." Serena's voice mumbles through the blaring noise, calming me down somewhat in the process.

There's not much that I remember from last night, but I do remember how she rode my dick when we came back to the room. Everything between meeting her and Aria in the lobby to her riding my cock like it was her own personal toy, is all a blur.

"Fuck." I tighten my arm around Serena before letting her go and reaching for my phone. Sure enough, it's the fucking culprit of the blaring noise.

Why is it so fucking loud?

"¿*Qué*?"

"Where the fuck are you? You were supposed to be here ten minutes ago," Santos growls from the other end.

"What the fuck are you talking about?" I don't have time for his bullshit. My head is fucking killing me and all I want to do is slide my cock into Serena's sweet cunt to forget about the headache.

"It's after nine in the fucking morning. On Monday. The meeting with Chambers is happening right now."

Fuck.

My eyes shoot open, instantly pulling my phone away from my ear and checking the time.

Fuck. Fuck. Fuck!

I overslept. I overslept and I'm late for that fucking meeting.

"Hold off Emilio as much as you fucking can. I'll be down in five."

"You better hurry. This bastard is going to take every chance he gets to turn this into his deal." He hangs up without another word, and I frantically get out of bed, searching for my clothes.

"What's going on?" Serena asks, sleep coating her voice. As she sits up, the bedsheet falls, unveiling her amazing tits. If I wasn't already late, I would devour them.

I would devour every single inch of her.

"I'm late for an important meeting. I got to go." I pull up my slacks and then reach for my shirt, buttoning it up haphazardly.

"What time is it?" Her voice having a bit of a rasp to it.

This is definitely not how I picture spending my last few hours with her.

"After nine." I grab my jacket and my belt and slide them both on, I grab my shoes and slide those on next. "I'll see you after twelve, okay?" I head to the bed and give her a quick kiss.

"Leo, no, you won't," Serena yells as I run to the door.

"What? Why?" I walk back to her.

"I'm heading home." She is looking at me like I'm losing my mind.

"What are you talking about? Your flight isn't until tonight."

She's shaking her head before I even finish the sentence. "It's at eleven-thirty, in the morning. I have to be at the airport in an hour."

Fucking hell.

This is definitely not the way I thought this morning was going to go.

My phone goes off again and a quick check tells me that it's Santos telling me to get my ass to the meeting.

"I really have to go." I approach the bed once again and give her another kiss, this time much longer so it will hold me off until I see her again.

If I see her again.

"Leo," she starts to say something else, but I stop her with another kiss.

"Leave your number before you leave. I'll call you. I promise." I leave the room without a second glance at the beautiful woman that let me be someone other than who I was raised.

I'll see her again.

Hopefully.

Racing down the hall and into the elevator, I count the seconds until the doors open again. And once they do, I'm running through the hotel to head to the hotel across the street.

I'm going into this meeting completely off-kilter, I don't even have my gun strapped to me. All I have is a knife that's on me at all times.

The only reason that I don't have my gun on me is because I was with Serena. Santos was strapped but I let my guard down and had a moment of weakness because of a woman. If my father were here, he would put one straight through my skull for letting a beautiful woman distract me from doing the job.

A good soldier would never be distracted by beauty.

I run across the Vegas Strip dodging cars and people left and right. When I finally make it to the hotel, I try to compose myself as much as I can before I step into the elevator.

The second I step into the small box, I become a different person.

I'm no longer the man that woke up next to a beautiful woman a few minutes ago.

No longer the man that would buy a dress and a purse all to see a woman smile.

No, I become the killer. The drug dealer and the thug that everyone in my world knows so well.

I'm fucking untouchable.

The elevator dings and I step out and make my way down the hall to Chamber's private conference room.

I guess it pays off to build your own hotel. You are able to have private meetings with the cartel whenever you want.

Turning the corner, I find Santos pacing the length of the hallway.

"I'm here."

I can see the anger on his face when he looks up, "About fucking time. The bastard put yet another deal on the table, one with a few million less."

Fuck.

On Friday morning, Emilio offered our product to Chambers for a few thousand under with supply coming from his family not from us. A million less than what we originally asked for would destroy the market and make us a running joke.

"This is what my father wanted. He wanted us to fail so that Emilio and his family could step in and get all the credit for bringing the top coke to Vegas."

"Get in there and fix this shit. Otherwise, Eli will have to step in, and we both know how Ronaldo feels about the Lane family."

He despises them.

"Open the door."

Walking into these types of meetings can be a wild card. They never go as expected, and sometimes the individuals that attend these meetings leave in a body bag.

"Gentlemen, I apologize for being late." Rule one, walk into every meeting like you're the king and own the place.

Rule two is always read the room, read the people, read their perception of you. Sterling greets me as if it were any other day, which tells me he wants this meeting to be done and over with. Emilio gives me a snarl, which tells me that he would rather have me killed than have me here.

The bastard is lucky that my father made a deal with his. Otherwise, I would have killed him on Friday morning when he derailed the first initial meeting, and I would kill him again for the shit he is pulling with this one.

"No worries, Emilio and I were just discussing this new deal put on the table," Sterling says to me, arching a brow, challenging me.

"And what deal would that be?" I take a seat across from Emilio, not taking my eyes off him. I don't trust the *pendejo.* Especially in a closed room.

Sterling goes on to explain what we originally discussed. If we wanted to work together, it would be a major shipment, but to find out that we can trust him to move the coke, he would get only a quarter of the product, move it and give us thirty percent of the profit. The quarter of product was worth 1.5 million dollars. A win for the cartel.

Emilio suggested ten percent profit and a discount for Sterling because we were 'friends.' The discount, one million dollars. His original offer was only twenty-five thousand discounted.

This fucktard is trying to take money away from the cartel and I won't have it.

"Frankly, I like the latest deal the best." Of course, he does. The man wants the fancy hotel and all the foot traffic, but he will go in the path that spends the least amount of money.

"And I think if that is the case then we should move along and find another businessman that won't screw us over." I finally move my gaze from the bastard in front of me to the one sitting at the head of the table.

"And what other businessman would want to work with thugs like you?"

Ah there it is, the racist side of Sterling Chambers.

To him we are just a bunch of drug dealers looking to make quick cash. He's the type of man that will always underestimate exactly what a cartel can do.

"Have you heard of Elliot Lane?" Sterling's face shows shock when I mention the name. "Funny enough, Lane and I go way back. He's willing to do business with us at a higher price than what we offered you, because he knows just how much notoriety our products hold. And of course, he would be set to walk away with three times as much money than what he would put in."

I can see his jaw go rigid when I mention how much Elliot will be making. The truth of the matter is, I would never make that kind of deal with Elliot. Especially not when it could jeopardize his family's business. He agreed to it, yes, but I would never follow through.

The reason I brought it up is because Sterling Chambers hates the Lane family. He wants to be the most powerful one and the only way to do that is to take everything the Lanes have ever built. He can try at least, but he will never succeed.

"I'll take whatever you offered Lane and I will take the

first shipment as soon as possible. I'll make sure to get you your money within three months."

"I won't torture you that much. Let's make it six months and I'll get your first shipment by the end of the week." If he doesn't have my money in six months, I will come to collect.

"Deal."

Sterling and I shake, sealing together our agreement. I even had a contract drafted up yesterday so that this agreement would be considered official.

"It was a pleasure doing business with you, Mr. Chambers."

"I guess I should say the same thing." He shakes my hand before giving me a smile. "I guess congratulations are in order."

I feel my eyebrows draw together. "And why would that be?"

"The wedding ring," he points down to my left hand. "You didn't have it on the last time we met, so I guess the nuptials happened over the weekend. Congrats."

What the actual fuck is he talking about?

I look down at my hand.

Holy. Fuck.

Adorning my ring finger is a black band with a small diamond embedded in the center.

When did it get there? It sure wasn't there last night when we went to dinner. And how in the actual fuck did I not notice it or even feel a ring wrapped around my finger?

"Who's the lucky lady?" Emilio asks, taking my attention from the ring. He has a smug look on his face, one I just want to beat off.

I compose myself as much as I can. "If you gentlemen will excuse me, I think the meeting here is done and I have more pressing matters to attend to."

Like catching Serena before she heads back home.

Leaving the conference room was the easy part, the hard part comes from trying to head back to the hotel room where I left Serena. It's as if I am in a daze as I make my way back. I honestly don't even know how I made it in one piece.

My heart is beating as I open the door and start calling out her name hoping that she would pop out, but the room is empty of her and whatever belongings she had last night.

"Fuck!" I pull at my hair, not believing that this is happening.

I married a woman that I met three days ago.

In fucking Vegas!

How stupid can I fucking be?

Her number.

I told her to leave her number when I left so that I could call her.

Looking frantically around the room, I try to find where she must have put it. Not on the nightstand, not by the TV or the little table in the corner.

No, it's on the pillow. Just like the note I left her on Saturday. I grab the paper and I can't dial fast enough.

The phone doesn't ring, it just goes straight to voice mail.

She's already on her way home.

Serena is on the plane home and all I can think about is if she knows that we got married.

Fuck.

What happened last night?

12

SERENA

I WOKE up disoriented and I feel it even more as Leo leaves the room in a hurry.

Leave your number.

Almost seventy-two hours since we met, round after round of amazing sex and our time together is over with him rushing out the door.

Leave your number.

Maybe if I do leave it, he will call like he promised. Maybe he won't, who knows.

I throw the sheets off my body and head to the bathroom. My body feels sluggish, I'm sure the result of all the alcohol we consumed last night. I do my business and then head to the sink to wash my face. I'll shower when I get back to mine and Aria's room to pack my stuff. The walk of shame will be strong with me this morning.

The splash of water that lands on my face feels like a refreshing ice cube, exactly what I needed to wake up.

Checking my face in the mirror, I see that I'm all puffy and my hair is a complete mess.

No wonder Leo left in a hurry; I look insane.

I start rubbing at the puffiness under my eyes, when something shiny catches my attention. Something shiny on *that* finger.

What the fuck?

Pulling my hand back, I stare down at a ring that absolutely wasn't there last night. It's a stunning emerald cut diamond sitting on a platinum band, and right beneath it there is a matching eternity ring.

It's a wedding ring.

There is a motherfucking wedding ring on my finger.

"Oh my god. Oh my god. Oh my god!"

Did Leo and I get married last night? I try to remember, but I don't remember much, just a few bits and pieces. I remember drinking at the bar, then we went to eat at a restaurant at The Bellagio. After dinner is where things get fuzzy, and my memory goes to walking Aria and Santos to the hotel before Leo and I came back to the one he booked Saturday. I remember the sex, but that's it I don't remember a freaking wedding.

I'm pretty sure I would remember a wedding especially one where I would be marrying Leo.

Wait, did I marry Leo? Or did I find another stranger and married him?

Oh my god, what the fuck did I do?

I rush out of the bathroom and frantically get dressed. I need to find Leo and make sure we didn't do something stupid. Or better yet, something we regret.

Do I regret it?

No clue, I don't think my mind is functioning properly to think about that at this very moment.

Grabbing my phone, I open the phone application and hover over the numbers. We didn't exchange numbers. He knew that when he told me to leave my number when I left.

Fuck.

Was I supposed to wait until he came back into the room, saw my number and called me? It could be hours. Also, there is a possibility that he won't call, and I will be stuck married to a stranger for the rest of my life.

If I didn't feel stupid already, I sure as hell do now. I'm about to slam my phone down on whatever hard surface I can find, when a message comes in.

ARIA: *Where are you?*

LOOKING at the clock I see that I have very little time before we have to head to the airport.

ME: *I'll be right there!*

I GRAB my stuff and once I have everything, I look around the room to see if I can find a piece of paper and a pen.

Opening the drawer of the nightstand, I find a pad and a pen and scribble down my number.

This piece of paper should contain more information than just my phone number. It should contain my full name, my address, anything that will direct him to me, but I don't write anything down. I don't know where we stand, if anywhere.

So, I place the piece of paper with only my phone number on the pillow and leave the room.

The whole way to meet Aria, I keep chanting the words 'please call' to myself over and over again. Painfully hoping that he will find the number and keep his promise about calling.

To say that I wasn't a chaotic mess when I walked into the room I shared the first night with Aria, is an understatement.

"Finally. I was about to just pack all your stuff and head to the airport without you." She gives me a glance from head to toe, her eyebrows bunching up. "Are you okay?"

"No," I yell out and start pacing the room.

"Did something happen? Did Leo do something to you?" Aria checks my body with her eyes and then her hands, making sure I'm okay.

Oh, I'm definitely not okay.

I shake my head, "If you don't mean me marrying him, then no, nothing happened."

"What?!" Aria exclaims loud enough that I'm sure the people down at the casino heard her.

I hold up my left hand for her to see.

The second her eyes register what I'm showing her, they go wide, and her jaw drops to the floor.

"Holy. Shit."

"I'm freaking out, Aria. Freaking. Out. What in the world did we do last night?" I start pulling at my hair as I continue to pace. I think I might be having a panic attack. How do I not remember anything from last night?

"Hey." Aria comes up to me and places her hands on my shoulder, stopping the pacing. "Calm down. We will figure this out. I promise."

"How? Do you remember anything after arriving at the restaurant?"

She takes a step back and I would too, because I sound crazy, and I probably look it too.

"Um, yeah. We had dinner and sometime around eleven, we left and went to the bar by the fountains and had a few more drinks."

We went to another bar after dinner? Why don't I remember anything about another bar?

"Was I wasted?"

"I think we all were, but we were having a good time and enjoying ourselves. I didn't see anything wrong with it."

I try to rack my brain for something that may trigger a memory about the wedding.

"We watched the water show," I state, the only thing coming to mind.

"We did," Aria confirms. "You and Leo were all wrapped up in each other, kissing, the works."

"What else do you remember?"

"We went to a club, danced a little and it was around two when we decided to head back to the hotel. You and Leo walked Santos and me here and then you guys left."

I try to piece everything together, trying to put Aria's memories and my fuzziness all in one place. I partly remember walking them to the hotel and then watching them as they both got on the same elevator.

From there, I remember turning to Leo and him smiling down at me, taking my hand and us just walking.

I remember being happy and just enjoying our time together and not wanting the moment to end, and I told him that. He responded by telling me that he felt the same way, that he didn't want it to end, then he kissed me. He gave me one of the best kisses that anyone has ever given me right there in the middle of the casino.

I felt like I was on a cloud, and all that mattered was Leo and me.

More and more bits and pieces keep coming back to me. After our kiss we walked hand and hand to the Aria hotel and walked through The Crystal Shops.

"The Crystal Shops," I state.

"What?" Aria asked, confused by my statement.

"We went to The Crystal Shops when we dropped you guys off. We walked around for a while until I made him stop in front of the Tiffany's window display." Oh my god. The display.

"If I were ever to get engaged, I would want that ring right there," I said, pointing to the emerald cut diamond ring that is displayed right in the middle.

It's simple and sophisticated and everything that a girl would ever want in a ring. It was simply gorgeous.

"Oh yeah?" Leo came behind me and wrapped his arms around my waist bringing my body closer to his.

I nod. "Yeah, and then if I were to get a wedding band to fit the ring, I would get that one." I pointed to the band that was filled with little diamonds. Like the emerald cut, it was simple and absolutely perfect.

"I think that both rings would look gorgeous on you." He moved my hair to the side and placed his lips against the skin of my neck.

"Really?" I melted more and more into his embrace.

"Really." He continued to kiss my neck, occasionally using his tongue to run along the veins.

"If only you were the one to give them to me." I meant it as a joke, because how else was I going to cope with never seeing him again.

He was silent for a second before he pulled back and turned my body so that I was facing him. He cradled my face with his hands before he spoke. "I would give you anything you wanted. Even this."

I kissed him then, I kissed him and a few minutes later he was calling someone to open up the jewelry store in the middle of the night. I kept telling him that no one was going to come, but somehow, I was wrong, because fifteen minutes later, an associate arrived and I was trying on the rings.

The rings that I'm currently wearing.

"Oh my god. Oh my god."

Was this my idea? I think it was.

"What?" Aria asks, a slight panic filling her voice.

"I showed him the ring. I showed him the rings and then he was able to get someone to go to the store. At two in the morning. All he did was make a phone call and someone showed up at two in the morning at Tiffany's." My head is literally spinning.

"Okay, who is this guy? Who even has the ability to do that?" Apparently, Leonardo Morales does, whoever the hell he is. "Do you remember anything after the jewelry store?"

I try to think.

Tiffany's.

Trying on my ring and then asking the associate if they had men's rings.

Leo trying on his one ring. I remember telling him that he looked good with the ring on, that maybe he should keep it so he could wear it all the time to remember me.

I remember the words he whispered in my ears. Words that made me shiver. Words that no one has ever told me before.

"*Marry me,* princesa*. Then you won't be a memory. I will be able to have you for as long as I live.*"

I said yes.

I said yes and once everything was paid for, we left the store, and he called an Uber to take us to a chapel that was open twenty-four hours.

Leo was still in his suit, and I was in the white dress that he had bought me and half an hour after he asked me the question, we were married.

"We left the store, and we got married." It feels like I'm having an out-of-body experience. I need to sit down.

Dropping to the bed, I try to control my breathing as much as I can.

I can't believe I did this.

"Hey, we'll figure it out." Aria comes to sit next to me, and I instantly get the urge to cry. I want to cry even more when the alarm on her phone goes off signaling it is time to head to the airport.

"I don't know if I can leave. I should wait for Leo to get back from where he went, so we could figure this out." No rational person would leave in a situation like this.

"What if he doesn't come back? What will you do then?"

I shrug. "I have no fucking idea."

"He has your number, right?" Aria stands from her spot next to me and starts gathering my stuff. She has a shift tonight, so she has to head back to Austin. Me on the other hand, I'm on summer break so I can stay behind if I need to.

I nod.

"Okay, so I say we head home and hope he calls you. Because there is no way in hell, I'm going to leave you in Nevada all by herself." She shoves my stuff into my bag as she speaks.

"What if he does show up?" Leo doesn't seem like the type of man to marry a stranger and just vanish.

"If he shows up, then he finds your number and he will call you and fly to wherever you are. If that man has enough money to open a jewelry store at two in the morning, then he sure as hell has enough money to fly to Austin."

She's right.

If Leo is the man that I think he is, he will find the number and call me, and we will figure something out from there.

After calming myself down as much as I can, I help Aria pack my stuff. Once I'm changed and look like a normal human being, we head to the airport to fly home.

The whole flight home I pray to God that Leo finds my number. That he finds my number and calls me so we can get this situated and start the process to end the marriage.

One can only hope it would be that easy.

13

LEO

"You were giving me shit for bringing women back to the suite, all while you were chasing your own string of ass. *Hipócrita.* I bet the broad was nice and tight if you married her."

It's one thing to call me a hypocrite, it's a whole other to speak about Serena in that way. Wife or not. He doesn't even know her.

I don't let Emilio finish before I charge at him and start pounding his face in.

Hit after hit. My fists land on his face, blood going every possible place it can. I don't stop until I feel arms on me, pulling me off my supposedly future brother-in-law.

"*Pinche Pendejo,*" Emilio spits out when he can finally sit up and can spit the blood pooling in his mouth.

"You're fucking lucky that all you have is a broken nose. Keep talking and you will have a lot more broken shit to deal with."

The fucker has the nerve to spit out more blood in my

direction and if Santos wasn't holding me back, the asshole would be dead. Fuck whatever deal he has going with my father.

"*Calmate.*" Calm down, Santos says to me. He knows Emilio is just trying to provoke me and it's fucking working. "Let's get going."

Santos pulls me along with him as he heads to the jet that is currently waiting for us about thirty feet away. Leaving Emilio groaning as he gets up from the floor and follows behind us.

It's been an hour since our meeting with Chambers and since I found out that I married Serena last night. There are no ifs about it. I did in fact marry her. The copy of the marriage license I found in my jacket pocket is proof of that.

I called her multiple times and there was no answer. After the fifteenth call went to voice mail, I left the room that we had to ourselves and went over to the room she had with Aria. I knew she wasn't there, but I had to try anyway. Maybe her phone was dead, and she was still here.

After a handful of hard knocks, I realized that nobody was going to answer the door and that they truly had gone home. I went back to the room I shared with Serena defeated, and I continued feeling defeated as I grabbed my things and headed back to the suite to meet Santos and Emilio for our flight.

My mind must have been all over the place when I first called Serena's number. It wasn't until we were in the car that I realized just how stupid I really am.

It was an Austin area code.

I should have seen it from the beginning but somehow, I missed it.

She told me that she was from California and had gone to school in San Francisco, so I automatically thought she lived there. Never did the thought that she might live in Austin come to mind. It wasn't even a possibility.

Now it is.

She has an Austin area code and there is a possibility. A possibility that I will be able to see her again and sort this fucking circus out.

Because in less than three hours, I will also be in Austin.

Now I can only hope that she answers my calls the second she lands, otherwise, I will have to find her another way.

The cartel way.

———

SERENA

YOU WOULD THINK that being on a plane for three hours would calm your brain a little bit.

Nope, being on a plane for three hours after you found out you were married after a night of drinking is the worst possible thing to do.

All you do is overthink and overthink and almost have

a damn panic attack because of said overthinking. If I wasn't completely hungover from the weekend, I would have snuck alcohol onto the plane and drank the whole ride.

It also didn't help that I was checking my phone every two minutes to see if a call came in. Then I remembered my phone was on airplane mode and then sometime two hours and fifteen minutes into the flight my phone died.

Now as we are getting off the plane, I have the urgency to find an outlet to plug in my charger. Somehow Aria convinces me to not be a crazy person and wait until we get home to charge my phone.

"You need to breathe," Aria tells me as we head to our apartment in an Uber.

"I married a stranger in Vegas. I'll breathe when I'm no longer married," I whisper-yell so the driver won't hear me.

"What if you stay married?"

I turn to glare at her and she holds her hands up in surrender.

"I'm just saying, it could happen."

"I met the guy three days ago. I'm not staying married to him." At least I think I'm not.

Would staying married to Leo be a bad thing?

Yes, because for one, I don't even know him all that well, and two, what if he doesn't even want to stay married to me?

This marriage can go in a lot of different ways, and if I am being honest with myself, I don't know which way I want it to go.

There are too many things to think about and I need to at least talk to Leo to make a decision.

That is, if he even calls.

I shake my head, trying to clear it before I start going into panic mode in the back of an Uber

When the driver pulls up to our building, I'm somewhat calm but the anxiousness comes creeping up again to charge my phone.

"I swear you need to start carrying portable chargers," Aria yells out as I grab my bag, leaving her at the Uber and head up to our place.

Five minutes is what it takes me to get to the apartment, run to my room, plug in my phone and let it sit until it turns on.

After what feels like forever, the little white apple finally appears, and the screen comes to life. I go straight to the phone app.

No notifications.

"Ahhh." I throw myself back on my bed, completely over this day.

"I'm guessing he didn't call?" Aria enters the room, and I feel the bed shift under me.

I nod, not bothering to respond.

"Maybe he will. Maybe he's still in his meeting and hasn't realized that you two are married." I hear a hopefulness in her voice, and I wish I felt the same.

Who knows, she might be right, and Leo is still in his meeting and hasn't yet realized we're married.

I want to believe that, but a part of me deep inside knows that most likely isn't the case.

Continuing to lie on my bed, looking up at the ceiling, I try to force myself to breathe. Breathe and think positive thoughts about the whole situation.

Ding.

Ding.

Ding.

I shoot up from the bed and look at Aria, afraid to even look at my phone screen.

"Okay let's be calm. It could be him, or it could not. Let's take a deep breath and we will check." I nod not sure if I'm able to form words.

I take a deep breath, close my eyes before I grab my phone. Turning it over in my hand, I finally open my eyes and see the notifications that continue to pop up.

Missed phone call after missed phone call pops up and for a second, I get confused when I see the area code for the number.

"It's an Austin area code." I say, not really sure what it means.

"Austin? Leo lives in Austin too?" She sounds surprised and honestly, I am too.

I shrug. "We didn't talk about where we live currently, so maybe?"

"Call the number back." She nudges me as if it's going to get my fingers moving.

"What if it's a random telemarketer or something?" It might be Leo, but I don't want to be disappointed if it's not. I don't know if I'd be able to handle it.

"And what if it is him? You won't know until you stop

being a pussy and call the number back." I sometimes wonder how this woman became my best friend.

Aria is right though. I need to put my big girl pants on and call the number back.

Taking another deep breath, I center myself before I press the number and bring the phone to my ear.

Ring.

Ring.

Ring.

Until the ringing stops and the line goes silent.

Did the call drop?

Did the other person answer? Do I say something?

I'm about to pull the phone away from my ear when a voice comes through the other line.

His voice.

"Serena?" At the sound of my name, I let out a breath that I didn't know I was holding.

"Hi Leo," I say his name with relief. I turn to give Aria a small smile and nod that the person that was calling was indeed my husband.

Fuck. My husband.

"We got married last night," I state, and I hear him let out a sigh.

"We did."

"What do we do?" Please say meet, please say meet.

I don't think I can handle the topic of divorce over the phone. FaceTime maybe but not over the phone like this.

"I'm going to take a wild guess that by your area code, you live in Austin."

I nod, even though he can't see. "I do and I would guess the same thing about you."

He lets out yet another sigh. "Something like that. Send me your address and I will head to your place later tonight so we can talk about it."

"Why can't we talk about it now?" That would be the logical thing, right? To get this situated as soon as possible. Why would we have to wait until tonight?

"Because I have to deal with my father."

14

IF I HAD it my way, I would be in the car driving over to Serena's apartment, not crossing the border into Mexico because my father summoned us to his compound.

As soon as our jet landed on the tarmac in Austin, my phone started to ring. My first thought was that it was Serena finally calling me back after my twenty calls that went unanswered. I wasn't so lucky, because instead of it being Serena, it was a message from my father calling me for an update on the deal with Chambers.

Definitely not something that I want to deal with right now since I have more pressing matters. But the more I thought of disobeying his orders, the more his voice started playing in my mind.

"Está familia y esté negocio serán las cosas más importantes de tú vida."

This family and this business will be the most important things in your life.

So without question, I got back on the plane and flew

to San Pedro with Santos and Emilio. It was when the plane was about to take off that my phone started to ring.

The number on the screen was one I had memorized because I had dialed it so many times in the last four hours.

Serena.

She was calling me back. It took me a second to collect myself, before I got up from my seat and headed to the back of the plane to answer the call. I rather not have this conversation in front of Emilio. Who knows what else the fucker will say.

I kept the conversation short, since this isn't the type of conversation that we should have over the phone. So, I told her that I would head to her place tonight. If I can escape my father that is.

Hearing Serena's voice was like a breath of fresh air, and I have no idea why. Sure, we got married after a drunken stupor, but I just met the woman. Hearing her voice shouldn't feel as good as it does.

After my call with my wife, I head back to my seat and the plane took off for its thirty-minute flight.

Soon we were disembarking at the San Pedro Airport, Ronaldo Morales' very own airport. That's right my father has his own, he's the kingpin after all.

The motherfucker.

If I would have known he wanted to see me, I would have flown here instead of heading to Austin first.

There is a black SUV waiting for us when we step out of the plane. Black cars that everyone in this town knows exactly who are in them, there is no secret that the

Muertos Cartel calls San Pedro home. The people of San Pedro are loyal to the cartel, or more so loyal to my father.

So loyal that if a *federal* would come to this town, no one would speak.

It angers me at times, how so many people could turn a blind eye, but then I look at it from the perspective of the cartel and it's the best business move out there.

The SUV approaches the compound, a compound that is surrounded by guards in every little corner. Not even the President of the United States is this heavily guarded.

Once we stop at the front of the estate, my door opens and I step out and make my way to my father's office where he is predictably waiting for us.

I walk through the house like I fucking own the place and in a way I do. It's right as I make it to my father's office door that I feel a hand on my shoulder, stopping me from going further.

Turning, I find Santos right behind me.

"Your ring." He whispers, his eyes on my hand.

Fuck.

I haven't made the effort to take off the ring that is adorning my finger. It doesn't bother me, and I might have forgotten that I was wearing it but walking into my father's office with a new piece of jewelry is going to bring up questions. Questions that I certainly don't have the answers to.

Swiftly I slide the ring off and pocket it before opening the door to the office.

My father is sitting at his desk, a stern look on his face, a glass filled with scotch in his hand. The one man in Mexico that drinks fucking scotch.

"Leonardo, Santiago. You're late." If I were one of my sisters, I would have rolled my eyes at the man.

"*Perdón, Apá.* The plane was late." It's better to ask for forgiveness for something he has no idea is true.

My father grunts and waves us in. Santos and I take a seat in the chairs in front of his wooden desk, while Emilio stands behind us.

Hopefully Ronaldo doesn't mention anything about Emilio's face.

"Tell me, is the deal with Chambers done?" His voice is stern and hard, and his accent thick as ever.

I give him a curt nod. "It's done, it took a little bit finessing but it's a done deal. If everything goes to plan, we should have the product heading to Vegas by the end of the week and should be seeing payment soon after that."

Ronaldo nods like my words are nothing of importance. Like we just didn't bring millions of dollars to his desk.

"Why did it take you three days to get the deal done? You're better than that, Leonardo." Of course, he's putting the blame on me and not on his future son-in-law.

My jaw goes tight. I'm meant to live this life but no matter what I do, it's not good enough for the kingpin himself.

"There were a few setbacks on Chambers' side, he didn't want to agree right away." It's complete bullshit, and it's the only way to protect his precious Emilio.

Santos lets out a noise, one of irritation which my father takes notice of. His eyebrows lifting in question.

"Is there something you want to add to this conversation, Santiago?" He leans forward, his focus on my right-hand man.

"No, Don Ronaldo." Santos sits back straight, not accepting the challenge from my father.

"What about you, Emilio? Do you have anything to say?" I stiffen at my father's question.

Who knows what Emilio will say, the fucker is probably trying to figure out how to tell my father the news of my spontaneous wedding.

"No, *señor*, I do not have anything to say." About time the asshole keeps his mouth shut.

"Not even as to why your nose looks like it needs to be seen by a doctor?"

I can hear Emilio shuffling behind me, but I don't turn to face him. I just keep my eyes on my father.

"No."

The room is silent for a long minute as Ronaldo stares down Emilio.

Finally, he nods.

"Good, now, before you get to work." He stands up from his desk, placing his drink down. "In celebration of this deal, I will be hosting a dinner party this Saturday. I expect you all to be there, we are *familia* after all."

Yeah, one big happy *familia*.

Without another word, my father waves his hand and excuses us.

I swiftly get up from my seat and am about to follow Santos and Emilio out of the office when my father calls out my name.

"I don't know what happened in Vegas, but I'm putting

trust that you and Santiago didn't let Emilio fuck up this deal."

And whose fault would that have been? It was his idea to let the fucker come with us on this trip. If he had fucked up like he intended to, it would have been my father's fault not mine.

"I promise you, *Apá*. Emilio had nothing to do with this deal, I put a stop to anything he had planned." And that's the fucking truth.

"Good."

With one final nod to my father, I leave his office and head to my wing to fucking change out of this suit before heading to the airport.

While I'm pulling on a clean shirt, there is a knock on my door. Thinking that it's Santos, I tell him to come in.

"Where are you going?" The voice of my sister, Isabella, stops me in my tracks.

I turn to see my sister standing by the door, giving me a questioning look. Eyebrows raised and all.

"I'm heading to Austin for a few days," I tell her grabbing a few things and putting them in a weekender bag.

"But you just got back. Why are you leaving again so soon?"

When it comes to our family, Isabella is the protective one. Like our mother, she worries every single minute we are not under the same roof. Given the life that we live, it's understandable. She doesn't want to get a call that I was shot dead somewhere. My mother was the same way, and after her untimely death, Isabella's worry has increased.

"I know, but there are a few things that I need to deal

with. I will be back on Saturday, I promise." I go to her once I'm done packing and place a kiss on her head.

"Did Dad tell you about what's going to happen in the next couple of weeks?" Her voice cracks a little at the end, and I can't help but feel sympathy for my sister.

"He did, and if there was any way around it, I would do everything I could to get you out of it." It's the truth.

My sisters both deserve something better than this life, than a life where one of them is set to have an arranged marriage to someone not worthy of her or her grace.

She needs someone strong, someone that would treat her like the queen that she is.

Someone like Santos Reyes.

Isabella nods at my statement. "Please be careful. I would rather go through this fucked-up arranged marriage shit with you there, than you six feet under."

I laugh. "I'll be back before you know it." With one last kiss to her cheek, I leave my sister and head out to deal with my own fucked-up shit.

It's time that Serena and I sit down and figure out what in the actual hell we will be doing with this marriage of ours.

Some real fucked-up shit.

15

SERENA

I DON'T KNOW how many times I pace the length of my room, waiting for some form of communication from Leo.

It's been a few hours since our phone call and I'm going insane just waiting for him to either arrive or call, telling me he's not coming.

My nails cannot take the stress any longer.

Aria left for work about an hour or two ago, so I'm by myself and it sure isn't doing anything to calm me down.

My thoughts are going haywire. Thoughts about what would be the best option to end this marriage, would it be divorce? Is annulment even an option? How do we go about this?

All of this is freaking me out.

I'm twenty-seven, I've never married a man spontaneously, I don't know what the proper protocol is here.

I don't even have siblings who I can talk to about it, the closest person to that title would be Aria, and she's all hopeful and shit. My parents could be an option but they're probably gallivanting somewhere completely forgetting they have a daughter.

I need a drink. A nice strong one to calm the anxiety running through my veins. Maybe ice cream will do. That way I don't make yet another stupid decision like I did last night from drinking.

I'm about to pull open the freezer, where my chocolate chip ice cream sits, when the intercom buzzes.

He's here.

Leo's here.

It could be a delivery, or the wrong apartment.

F-off mind, I don't have the patience for the mind tricks today.

Putting the ice cream back in the freezer, I head over to the intercom and take a deep breath before hitting the call button.

"Hello?" My voice feels shaky, like I'm afraid of who's going to respond.

Maybe I am.

"It's me." His voice is thick and raspy, and it takes me back to how it sounded this morning.

No, I can't go there not right now.

"Come on up."

Forty-five seconds. That's how long it takes Leo to arrive on my floor, find the apartment number I sent him earlier and knock on my door.

Like I did earlier, before pressing the call button, I take a deep breath before opening the door. On the other side, Leo is standing there, his hand on either side of the doorframe. The suit he was wearing earlier, gone and in its place is a t-shirt and some worn jeans.

All weekend the only time I saw him out of slacks and a button-down was when we went to the pool or in the room. I haven't seen him dressed so casually, and I might prefer it to the suit, even if he looks mouthwatering wearing one.

But it's not the T-shirt and jeans that made the words not come out, it's his eyes. They're intense, so intense that they look almost black instead of brown. Just looking into them makes me want to forget everything that has happened today and fall deep into the dark pools.

"Hi, *princesa*,"

God his voice.

"Hi," I say shyly where I shouldn't.

This man has seen me naked and on my knees in front of him with his cock in my mouth. There is no need to be shy.

I open the door wider for him to come in and he gives me a small smile before walking into my tiny apartment. The apartment is perfect for Aria and me but with Leo standing in the entryway, makes it feel a lot smaller. Like his presence demands a lot more space.

"Would you like something to drink?" My offer is awkward, but I needed to say something to break the thick silence in the room.

"I'll have one if you'll have one," he says, giving me yet another small smile.

Nodding, I head to the kitchen and grab some bottles

of water from the fridge and head to the living room, where Leo now stands.

"Here you go," I offer him the bottled water, taking his attention away from the framed pictures that are taking over the wall next to the TV.

"Thank you." Now it's my turn to give him a small smile before taking a seat on the couch, Leo following suit and sitting a few cushions away.

We sit in silence for a few minutes looking from the water bottles in our hands and to each other. Like we are two complete strangers and didn't just spend the weekend under the sheets naked.

In a way, we are complete strangers.

"So," I start, trying to break the ice.

"So." So much awkwardness. You would think a man like Leo would know how to start this type of conversation.

"Do you remember anything from last night?" Everything started coming to me throughout the day, every touch, every word, every kiss. Everything came crashing in, and I couldn't help but wonder if Leo remembered the things I did.

"Bits and pieces, but the important parts are there." He leans forward, placing his elbows on his knees.

"And what are the important parts?" I ask him. Maybe to him, the important parts are the wild fucking we did once we went back to the hotel room.

"The jewelry store, how beautiful you looked when the ring was on your finger. Parts of the ceremony."

His eyes are intensely on me, like he wants to see into my soul.

"I remember that too." My words come out as a whisper, the intensity of his gaze putting a small ounce of fear in me. "What do we do now?"

The question had to be asked.

We can't continue circling the subject and not talking about it. We got married in Vegas after a drunken night, we have to put an end to it, we can't stay married.

Or maybe we can.

No, ending this would be the best option.

At least I think it is.

"Whatever you want to do I will go along with."

That's it?

He's leaving a humongous decision up to me?

"What *I* want to do?" I can hear the disbelief in my voice, and I know he does too. Leo gives me a curt nod and doesn't say a word. I scoff, "And what if I say I want to stay married?"

"You don't want to stay married to me, Serena. The life that I live." He stops short, not finishing his sentence. His face turns hard, like the idea of us staying in this marriage disgusts him. "The life I live isn't for a woman like you. Staying married to me would be the last thing you would want."

What does that even mean?

"And what kind of life would that be? You never told me how a man like you can call someone and be able to open a jewelry store at two in the morning."

Or maybe he did and with my drunken stupor, I don't remember.

"A life that would have you running as far away as possible from me, if you knew even an ounce of it."

The growl in his voice alone should make me run, along with his words but being the stubborn person I am, I don't move an inch.

"What are you a serial killer in your free time?" I sarcastically ask, standing up from the couch and making my way back to the kitchen.

I hear his footsteps behind me, but it's not enough time to register his next move. One second my back is facing him and the next, it's against the refrigerator, with Leo standing in front of me with one hand on my neck and the other on my hip. He draws his face closer to mine and once there is only an inch of space separating us, he speaks.

"I may not be a serial killer, *princesa*, but there is more blood on my hands than what you have running through this tight little body of yours. So, when I tell you that you don't want to stay married to a man like me, trust my words."

The pressure on how he is holding my body grows slightly. Not enough to cut off my air circulation in my neck but enough to feel his fingers on my skin. There is no force behind what he is doing, no malice. He is simply doing this to show me who he is and what he might be capable of.

"Who are you?" A simple question, one that I'm not sure I want the answer to.

"A heinous man that you shouldn't get into bed with." His words are a slight whisper against my lips and all I want to do is lean in and feel his full lips against mine.

"I've already gotten in bed with you." I shift my body, my lower region rubbing against his.

"And as my wife, I'm telling you to leave it. My bed is no place for a woman like you."

Wife.

He called me his wife.

Everything that we did last night has just gotten more real.

His fingers tighten slightly around my neck as he leans closer, his lips ghosting against mine.

Then Leo pulls back before his lips touch me, dropping the grip he had on my neck as well as the one on my hip. He backs up until he is leaning against the counter in front of me.

"You never answered my question. Who. Are. You?"

He crosses his arms over his chest and looks down at me with a hard expression, one that I can't really place. Not saying a word, he continues to look at me, eyes on my face.

He finally sighs when he realizes I'm going to stand my ground.

"Do you really want to know? Do you really want to know who I am and why I'm telling you that you should be afraid of me?"

Do I?

Do I really want to know who the man standing in my kitchen is? Do I want to know why he told me he's the villain of the story and not the prince?

Yes.

Yes, I do.

I don't voice my response; the words are having a hard time forming and leaving my mouth. So instead, I nod, I nod for him to tell me exactly who he is.

Leo continues to stare at me with a look that I should fear, and I do, but I will not show him that. Not when he might see it as a weakness.

"My name is Leonardo Morales, son of Ronaldo Morales, the head of the Muertos Cartel. He's the most feared and dangerous man in Mexico. I'm the second. I've killed, I've called hits, moved bodies and countless drugs, and there have been times where I don't regret a single one of my actions."

A cold chill runs through the length of my whole body.

The Muertos Cartel.

Living in Texas, so close to the border, you hear rumors of the cartel and all the bad things they do.

You hear about the drug trades that they are involved in, the number of dead bodies that are found dismembered that point back to them. All sorts of rumors that in the back of your mind you wonder if they are true.

I've heard of the cartel, how could I not? I've also heard of Leo's father, Ronaldo, but people talk about him as if he were a myth, an unknown figure that no one has ever laid eyes on.

The most dangerous man in all of Mexico, and I married his son in Las Vegas.

Holy fuck.

The same son that is currently standing a few feet away from me. The same son that has touched every single inch of my body.

I married the second most dangerous man in Mexico.

Leo watches me as I digest his words. His stare is empty and void of any emotion. He doesn't even move to come closer to me.

I watch him as I try to comprehend what he just told me.

The man standing in front of me certainly does not look like the son of a drug lord. He looks like any other man. The only difference between him and other men, is that he is built like a god and could make any woman drool.

He doesn't look like a man that can work in the drug world or even kill people. Put fear in people absolutely, but the man standing in front of me and the one that I spent the weekend with, is not a killer.

"Now you know why I told you that I was no prince. Why a woman like you shouldn't be married to a man like me?" he growls, his whole demeanor changing. "A woman like you doesn't deserve to live a life like this, a life filled with constant fear, filled with death and blood. You deserve more than a fucking marriage after a drunken night in Vegas. You don't belong in this fucked up world I live in."

I continue to stay silent, not saying a word, not even moving from my spot in front of the fridge. I do nothing but just stand there, not moving my gaze away from him.

Should I move away from this man? Will he hurt me?

I don't even have to think about it, because the answer is no.

Leo won't hurt me.

I'm not afraid of him, because to me he's not a drug lord's son. He's Leo.

He releases a long sigh before he nods his head and starts to leave the kitchen.

"I will have a lawyer draw up divorce papers and have them delivered to you by the end of the week. I'll try to see what can be done to speed up the process so you're not waiting sixty days to cut all ties with me."

Without another word, he walks out of the kitchen and heads for the door.

He's leaving.

This is it. This is how my less than twenty-four-hour marriage is going to end, with him walking out and him making the final decision.

It's what needs to be done. We need to end this marriage because we are two complete strangers and like Leo said, I don't belong in this world.

He's a part of the Muertos Cartel and he is dangerous.

But why does it hurt watching him walk away?

"No."

The word comes out on its own, and I don't do anything to stop it.

I watch as Leo stops with his hand on the doorknob, ready to pull it open. He slowly turns around to face me, his dark brows coming together in confusion.

"No? What do you mean 'no'?" There is a harsh undertone to his question and interesting enough after everything that he has told me, that's what makes me jump.

Why did I say no?

What the hell am I even doing?

"I mean no, I don't want you to draw up divorce papers, not yet at least."

"Why the fuck not?" He's angry now, and he has every right to be. He is telling me to leave without looking back, and here I am running straight into the abyss.

"Because something deep inside of me is telling me that you are not the person you keep saying you are."

"Serena."

"No, let me talk. Yes, I know who your father is, I know you're a part of the Muertos Cartel. I know that and I get it, but the person I met on Friday is not that person. The person you describe is not the person standing in front of me." He's not that person he said he was, I know he's not.

"Knowing me for seventy-two hours doesn't tell you who I am. The only thing that our time together did was paint a fantasy, a fantasy that doesn't fucking exist," he snarls, trying to show me a different side of him.

"Then show me. Show me who you really are, and if I'm wrong, I will go to the lawyer myself and draw up the paperwork to end this marriage." I stand my ground, not backing down from this.

All Leo does is continue to snarl by the door, not saying anything, just continues to stare at me like I'm the most insane person in the world.

Maybe I am.

After what feels like forever, his posture and facial expression relax a bit and he lets out a sigh. "This is what you want? To see who I really am?"

Is it?

"Yes."

He continues to stare at me for a while longer as if he is trying to see if I'm lying.

"Fine. We'll do it your way. I'll pick you up Saturday evening. Dress to fucking impress."

With that he opens the door and storms out like a hurricane. The second the door slams shut; my head begins to spin.

I married into the Mexican cartel and just turned down a divorce.

What in the hell am I thinking?

And what in the fuck is happening on Saturday?

16

It's been a fucking long week. If my presence wasn't required at the San Pedro estate, I would skip my father's celebratory dinner and drown the week in whiskey.

I'll probably be drinking whiskey anyway, given that Serena will be with me at the dinner table.

Fucking Serena.

Never in all the fucking wildest dreams in the world, did I think that I would leave her apartment telling her I was going to take her to my father's estate. My sole intention when I walked into her apartment was to follow through with whatever plan she wanted.

Serena was a smart, independent woman. No way would she stay married to a guy like me. I thought when I walked in, we would immediately start talking about divorce.

Never did I expect her to challenge me into telling her who I really am.

She knew who I was when I said my father's name, I

saw it in her eyes. She lived in Texas after all, She had have heard of the Muertos Cartel and knew what they were capable of, and yet she didn't show fear.

Not an ounce of fear swam through those beautiful eyes of hers when I told her my ties to the cartel and who I was. No fear when I told her that at times, I had no regrets for the things that I had done.

Nothing.

A part of me thought that she would push me out of the apartment and demand a divorce right there and then.

Yet she didn't.

She told me no. No divorce papers yet. Not until she makes me believe that I'm not the man I depict myself to be.

She will never be able to prove me wrong though, but in the meantime, I will humor her, and when she's ready I will sign the divorce papers.

Happy wife and all that fuckery.

Since I left her apartment on Monday night, I haven't seen Serena, but I have talked to her. Through text messages, but it's some form of communication at least. The conversations haven't been long, mostly about the dinner and what exactly I meant by "dress to impress".

The number of dress pictures that I have gotten in the last few days is bat shit crazy. They weren't even pictures of Serena wearing the dresses, it was all pictures of said dresses on hangers.

If this is what it's like to have a wife, I may lose my fucking mind. It hasn't been a week and this woman is already giving me grey hair.

Maybe after dinner tonight, she will see that I'm right about her not belonging in this world and will ask me for the divorce. Especially if she's around for the conversation that I have to have with my father regarding not finding any information out about the DEA's investigation on the cartel.

Not knowing any information can be deadly.

Deadly enough that I hope Serena gives me this divorce. It would be the only way to protect her. The only way to keep her alive.

I shake my head, clearing my mind of all the possible blood shed to come and try to concentrate on the task at hand.

Picking up my *wife* for dinner at my father's estate.

That's a weird combination of words to say. Especially since the only people at the dinner that know that I'm currently married are Santos and Emilio. My sisters will definitely be shocked when they find out. As for my father, well he might have a heart attack because I didn't follow Mexican or catholic tradition.

I guess I will deal with it when the time comes.

"We're here, *señor*," Arturo, my driver, tells me as we pull up to Serena's apartment building.

"*Gracias.*" I push open the door as soon as he is parked and make my way to the building. After getting buzzed up, I head up to the apartment.

When I knock and the door opens, I'm surprised to have Aria greet me instead of Serena.

"Hello, Leo." She gives me a tentative smile, opening the door wide enough for me, inviting me in.

"Hi, Aria. How are you?" I nod to her before walking into the apartment.

"Good. Well, good as can be since my roommate and best friend is about to go to dinner with the son of a drug lord, whom she also married." She eyes me as if I were the prey and she were the hunter.

I should have known that Serena would have talked to Aria and told her everything that left my mouth.

After an intense stare-off, I finally let out a sigh, conceding, "I gave her the option for a divorce, and she said not yet."

Aria nods, "I know, she told me. If something happens and she gets hurt..."

I don't let her finish. "I won't let that happen. We may have only known each other for a week, but I will never let anything happen to Serena. You have my fucking word on that."

She continues to look at me like she is trying to find the truth in my words and after what feels like a five-minute stare-off, Aria nods.

"I will hold you to that. Let me go get her." Without another word, she turns and heads down the hallway where the bedrooms must be.

I try to collect myself as much as possible before I hear a set of heels walking along the wooden floor. I don't need to look up to see that the woman making her way toward me is going to look beautiful.

And I'm right.

Dressed in an emerald green satin dress, Serena looks mouthwatering. Breathtaking in every sense of the word.

Her dark hair is in waves down her back and her eyes are surrounded by a dark shadow that makes them pop. She looks like a vixen, one that I wish was going to end up in my bed at the end of the night.

"Hi," she greets me shyly, moving from foot to foot, not really knowing what to do.

"Hi." I can't seem to form actual words.

"You said to dress to impress, I hope I got it right."

Fuck yes, she did.

"You look absolutely perfect." A slight blush covers her cheeks at my words, and she awards me with a timid smile.

Breaking the tension between us, I close the distance between us and place a kiss on her cheek.

Serena gives me another smile when I pull away from her. This woman doesn't even know just how gorgeous she is. Just looking at her now makes me want to really skip dinner and have her as my meal instead.

"Ready to go?" She gives me a nod, and after she grabs her clutch, the one that I bought her in Vegas, and says goodnight to Aria, we're off.

She lets out a slight gasp when she sees the dark SUV parked out front with Arturo standing by the door. I chuckle at her reaction. Wait until she sees the jet she's going to be on in twenty minutes.

"Does your father being the head of the cartel mean you're rich?" Serena whispers when Arturo closes the door behind me after we climb in.

"Something like that. Being in the position that I'm in, gives me some benefits." I don't give her any more details.

She saw for herself in Vegas, and she will see again in a few, no need to bore her with it.

Once Arturo is situated in the driver's seat, we are off to the airport.

I watch Serena as we make the drive and as she gazes out the window. Occasionally she turns to look at me, with a questioning look, but I stay quiet for most of the ride.

It's when we are about to drive through the private terminal at the Austin airport that she finally speaks.

"Where are we going?" Her question has a confusing tone to it, it's like she's curious but also fearful as to where I might be taking her.

"You'll see soon enough," I tell her, and I watch as she tenses up at my words. As we drive through the terminal, her leg starts to shake, and I can feel the nerves radiating off her.

I scoot closer to her and place my hand on the part of her thigh that is uncovered by the slit in her dress. I give her thigh a reassuring squeeze and rub small circles with my thumb against her skin, as we make the rest of the ride to the jet. Silently telling her that she has nothing to fear.

It doesn't work much, since her leg is still shaking once we reach the plane. Not only is she nervous, she's also in shock given how her mouth hangs open as she looks out my window.

"Holy shit," she whispers, not taking her eyes off the plane in front of us.

"Let's go." I hold my hand out to her, and she hesitates for a moment before taking it and following me out of the car.

I guide her up the stairs and once inside the cabin, she just stands there not knowing what to do with herself.

Placing my hand on her lower back, I guide her to one of the seats and take the seat right next to her, my hand going to her thigh again.

"Do you own this plane?" She leans closer to me to ask her question, not wanting the flight attendant to hear our conversation.

I nod. "It's part of the deal." Everything is part of the deal and as long as we are married, she will get a part of all of it. That's why I need her to sign the divorce papers. I need her to get as far away from this life as she possibly can.

The flight attendant comes over and asks if we want anything to drink. Serena shakes her head no, but I ask for two glasses of champagne. She needs to relax, and alcohol might be the best bet.

Soon we have our flutes and getting ready for takeoff and even with the alcohol, Serena still hasn't relaxed one bit.

She is sitting up straight, like she doesn't trust her surroundings.

I need her to relax. She can't be this rigid during dinner, my father will eat her alive.

There is only one way I can think of to get her to completely let go.

Knowing that the flight attendant is up front with the pilots, I make my move.

Leaning toward her, I move her hair behind her shoulder and place my lips on her neck.

"Relax, *princesa*. I will take good care of you." I move my lips along her skin, running my tongue along her pulse point.

The hand that's on her thigh travels up, exposing more skin as I push up her dress, making my final destination known.

"Leo," Serena pants out, squirming under my touch.

"What is it, *princesa*?" I nip at her skin, savoring the sweet little moan that she releases.

"You need to stop," she says, making no move to pull away from me. I hold her in place by tightening the grip I have on her thigh.

"And why would I do that, baby? Because there are people around or because you want me to?" I dip my finger into her thigh, as if I were marking my territory, as if I wasn't already doing that with my mouth.

"There are other people around," she lets out before she moans as my fingers travel up her thigh even more and meet her core.

"Do you want me to stop?" If she tells me yes, I will pull away right now and stop this before it has time to even start.

"No."

"Good." I move my mouth from her neck down to her collarbone, sucking on every inch of skin as my fingers are stroking her pussy through the flimsy fabric of her panties.

"Oh my god," she groans when I move the fabric to the side and slide my finger through her wet folds.

"Did you miss me, baby? Because I fucking missed you.

I missed you, especially seeing you on your knees taking my cock in that pretty mouth of yours."

I slide my finger into her tight cunt and Serena lets out a sweet moan. One that fills my ears and one that I'm sure the whole cabin crew heard.

With a smile, I pull my face out of the crook of her neck and place my mouth on hers. She lets out another delicious moan when my tongue meets hers, and another when my fingers start to move in and out of her.

"Answer the question, Serena. Did you miss me?" I growl against her lips, taking her bottom one between my teeth.

She nods. "I did. I did miss you."

I don't say another word, I just give a smirk before my lips land on hers again. As our tongues dance together, I spread her legs wider, giving me access to finger fuck her.

"Only three days with you and I can't even go a week without feeling you tighten around me," I say the words as I feel the plane taken off and leave the ground.

She must not feel it because when I pull back once again, her eyes open and are filled with a euphoric gaze. One that pulls me in, making me want to give everything and anything.

"Leo, I can't take anymore," she pants out, meeting my stare, her lips opening up in a perfect O.

I flick my thumb against her clit, moving my fingers faster until they are slick with her arousal and the only thing that I'm able to hear is my hand slapping against her skin.

At this very moment, we aren't up in the air, on our way

to my father's estate. There aren't three other people on this plane. It's just the two of us, in our own little bubble.

I can feel Serena tighten around my fingers, telling me that she is almost to the point of combustion.

"Come, baby. Coat my fingers like I know you want to. I promise you that later tonight I will pay you back for the fast finger fuck and treat you like the princess you are, with my cock and my mouth."

I hit her G-spot and when I do, she immediately tightens, holding my fingers in a vise, her release taking over her whole body.

"Fuck. Leo." She squirms as I continue to move my fingers as quickly as possible before slipping them, slapping my hand against her slick pussy.

Pulling back, I slip my fingers into my mouth savoring the taste of her release on my tongue.

Even better than I remembered.

She watches me as I lick my fingers clean, releasing another moan in the process. I will die a happy man if I could hear her moans every fucking day.

"So beautiful." I lean in, whispering the words against her lips as she continues to come down from the orgasmic high.

As we kiss, I adjust her panties and her dress, covering her up. The flight attendant, who has worked on my flights before, knows to not come to the cabin unless asked. She wouldn't have seen anything, but Serena doesn't know that, so I will cover her up to let her feel more comfortable.

For the rest of the flight, we kiss like two out of control teenagers. Some very heavy petting might have been involved, and if we weren't on our way to dinner with my family, Serena would be fixing a lot more than just her lipstick.

By the time that we land, Serena is definitely more relaxed than what she was when we first stepped on the plane. Her lipstick is fixed, her dress is formed to her body, and she looks like she is ready to conquer the fucking world.

I take her hand in mine as we walk off the plane and head to yet another black SUV that is sitting stand by waiting for us.

"*Buenas Tardes,* Don Leonardo," the driver says as he opens the door for us and I guide Serena in. I nod a greeting to him before climbing in and closing the door.

"Where are we?" Serena asks once she gets settled in her seat.

No need to hold information from her anymore, she has to find out eventually. "Mexico."

"Mexico?" Her eyes go wide with shock.

I nod. "San Pedro to be exact."

"And what are we doing here? I thought we were going to dinner." Her voice goes up an octave at the end of her sentence.

"We are." I don't say anything more as the driver gets in and drives away from the hangar. The ride to the compound is quiet and once we drive through the gates of the estate, I feel Serena's gaze on me, asking silent questions.

When the car pulls up to the front of the house, I

finally turn to her, and I find her looking at me with curiosity in her eyes.

"Where are we?"

I give her a smile, trying to show her calmness, because once I say the words, her nerves will be back in full swing.

"My father's estate. We are here for a family dinner." I open the door, stepping out and holding a hand out to her.

"Family?" I was right, the nerves are back. There is a shakiness to her voice that I expected.

I nod, "Yes, my family." I see the hesitation in her face, so I try to reassure her. "I promise nothing bad will happen."

Her hazel eyes bore into mine, and after a few long minutes, she finally relents and takes my hand.

Once she has both her heels on the ground, I take her face in my hands and place a soft kiss on her lips.

"You will always be safe with me. I promise you that. Married or not."

She nods at my words, probably afraid to say anything. I give her one last kiss before taking her hand and guiding her inside the house.

There is light music playing in the background as we walk to the patio, and as we get closer, I hear voices coming through. A few laughs here and there.

This dinner is supposed to include my sisters and a few of my father's men, with Santos, Emilio and me. From the sound coming from the patio. I will say everyone might already be here.

And that's what it looks like when we arrive at the

patio. Serena and I stand just outside the French doors when all the talking suddenly stops.

Everyone turning their heads in our direction, all looking at Serena wondering who she is and what she's doing here.

I tighten my grip on her hand before I speak.

"Everyone, this is Serena. *Mi esposa*."

17

SERENA

WHEN LEO TOLD me we were going to dinner, I should have said no.

At the very least, I should have said no when he told me that we were having dinner with his family. That should have been where I drew the line and stayed in the car, or better yet, on the plane.

But no, here I am with ten different sets of eyes looking right at me. All while I try to hide behind Leo.

It's uncomfortable.

Definitely awkward.

"Wife? I'm sorry, did you say *wife*?!"

My eyes travel to the woman that asks the question.

She is dressed in a white form-fitting dress that looks like it was made specifically for her. Her dark hair is curled in loose waves that makes my hair look like amateur hour. She's stunning and absolutely holds power, and by the way that everyone in the courtyard looks at her, everyone knows it.

"Yes, I said wife." Leo squeezes my hand in reassurance as he addresses the woman.

"When in the actual fuck did you get married?" This time the question is asked by another woman. This one is a lot younger than the first and instead of dark hair, she has almost ashy blonde hair that matches her complexion perfectly. She too is just as beautiful, dressed in a black dress that accentuates every one of her curves.

If I had to take a guess, I would say these beautiful women are Leo's sisters.

All three of them have the same dark eyes and some of the same facial features. The only difference is that Leo is more masculine whereas the two women have a softer touch to them.

Leo lets go of my hand only to pull me to his side and wrap an arm around my waist. "We got married this past Sunday. In Vegas."

His fingers dig into my hip like he is trying to make a point to everyone standing in front of us. I just don't know what that point happens to be.

Somewhere a piece of glass breaks and all eyes turn from Leo and me to a man standing by the dinner table. He's surrounded by other men but he has this power that would make any normal person feel afraid.

Afraid.

Terrified.

Take your pick. Whatever you choose, this man channels that and more.

Especially when his eyes are centered on you.

Like they currently are on me. If Leo wasn't holding me

like he is, then I would be running back to the car. Away from the man that the more I look at, the more I figure out who he is.

Ronaldo Morales.

Leo's father, and the head of the Muertos Cartel.

I take an audible swallow and move my body more toward Leo, as if he would be able to shield me from his father's murderous glare.

"*Puta madré*," Ronaldo growls out, still not taking his eyes off me.

I know enough Spanish to know that *Puta madré* means motherfucker. He's angry, I just don't know about what. The situation, at his son or at me. It could be all three.

"We don't marry *putas,* son, and we definitely don't bring them to my fucking house!" Ronaldo abandons his position by the table and stalks over to where we are standing.

I jump when he is only a few feet away from us.

"Don't call her a fucking whore." Leo lets go of my hip and goes to stand toe to toe with his father. He stands a few inches taller and has broader shoulders than him but at this distance, you can see the family resemblance.

"That's what she is. Just another *puta* you met in Vegas. One that doesn't belong here and never will."

I see how Leo's back tenses at his father's words. I see how his fist balls up at his side and how he tries his hardest to not do something that he will probably regret.

Like hitting his father.

Would that be something that he would do? Would Leo hit his father to defend me?

I step closer to the pair before it escalates that far.

"Leo," I whisper, placing a hand on his back.

He tenses even more at my touch, and barely turns to look at me, before he turns back to his father.

"Camila. Isabella. Take her inside and keep her there until I say otherwise," he growls out with authority.

The two women that I figured out were his sisters, walk over in a hurry and each of them takes one of my arms and drags me inside the house.

More like a mansion, than a house.

I don't watch where they drag me to. My eyes stay on my husband of a week. Watching as he steps as close as he can to his father.

"Come on," one of the sisters says, pulling me further until I can no longer see what is happening outside.

I continue to let Camila and Isabella drag me through the house until we reach a side of it that smells oddly like Leo.

His cologne, one that I got accustomed to and absolutely fell in love with in Vegas and also his natural scent. One that is all man, and everything that Leo encompasses.

This must be his part of the estate.

"We'll wait here until their, um, discussion is done," the blonde sister says, finally letting go of my arm, going deeper into the room.

I try to take a step forward, needing to sit down before I have a panic attack and collapse but the dark-haired sister tightens the grip she still has on my arm.

My gaze turns to hers. Her eyes are dark and filled with anger and what I think is mistrust swimming in them. It reminds me of the look her father was giving me.

I feel the urge to step back from her, but her grip is keeping me in place.

"You have one minute to tell me how in the hell you married my brother? Who the fuck are you? Are you just some whore who is after his money? Because if you are, I'm telling you this right now, sweetheart, you will not leave this room alive."

Her eyes narrow, her grip on me getting tighter and tighter. So tight, I'm sure I will have marks from her nails on my forearm.

This woman is my same height, but the way she is looking at me, makes me feel like I'm two feet tall.

"Bella, you're scaring her. Bring down the scary bitch mode a few notches."

Bella.

So, the sister digging her nails into my skin is Isabella, and the blonde is Camila. Right now, I think that Camila is my favorite sister.

"You don't even know who she is!" Isabella yells over to her sister, swinging her death glare over to her. "She could be working with federal agents for all we know. She could be here to destroy our family."

Does she really think I would be capable of that? Even if I was, would I have it in me to do it?

No.

Yes, it freaked me out when I found out who Leo was and who his father was, but never did it cross my mind to contact the FBI or whoever deals with this type of stuff. I doubt the Austin police department would have those types of resources.

"I would never do that." I whisper, ending the stare-down between the sisters.

Isabella snorts, giving me a smile like she doesn't believe me. "Of course, you wouldn't. Tell me, did you see my brother, found out who he was and decided to dig your nails into him? Came up with a plan to marry him?"

I'm shaking my head before she can even stop talking. "That's not what happened. I didn't even know who he was until after the fact."

"You see, I don't believe you." She finally lets go of me and comes closer. My instincts telling me that if she could slap me, she would.

"Bella," Camila tries to warn her sister off, even leaving the spot on the bed and coming closer to us.

"Tell me, Serena. Tell me exactly what your plan is and I will let you walk out of here alive. Of course, with some bloodshed, but alive nonetheless."

If I wasn't in the situation that I was in, I would think that she was joking. Yet given who her father is and the title that her brother holds, I know she is completely serious.

I have words on the tip of my tongue, but the sound of his voice stops the words from coming out.

"Enough, Isabella." Leo's voice roars through the room, making me jump. The tone of his voice doesn't even affect Isabella.

"You don't even know her." Isabella says through her gritted teeth, not taking her eyes off me.

I try to keep my facial expressions as neutral as possible, not wanting to show just how much this whole night is affecting me.

"I know enough. Now back off before the person leaving this room with a few drops of blood is you and not Serena."

I turn to look at my husband when I hear his words.

Did he just insinuate what I think he did? He wouldn't put his hands on his own sister, would he?

If he were able to touch his sister like that, what makes you think he wouldn't do the same to his wife?

"You would never lay a hand on me. It's not who you are. Not to women." Isabella finally turns to her brother, her words taking me out of the dark turn my mind was heading.

"No, I wouldn't. But just because I wouldn't, doesn't mean that my wife wouldn't either." I wouldn't, I think Leo knows that, but Isabella doesn't.

"Now back down," Leo growls once more.

With one last look of disgust in my direction, Isabella finally takes a step back. She looks me up and down before she turns and leaves the room.

"Camila," Leo says to his other sister still in the room and when I turn to her, she's nodding. He's dismissing her.

Before she leaves the room, she turns to me and gives me a small smile.

"If it's any consolation, I believe you. Bella will come around to this marriage eventually, just give her time. Congratulations and welcome to the family, I guess..." She takes my hand in hers for a quick second and gives it a squeeze before she follows her sister out of the room.

It's silent for a few minutes after his sisters leave. the two of us just stand there in the middle of what I think is his room, just looking at each other.

He looks angry, not directed at me, but at someone else. At this point, it could be a number of people. As I watch him, I notice an angry gash on his top lip. It's red and fresh, looking like it definitely stung when it happened.

Without a word, I make my way over to him and I let my hand travel up to his face, running a fingertip along the cut. It's small, but even the slightest touch has Leo cringing slightly.

"What happened?" I ask softly, moving to cradle his face, and being a little surprised when he leans into my touch.

"My father didn't take the news of our nuptials very well. The anger got the best of him, and he clipped me." At least he is telling me the truth and not giving me a bullshit answer.

All I do is nod, not being able to find words to say. His eyes stay on mine for a few seconds until they travel down my arm and land at the crescent moon marks that were left by Isabella.

Leo pulls my arm back and inspects it. Like his lip, the marks are red and slightly fresh, the only difference is that my marks aren't cleaned up. There are a few specs of dry blood surrounding each individual mark.

He looks at the marks, getting angrier as he continues to run his fingers along them.

"She didn't mean it," I whisper, trying to calm him down as best I can. I don't even know why I'm protecting Isabella, but it seems like the right thing to do.

"She left marks on your arm. You don't need to protect her." His tone is harsh, and I have to swallow my emotions down.

"She was trying to protect you. You're her brother, and she loves you and wants the best for you. Us getting married in Vegas, probably shocked her enough to pull up her defenses. I get it, I wouldn't trust me either if I was her, especially with a family like yours."

I see as he takes in my words and thinks about what I said.

He knows I'm right, and he finally admits it when he nods.

"You're right." He lets out a sigh before he continues. "Are you ready to sign the divorce papers yet? Now that you met my family."

Am I?

Did his family scare me enough to ask for that divorce he so easily wants to give me?

I look at the marks on my arm and then at the gash on his lip, then at the man standing in front of me.

The way he is looking at me is enough to tell myself, no. I'm not ready to sign my name on the dotted line just yet.

I shake my head. "No, they haven't made me run for the hills with one dinner."

"They will. If not my family, then this life." Leo takes a step back from me, looking at me like he doesn't understand why I don't walk away from him.

"Maybe, but until that day comes, I will show you that you are not the person you think you are." I walk over to him and place a small kiss on his cheek.

He doesn't lean away from my touch; he just continues to stand there looking at me.

I pull back and give him a small smile. "I'm sorry, I ruined dinner."

"You didn't ruin it." He steps closer to me, brushing a few strands of hair away.

"What do we do now?" Can we go back to the courtyard and have a normal dinner? I highly doubt it.

"Want a tour of the estate?"

18

LEO

I SHOULDN'T HAVE BROUGHT her here.

That's a bad decision on my part, I should have thought about it more and put together what their reactions would be.

But I didn't.

I wanted to show Serena a part of this life that would ultimately give her the idea to walk away from me.

To see the people that are around me on a daily basis.

I expected my father's reaction. Since I was eighteen, he has had it engraved in his mind that I needed to find a woman that acts more like a puppet and caters to my every needs. The traditional housewife that doesn't ask questions and does what she is told. A wife that is fearful of her husband and stays in the shadows.

The type of woman my mother was.

The type of wife Isabella is set to be.

Not the type of wife that would stand at his side and

make him stronger and more powerful. Not a wife that has strength of her own and commands a room.

Because that's what Serena is, a woman that commands a room. A woman that adds to the man that's on her arm.

Last night, even with fear running through her veins as to what the night would bring, she stood tall. Her head was held high, and she conveyed power that made everyone that was in that patio look at her.

There was nothing about her last night that said that she would hide in the shadows. That was the first thing my father noticed. He noticed, and it terrified him.

Here was a woman that hadn't been vetted, hadn't been threatened with her life, standing in the middle of his estate, married to his one and only son. A son set to take over the throne when he was no longer standing on this earth.

My marriage should have been an event, not something done in Las Vegas.

With a *puta*.

A *gringa*.

Because someone that isn't of Mexican descent is always considered a whore in his eyes. An even bigger one when she marries someone after only a few days.

I expected the reaction my father would have to the news, what I didn't expect was my reaction to him. Anger boiled inside of me when he called my wife a whore and the second my sisters had Serena out of sight, I charged.

Hits were landed, both on him and on myself until someone pulled us apart.

"*Desgraciado. Vete con tú puta esposa.*"

Getting called a fucking idiot by my father warranted me leaving the patio and go looking for my wife. Not before I cleaned up my face from the scuffle.

I wasn't surprised to find that my sisters took Serena to my wing. What did surprise me was the way Isabella, my younger sister by only three years, was looking at her. There was anger in her eyes, and I didn't like it, not one bit.

Serena still had her head held high, not succumbing to my sister's glare.

When my sisters left the room, I thought for sure she would ask for me to take her home and hand over the papers. But she surprised me yet again and said not just yet.

This woman is going to keep surprising me and I won't know what to fucking do.

After that, the smart choice would have been to leave, and take her home, but like my father said, I'm an idiot and showed her around the estate.

Thankfully everyone who was set to attend the dinner either left the compound altogether or retired to their quarters. We walked around the compound and I told her stories of the adventures that I would take with Santos and my sisters when we were kids.

She took in every word and when I would turn to her, she would give me a smile. One that I wouldn't mind seeing every day.

We finally ended up back in my wing, and for a few minutes I contemplated taking her back to Austin. For some reason though, I didn't voice it. I just stood there as she took off her strappy heels and got comfortable in my bed, falling asleep within a minute or two.

She didn't even undress, but seeing her lying there, innocent and angelic, did something to me. Something I don't ever remember feeling before. So, I let it be, after undressing I laid right next to her and tried to let sleep take over.

It didn't happen.

I spent most of the night staring at the woman lying next to me and trying to figure out how to get her out of this.

Nothing came.

Now I'm sitting in a chair in the corner, watching my wife sleep, as the light of the morning fills the room.

I don't know how long I sit here, but it's enough time for Serena to stir. Her sleep-filled eyes search until they find me in the dark corner that the sunlight hasn't hit yet.

"Good morning."

"Morning."

Just like her eyes, her voice is filled with sleep. It's raspy and it brings back memories of our time in Vegas. Memories that make me want to go to her and devour every single inch of her.

"How did you sleep?" I ask, trying to control my dick from taking charge and pouncing on her.

"Good, your bed is very comfortable." Her words are like a purr, making it even harder not to go to her and rip off her dress so I can fuck her.

I nod. "That's good. I'm glad that you slept well."

She gives me another sleepy smile before she pushes up. "Did you? Sleep well, I mean."

I don't respond, I just sit there, watching her. My silence must have provoked something in her because she swings her legs over the edge of the bed and makes her way over to me.

Her hips sway at the motion, giving me the urge to grab her and situate her on my lap. She does just that when she finally makes it over to me.

My hands automatically go to her hips, while hers wrap around my neck.

"Why weren't you able to sleep?" I feel her fingers playing with my hair and I try not to get lost in the feeling.

"And how do you know I wasn't able to sleep?" I dig my fingers into her hips, wishing that the material of her dress wasn't in the way.

"You have bags under your eyes," She runs a finger along my undereye as to prove a point. "Your hair looks as if you've been running your fingers through it all night."

I let out a sigh. "I kept thinking that bringing you here was a bad idea."

"But you wanted me to see this life. To see it and make my own conclusion."

This woman is way too smart for my own good.

I nod at her, "Yes, but it could have gone very differently than what it did. There could have been a lot more bloodshed."

Serena's body stiffens at my words, knowing exactly what I'm trying to say.

"Us getting married, just how bad can it turn out for you?"

Her hands stop moving through my hair and the one that was touching my face drops. I debate for a long minute whether to tell her the truth or to straight out lie.

Might as well go with the truth with her.

"This family is all about tradition. Especially when it comes to marriage. My father put it in my head at a young age, that I had to find a woman like my mother to marry. A woman that depended on the man and didn't do what she wanted, one that asked permission from her husband. A woman that took care of the house and the kids, while her husband was out running the cartel and fuck any piece of ass he wanted. A woman that didn't ask questions and turned a blind eye. When it came to marriage, that was what was expected of me, and it's expected for my sisters to follow in my mother's footsteps and become the doting housewives. I'm supposed to marry someone that isn't a weakness, someone I wouldn't care about if they died. Getting married the way we did, opens up the opportunity for people outside of the family or even within these walls, to view you as a weakness."

The whole time I speak, Serena looks as if she is in another world. As if she is listening to the words that I'm saying but not really processing them. I rub little reassuring circles along her hip.

What I wouldn't give to feel her skin against mine, to slide into her and forget about every single worry in the world.

"What type of weakness would I be?" Her voice is

timid, filled with hints of fear.

I tighten my grip on her, "A weakness that they can use to kill me. If anyone gets word that I got married outside the traditional way, outside the arranged marriage way, they will use you. They will go after you to get to me, possibly killing the both of us in the process."

"Why would they go after you? It's been a week. My presence in your life shouldn't have that big of an impact."

Does she really not see the effect that she has on me?

My father saw it and all it took him was sixty seconds.

"Because in all my adult life, I have never shown interest in even marrying a woman. Whenever my father brought it up, I turned a blind eye. You somehow, in a short period of time, have wedged yourself within me. There is something about you. Something that I can't pinpoint. My father saw it last night and he wasn't the only one. In their eyes, you made me weak already. And they will go after you to make me weaker, to destroy me."

I let go of her hips and take her delicate face between my calloused hands. Her eyes are still filled with fear and I want to make it leave.

"I promise you, Serena, I will protect you no matter what. It doesn't matter if we get divorced or not, I will protect you at every turn. Killing anyone that dares to touch a hair on your head."

I will protect her in a way my father never protected my mother.

It doesn't matter what Serena is to me, I will kill anyone that tries to harm her.

No matter what.

19

SERENA

Do you sometimes wonder what has your life turned to? Like do you ever stay up late at night staring up at your dark ceiling and ask yourself, how in the actual fuck did I get here?

Over the past month, I've been doing that a lot more often than I would like to admit.

There have been nightly questions where I ask myself everything under the sun.

Will my kids in the upcoming school year be good kids or will they be little jerkfaces?

Do I need to go shopping for a new wardrobe?

But the most important question I ask myself is how in the world am I still married to the second in command of the Muertos Cartel?

Yup, you heard that right. A month after my spontaneous, very drunk wedding in Vegas, I'm still married.

If I could, I would stay married to Leo for the eye candy alone, but that's just me.

Okay, that's a lie but hey who wouldn't want to stay married to the man? He is hot as sin, tattoos that I just want to lick and his voice, god, his voice. It's rough and smooth with a hint of an accent and so freaking hot. Add the things he does to my body, and I will be forever in heaven.

Wait, what was I saying?

Oh yeah, that a month after our Vegas wedding, we are still married.

The day after the failed dinner at the Morales estate, Leo brought me back to Austin and told me that he was only a phone call away if I needed anything. After a quick kiss to the forehead, he was gone.

It threw me off a bit, but I didn't question it when he left. I didn't question it for a few days actually, until after about four days, I finally gave in and texted him to see if he wanted to meet up.

After about two days, he responded, telling me he couldn't, and we've been texting ever since. That's all that our communications have been, text.

We've talked about everything. How our days are going, what we ate that day, and he ends every conversation by asking if I'm ready for a divorce. Because he wants to protect me, and not be involved in this life.

Every time my answer is still the same.

No.

Other than that, we haven't talked in person. I don't know why but I don't like it. It makes me feel like he doesn't want anything to do with me. And maybe he doesn't and I'm here trying to throw myself at him. This past month has made me think about that more and more.

Maybe I'm overreaching and should give up this whole charade I have going on in my head and take the divorce that he so kindly is handing me.

We don't know each other. A month of texting doesn't make a relationship, it doesn't tell you much about a person either.

I should just send a text that tells him to start the paperwork already so we can go our own ways. That way he won't have to worry about anything happening to him or to me and I can go back to filling my loneliness with pencil dick jerks.

Because that's what you want.

God, I need a distraction or something to get my mind off whatever my relationship with my husband is.

It's a good thing that I go back to work in two weeks, that would be all the distraction that I need.

After starting my lesson plan for the first two weeks of the school year, I decide that I need a break. So, grabbing my purse and my phone, I make my way over to the store to get some art supplies to start the year.

Walking into the cool air of the store, I feel an instant sensation of relaxation. Who knew shopping for art supplies could be so calming, usually I'm stressed at the start of a new school year.

Once I have all the supplies that I was looking for, I decide to do another walk through the store to see if anything catches my eye.

It's nice to actually do something with my life other

than to stress about when my husband will get in contact with me.

I make it through the whole store and when I make it to the women's clothing section, a weird sensation comes over me.

One of those feelings that tells you that someone is looking at you.

Looking around the section, I don't notice anything out of the ordinary. There's a worker over by the dressing rooms folding clothes, and a young woman by the swimwear, both minding their own business. Must have been someone walking by that just looked in my direction.

Brush it off, Serena. Stop being crazy.

I continue looking at the clothes, but when I pull down a dress from the rack, I get the feeling again.

This time when I look up, I see two men by the men's section. One has their eyes on the T-shirts in front of them, the other is looking right at me.

He doesn't look overly familiar, but the more I look at him, the more I realized that I have seen him more than once today. He was in the art supply section and then I saw him again when I went by the shampoo aisle. I chalked it up to pure coincidence, but as I think about it, I don't think it is.

Are they following me?

Getting a bad feeling in the pit of my stomach, I turn away from the man, and with the dress in hand, I walk toward the dressing room.

Sure enough, as I move to the end of the section of the department, so do they.

Okay, they're definitely following me.

Or at the very least up to something.

I need to find a way to get my head straight so that I can think of a plan to get as far from them as possible.

"Excuse me? Can I try this on?" I ask, holding up the dress in my hands to the employee at the dressing room. She nods.

I abandon my cart, grab my purse and follow her as she walks me to a room.

Turning slightly, I watch as the men stop just outside the dressing room. Taking a deep breath, I continue to follow the worker.

As soon as she leaves me in a room to myself, I close the door and lock it.

This is a stupid idea. I should have gone to the front of the store and notified someone about my suspicion, or at least told the worker. Maybe then the men would have left and the police would be called. Now here I am, in a dressing room at the back of the store with no one to help me.

Stupid. Stupid.

Okay think, Serena. What should I do?

For all I know, the employee went about her business and the men could be standing right outside, waiting for me.

I really should have said something to the worker.

I can feel myself start to panic, so I grab my phone and with shaky fingers, I dial the one number that comes to mind.

Not Aria.

Not my parents.

Not the cops.

No, I decided to call my husband.

I bring the phone up to my ear and hear it ring until after a long minute, it goes to voice mail.

Fuck.

Trying again, I get the same result. In the month that we've been married, I only called him the day we got back from Vegas. Everything from there has been text. Certainly, he knows that something has to be wrong if I'm calling him, right?

My body starts to shake and tears spring in my eyes as I dial his number for the third time.

Please pick up.

Please pick up.

When I'm about to throw my phone against the dressing room door, the line goes silent. I prepare myself to hear his voice mail when I hear his voice instead.

"Serena?" I let out a sigh of relief at the sound of my name coming from the other line, the tears finally releasing.

"Are you in Austin?" I ask instead of greeting him. There's an urgency in my tone that I know he hears, because his next words feel weighted.

"Serena, what's going on?"

"Please tell me you're in Austin." I know he spends his time split between Austin and San Pedro, but I really hope he's here. I don't know what I would do if he's a three-hour drive away.

"I'm in Austin. What is wrong?" I hear him shuffling around and keys rattle.

"I think someone is following me." I whisper into the phone, just in case the men are on the other side of the door. "I came to the store to get some things, and I got this strange feeling that someone was watching me. When I looked up there were two guys, and one of them was looking right at me. Then I came to the dressing room, they came closer."

The line goes silent, and I have to pull the phone back to see if the call dropped.

"Leo?" I whisper, slightly panicked.

"I'm here, baby. Where are you?"

I rattle out the store that I'm at, all the while I hear a door slam shut from his side.

"Listen to me, Serena. I'm on my way to you, but I need you to compose yourself. Compose yourself as best you can and leave the dressing room as if nothing is wrong. Smile and once you leave the store, I will be out front waiting for you. Act as if it were an Uber picking you up."

Does he seriously think that I'm mentally able to even leave this room? I don't even know if I can open up the door.

"I don't know if I can do that." I can feel a sob trying to come out, but I try to hold it in. No way in hell am I going to have a mental breakdown in a dressing room.

"You can, baby, and you will. I will be outside waiting for you." His tone is a lot calmer than it was a few seconds ago and I know it's for my benefit.

"But why can't you come in?" I would feel safer that way, but I don't voice it.

"Because if they see me, it might become a dangerous situation for everyone."

A strangled sob forces its way up my throat, I slap a hand over my mouth to stop it from escaping.

"Who are these men, Leo?" Are they connected to the Muertos? Are they men that know Leo? Or are they strangers that are after me just to kidnap someone?

"I don't know. Just do what I fucking say, Serena, please. I will meet you out front." His voice roars through the phone as if he were right here next to me.

I take a deep breath trying to keep the fear at bay. The fact that I have Leo on the line is helpful.

"Okay," I say after a long minute. "Okay, I think I can do it."

"You can, baby. Remember, nothing is wrong and everything will be okay." I nod even though he can't see me.

"You'll be outside?" He has told me this over and over, but I need to make sure.

"Yes, I will be outside." I nod once more, this nod more for myself than anything and pocket my phone without ending the call.

No way in hell am I going to walk through this store, let have something happen and not let Leo hear it. I collect myself as best as I can and wipe at the tears that were able to escape. After a long minute of more calming breaths, I open the dressing room door slowly, looking to see if anyone is around.

Thankfully, nobody else is in the little hall but as soon as I step through the entry door, I see the two men standing a few feet away, perusing a rack.

I turn my head quickly, before making eye contact with one of them and start walking out of the women's department.

"Did the dress work out okay?" I jump when I hear the employee's voice. She gives me a bright smile when I turn to look at her.

I take a big gulp. "Actually no, it fit too small. I was going to see if you guys had it online so I can order it in a different size." It trips me out just how well the lie fell off of my lips.

She nods. "Yeah, that might be the safest bet. I can take it for you. Did you forget about your cart?" She points over to my abandoned cart, the same cart that is about ten feet away from the suspicious men.

"Right. Silly me." On shaky feet, I walk over to the cart, making eye contact with one of the men, and walk back out of the section.

I hear the footsteps coming a few seconds later. I try to keep my composure as best I can, reminding myself that all I have to do is walk outside and Leo will be there waiting for me.

Deciding that I need to distract the men somewhat, I don't walk straight to the door. I divert myself to the toy section abandoning my cart along the way before heading back to the front of the store. Chancing a glance, I see that they aren't right behind me, getting stuck behind a group of teenagers that are killing time.

That's when I start walking faster. With a grip on my purse, I walk out the doors and reach for my phone right away.

"Leo?" Please tell me he didn't hang up.

"Pulling up right now," A black SUV screeches to a halt a few feet in front of me, the back door swinging open, and once I see Leo, I jump in.

As soon as I hear the door close behind me, I wrap myself in his arms and finally let out the sob that had been brewing in me.

"You did good, Serena. You did good," he says into my hair, consoling me as I cry into his chest.

I don't know how long I cry for, or even how long he holds me, but it was enough time for me to calm down a little.

That is until I feel the car speeding through the Austin traffic.

Before I can ask anything, or even pull away from Leo, his driver speaks, and even though his words are in a different language, I know there is something wrong.

"*Nos están persiguiendo.*"

I pull back to look at Leo for answers, but he's not looking at me or at his driver, he's looking at something through the back window.

Right then, I don't need to know a whole lot of Spanish to know what is happening.

We're being followed.

20

I was protecting her by staying away.

Me staying away from her, meant that no one and their fucking mothers would know that she existed. No one would see us out together, no one would see her on my arm and abso-fucking-lutely no one would go after her.

Staying away from her was in her best interest.

I didn't give a shit if we were married. I was keeping her alive.

Yet I stayed in Austin, only going to San Pedro when needed and staying close to her. Just in case she needed me for something.

Hanging up a TV. Opening a jar of pickles, I didn't give a shit.

If Serena called and told me she needed me for something, I would have gotten in a car and drove to her.

Never in my wildest fucking dreams did I think she would call me because she thought that some fucking bastards were following her while she shopped.

The second I heard the fear in her voice, I knew something was wrong. I knew it deep in my fucking bones. Thankfully Arturo and I were at a restaurant nearby and we were able to get to her quickly.

Now the motherfuckers are following us as we drive through the streets of Austin.

I have no fucking idea who they are, but they won't live long to see out whatever plan they have. That is, before I find out how in the hell they knew about Serena and how to find her.

"Lose them." I order, making Arturo nod all the while he presses a heavier foot on the gas.

Serena pulls herself away from my hold and looks over the back seat to see who might be following us.

"It's the men from the store, isn't it?"

As much as I want to keep her out of this, I can't. She's involved now and if these people are really after her, she has a right to know, no way will she let me keep this from her.

We may have only known each other for a month, but it's enough time for me to know certain things about her.

"I don't doubt that it isn't. They probably have been keeping an eye on you and finally saw you alone, so they took their shot."

They probably have been watching her for a while now. Since she rarely leaves her apartment without Aria, now was probably as good a time as any to go after her. I also don't mention that I've also had a man watching her, for my own sanity and her protection.

The one day, I tell him to leave post, this fuckery happens.

"Do you think they saw you when I got in the car?" Her eyes go wide with worry.

I shake my head and speak through my teeth. "If they did, they wouldn't be following us."

Turning around, I see that the dark pickup truck I saw earlier, is now only a few cars behind us. Too far away to make out the driver.

"How did they find me? Or even know who I am?" Very good fucking questions.

"I don't know, but I will find out before I put a bullet in their heads."

Serena flinches at my words and she has every right to, because I don't plan on going against them. These fuckers came after my wife, and they will pay.

"Don," Arturo says, taking my attention from Serena. When I turn to look at him he nods toward the rearview mirror, turning back to look at the pickup, I see now that they are right on our ass. The windshield still too dark to see through.

There is no way we can lose them now. Might as well play their little game.

Reaching under the seat, I grab the semi-automatic that I have stashed. Once it's loaded with the magazine that I have hidden in the center console, I place it between Serena and me. I don't look at her, and I don't look at her when I reach for the holster that is hidden by my suit jacket.

"Ever shot a gun before?" I make sure the gun is loaded

with one round ready to go in the chamber. I'm met with more wide eyes when I hand the gun over to her.

Her eyes travel from the gun to me, shaking her head the whole time.

"Here's the safety." I grab her hand and wrap it around the grip of the gun. "If anyone besides me or Arturo comes at you, you flip the safety and you pull the trigger. Do you understand me?"

"Leo." She continues to shake her head, more tears forming in her eyes.

"Do. You. Understand. Me?" If asking the question through my teeth makes her realize the severity of this, so fucking be it.

Serena nods after a long minute of silence, tears running down her cheeks. "Yes."

The way she is looking at me breaks me. I reach over and wipe away the tears on her cheeks before pulling away and facing Arturo.

"*La bodega.*"

He doesn't even question it, he just swerves through traffic and heads in the direction of our warehouse.

There will be blood, and I won't drain it on the streets of Austin, especially with the DEA on the cartel's ass.

As expected, the pickup truck continues to follow us all the way. They are probably thinking that Serena is stupid enough to lead them to a Muertos Cartel warehouse. Little do they know it's not our main facility and I'm in the car.

Arturo makes it into the building seconds before the pick-up.

We sit in silence, waiting for something to happen.

Five seconds.

Five seconds is all it takes before the sound of bullets hitting the SUV start filling our ears. The three of us duck in our seats, as Serena's screams of fear ring out.

It's her screams that have me grabbing the semi-automatic that sits on the seat and pushing the door open.

"Leo!" Serena yells for me, but I close the door to the car as soon as I step foot on the concrete. If anything happens to me, Arturo will drive her away.

I press my body against the walls of the SUV, letting it shield me from the bullets flying everywhere.

Whoever is shooting, hasn't noticed that someone stepped out of the vehicle, so when I get trigger-happy in their direction, it takes them by surprise.

There are three men. Two who, I'm guessing, were following Serena while she was out and then their driver. They all look young, share the same complexion and dark hair. Undoubtedly, they're Mexican but they aren't any of my men. No, these are hired help.

But whose?

Not knowing who sent them doesn't stop me from shooting at them. For a second or two, their attention is on me instead of on the car covering me. It's in those few seconds of distraction that I'm able to get a few good shots in.

One bullet travels and hits one of the bastards in the chest. Another flies and hits the one hanging out of the passenger side window. Only leaving the driver to get taken care of.

He makes eye contact with me, and instantly I can see the fear in his eyes, see the blood draining from his face.

He wasn't expecting me to be here. Yet I am, and now this fucker knows that he is near death. He knows he won't be walking out of here alive, so he stays rooted in place, dropping his gun, just waiting for me to shoot him.

The closer I get to him, the more I'm able to see just how young he is.

When I'm only a few inches away from him, I slam the butt of the semiautomatic against his head, making him drop to his knees.

"*¿Quién te mandó?*" Who sent you?

He doesn't say a word, just whimpers on the ground. I place the end of the barrel against his skin, but he still doesn't speak.

"*¿Con quién estás trabajando?*" Who are you working for?

The bastard has the gall to shake his head at me, giving me a good view of the tears falling down his face.

"*¡Dime!*" Tell me!

He whimpers again, but this time instead of tears escaping, a wet puddle surrounds his legs.

Great, he's pissing himself.

"I don't know." He is able to let out in broken English. "We were just told that we needed to follow the lady and take her to an address. That's it."

"What address?" I growl out, shoving the barrel deeper into his skin.

"I don't know," he sobs out, finally making eye contact with me. "He was going to send us the address when we told him we had her."

"*¿Quién?*" I'm tired of the no-answer bullshit, I need to know who the fuck sent them.

"*No sé!*"

"Not fucking good enough." I pull the trigger, the bastard's body falling back from the impact, but not before all the blood spatters gets everywhere.

Three dead men and no fucking answers as to who went after Serena.

I hear the car door open and slam shut, followed by heavy footsteps.

"Burn them and the truck and then clean up," I order Arturo, who gives me a nod and getting right to work.

The only saving grace about this whole thing is that it happened on our own turf. Otherwise, it wouldn't be such a pretty sight.

I make my way to the car, not even caring what I might look like when I open the backseat door. I know there is blood somewhere on me and that my face may be in a scowl. Not giving a shit either way, I open the door and instantly, Serena cowers as far away from me as possible.

She just witnessed me shoot three men dead, of course she fears me. She should fear everything about me.

Without saying a word to her, nothing reassuring directed at her, I place the semi-automatic back in its place and close the door before hopping into the driver's seat.

No words leave either of our mouths as I pull out of the warehouse, leaving Arturo to deal with the carnage of my actions.

I drive us in the direction of the airport and when I take the exit, Serena finally speaks.

"Where are we going?" Her question is low, almost a whisper and not a tone I'm used to hearing from her.

"San Pedro," I state, turning into the airport.

"What? Why?"

"Because you're not safe here. Who knows who else knows that you exist and is planning on coming after you." I need to find out who sent those men, but first I need to talk to my father.

I need to see if he spread news of my marriage and if he did, to whom.

"I can't leave. What if whoever it is, goes to the apartment and finds Aria and goes after her?" There is an urgency to her voice, and I have to remind myself that she would be devastated if something were to happen to her friend.

"Call her and tell her to get a hotel or stay with a friend or family for a few weeks. Just long enough for us to know it's safe."

"And what about me?"

What about her?

Bringing her to San Pedro is just as dangerous as having her stay in Austin. Whoever is after her can find her in either location, but in San Pedro she will be protected in a heavily guarded place. Whereas in Austin, she will be free game.

"You will be staying with me for as long as I say. I don't give a shit where you have to go, you will stay by my side at all times."

At least until I kill every single motherfucker trying to get their grimy hands on her.

Maybe then I will let her leave.
Or she will walk away on her own.

21

SERENA

Gunshots.

Blood.

Dead bodies.

Three things that up until a few weeks ago I never thought I would hear or see. Yet in a matter of minutes, I saw all three together and I don't know if I would be able to unsee it.

I won't be able to unsee the blood or the lifeless bodies or the fact that it was my husband who had pulled the trigger that ultimately ended the lives of those men.

It's one thing hearing the words he used to describe himself, it's a whole different thing seeing that description come to life.

Seeing his facial expressions change from one of a caring man to one of a killer, made my stomach churn. There was a hardness to his eyes that I hadn't seen before and quite honestly it scared me.

No, actually, it terrified me.

Something in me told me to run. Then I had to ask myself, why did he kill those three men?

Because he was protecting me.

I heard it all.

The moment that the shoot-out ended, I opened the door. I opened the door because curiosity got the best of me, and I wanted to know what was happening. It was the stupidest thing I could have done, but I did it anyway. Much to Arturo's dismay.

I was able to hear the man say that they were hired to grab me and then take me. My mind went haywire just thinking about what they could have done to me had I not reacted and called Leo when I did.

Before I even was able to close the door, the shot rang out.

Blood splatter everywhere, a limp body on the floor.

I wanted to scream, but I held it in. I held it in as I saw the man fall to the side, straight into a pool of his own blood.

I had just witnessed a man I barely knew, a man that I was married to, murder a man point-blank and all I did was sit back in my seat and close the car door.

Running should have been my first option at that point, but instead I just sat there waiting for something to happen. Arturo got out of the car and then a few seconds later, Leo was back driving us away.

It took me longer than expected to be able to find my voice, but when he took the exit for the airport, I was finally able to speak.

When Leo told me we were going to San Pedro, everything inside started to panic. The panic got worse when he told me to tell Aria to not stay at the apartment.

Now here I am a week and a half later, trying to not die of boredom here in the Morales estate. This place might be big but when you can't do anything without your husband, having all this space is useless.

Whoever is after me is out there, and until we find out who it is, I will be at Leo's side.

Every minute of every day, I'm within a few feet of Leo, and when he's gone, I have six or seven bodyguards watching me at all times.

Take right now, for example, I'm currently in the library of his wing, yes, this man has his own wing, staring at him as he does something on his laptop.

His dark hair is all over the place and he has stubble covering his jaw that I bet would feel amazing between my legs.

I really need to figure out what to do with myself, besides fantasize about my husband.

In the time that I have been here, I have been working on lesson plan after lesson plan so that I have everything set for the first four months of school. You heard that right, the first four months of school. That's just how much time I had on my hands since we left Austin and had my laptop delivered to me.

"Hey, what's going to happen when I go back to Austin?" It's a question that has been playing in my head for a few days now. Since school starts Monday and it's Thursday, might as well ask.

"You're not going back to Austin." Leo answers, not looking away from his computer screen.

Is this what corporate wives deal with on a daily basis? Their husbands talking to a screen more than them?

I take in his words. "What are you talking about? Yes, I am. I start work on Monday."

"You can work from here." He cannot be serious, can he?

"I'm a teacher. I can't work from here; I have to actually step foot in a classroom." I've done online schooling before, it's not easy, especially when you teach second grade. There are a handful of kids that aren't able to thrive unless they are being taught in person.

"Then get a substitute or whatever. Or better yet, quit. You're not leaving my side."

He did not just suggest what I think he did.

"I'm sorry, quit?"

Leo finally looks up from his screen, his eyebrows bunching up in confusion at my tone.

"Yes, quit. I can't have you going back to work. It's too dangerous for you."

"Then put security outside of the school or inside for all I care, because there is no way in hell that I will be quitting my job. I will be going back."

His jaw tightens, I can see it from where I'm sitting. "Serena."

My eyes narrow. "Do not 'Serena' me, Leonardo. I will not quit my job."

Of course, the first time I use his full name is when we are having a disagreement.

He gets up from his seat, slamming his computer shut. "I'm trying to protect you."

The way he says that through his teeth is so hot.

Not the time to be thinking how hot he looks.

Right.

"And I'm letting you. I let you take me from my home and bring me here. I let you keep me closed off for almost two weeks. No questions asked. Now the one thing that I'm asking for, you're not going to give me?"

This is such a ridiculous conversation. Do men seriously think that women will just quit their jobs because they tell them to?

Nope, sorry. That's not me.

I stand up from my seat, and if I was a childish person, I would be stomping my foot to drive my point even more.

We don't say anything to each other, we just stare, trying to make the other person cave. I can see that he's fuming, waiting for me to be the first one to break. I won't.

"Fine." Never underestimate the power of a woman's stare, it will never go the way you want. "Don't quit. But we will be coming back here every single night. Do you understand me?"

Not ideal and probably very expensive but he's going to let me work, so I will take anything that he gives me.

"Deal." I give him a sweet smile before walking over to him and placing a kiss on the cheek. "Was that so hard?"

"You're a stubborn woman," he sighs.

I shrug, "My stubbornness is probably why you decided to marry me in the first place."

Leo shakes his head before placing a hand on my hip.

"I'm sure that wanting to marry you had more to do with the fact that one weekend in Vegas with you, would never have been enough."

My breath hitches at his words. He drives them farther when he places a hand against my cheek and slides his thumb along my lower lip.

"Really?"

He nods. "Among other things, but that has to be number one."

I lean more into his touch, closing my eyes, loving the way his hand feels against me. "What are the other things?"

"In those few days, you made me want to finally tell my father I was done with this life."

That statement has my eyes springing open.

"What?"

Leo doesn't answer, he just continues to move his thumb along my lip, looking down at me with earnest eyes.

"You thought about walking away from this life? From your father?"

Would it be possible for him?

He nods. "It's been something that I've thought about for probably half my life. Getting out of this lifestyle. Going out into the world and being able to live a normal life. I made a deal with my father when I was eighteen, I will hold the heritage that I was raised in with honor. Everything else can go to fuck. I would go through the motions of the things that were expected of me, but once the time came, I would walk. As time went on and I got older, the possibility of living a normal life got smaller and smaller. I became a different person; I essentially became a younger version of my father." He drops his hand from my face, his face contorting into one of disgust. "I essentially became the person that at times I hate more than I hate myself."

"You hate your father." It wasn't a question, but a statement.

"Wouldn't you? If your parents, the people who were supposed to mold you into something great, made you into a killer? A drug dealer? All I ever wanted was to live a normal life, one where everything I did didn't bring the FBI or the DEA to my front door. One where I can use my real name and not have people cringe when they hear who I'm related to. One where I don't have to hide."

I can feel the pain in his words as he goes on. I can feel it deep inside of me. A part of me wants to close the distance between us and wrap my arms around his waist tightly.

"Is that what you felt in Vegas? The normalcy?"

The Leo I met in Vegas versus the one that is standing in front of me right now are two completely different people. It's as if he changed the second, he left the hotel room that last morning.

After a few seconds, Leo nods. "I was able to be someone completely different when we were in Vegas. And when it was just the two of us, I could drop the mask and actually be me. You gave me that normalcy that I was craving. You made me see that there was life outside of the cartel and I could leave it, even if it was for just a small amount of time."

This time I don't think about not going to him and wrapping my arms around him, I do it and after a few seconds of hesitation, he wraps me up tightly.

"Maybe one day you will be able to live a normal life," I say against his chest.

His arms tighten around me even more. "That will only happen on one or two occasions."

"And what would be those occasions?" Do I want to know the answer?

"Either my father dies." He takes a long pause and tightens his arms in the process.

"Or I do."

22

THERE IS ONLY one way out of this life, and that is with death.

Sure, serving time in prison can be seen as a way to escape the cartel. It's not, because you either die behind bars or you get released and get back to the same life and end up dying on the battlefield. There is no way to escape death with the cartel.

No matter who you are.

I knew from a very young age that the only way that I would be able to leave my father's choice of life would be in a casket. Whether it was me in it or him, it would always end with a casket.

If it makes me a bad son for wishing my father goes first, then so be it. Then I will be free of him, free of this cartel, free of this life and maybe then I wouldn't be afraid to have a wife in this world.

Maybe then I wouldn't be trying to convince my

current wife into a divorce, one that I know she doesn't want. Which by the way blows my mind.

It's been two weeks since the conversation Serena and I had in my study.

Two weeks since I told her some of my darkest secrets, and two weeks since I fucking agreed to let her go back to work.

To say that the thought of tying her to the bed and locking the door didn't cross my mind is the understatement of the fucking decade. I don't know what it is about this woman, but everything about her makes me want to throw all my shit through the window.

It's because you are falling for her.

As much as I would like to deny it, there is a high percent chance that my subconscious is right. I might actually be falling for the drunk brunette beauty I married in Vegas.

And I'm falling hard given just how much of a pussy I have become in the last few weeks alone.

I'll give right now for example. I'm currently sitting in the parking lot of her school waiting for her day to end.

I'm a sad little puppy and she's the one holding the bone.

This has been our routine for the past two weeks. We leave San Pedro in the morning, making it to Austin half an hour before Serena starts work. While she works, I head to one of the warehouses making sure that all our shipments are in order and all the men that work for me are doing what they are supposed to.

And on top of that, I am still trying to find the bastard that is after Serena.

In the nearly four weeks since the attempted kidnapping and the shoot out, I haven't been able to find a single clue as to who could be after her. I've heard ramblings that I was married or at the very least engaged, but I haven't heard anything revealing Serena's identity.

Nada.

I even asked my father for help and yet I still can't come up with a single thing.

It's frustrating as fuck.

So, every day after I'm done with my duties, I make my way back to the school before the day ends.

Like clockwork the bell rings, and the herds of children come running out. And also like clockwork, I see the beautiful brunette follow the children with a bright smile on her face.

She looks in her element, free and happy and absolutely stunning. This is the side of Serena that I wish I could see more often.

Just seeing her like this makes all the bullshit I get daily go away. It's like she's a little light to this vicious life that I live, and I never want to turn it off.

I continue to watch this woman that is somehow my wife as all the kids leave one by one. When there are no more kids running loose outside, she heads back into the building, which is my cue to follow.

Even though I have a team of six armed men watching the school at all times, I'm always the one to collect Serena and walk her to the car.

I knock on her classroom door to announce my presence and when she looks up, she gives me a bright smile.

One I don't deserve.

Especially not after what she has seen me do.

"You're right on time," she says to me as she stuffs her laptop into her bag.

"Have a good day?" I don't approach her, I stay rooted right by the door. Not wanting to do something stupid like kiss her and devour her on her desk.

Serena nods. "Yeah, it was fun. The kids are getting the hang of things so quickly, it makes me so happy." She does a little dance that brightens her smile some more.

"That's good." What else do I say? I'm so out of my element here.

Placing a hand on her lower back, I guide her out of the building and to the car.

Is it dangerous for me to be doing this?

Abso-fucking-lutely.

Am I going to stop doing it?

Fuck no. Not as long as this woman is my wife, because that's what she is. My wife.

"Do you want kids?" That is not a question that I was expecting as I close the car door behind us after getting in.

Pretty sure if I was drinking something it would have been all over Arturo's head.

"Um." I scratch the back of my head, trying to come up with an answer.

Do I?

"Sorry, it's just that you look a little awkward whenever you come to pick me up. I thought that I would ask if you ever saw kids being a part of your life." She gives me a sheepish smile before shaking her head. "You know what? Forget it."

I lean over and take her hand in mine. "I never really thought about it."

It's the truth, I haven't. Why would I bring a kid into this world?

"You haven't?" Her hazel eyes turn to me in wonder.

I shrug. "Not really, I know having kids is always a possibility, but it's not really a world I would like to bring one into. At least not right now."

Serena seems to accept my response because she nods and drops the subject for the rest of the trip to the airport.

It's not until we're in the air that Serena finally breaks the silence.

"I think that you'd make a good father." Again, she takes me by surprise, and I have no idea how to respond.

So I don't.

Is she right?

Would I make a good father?

It's not like I'm surrounded by men that give me the aspiration to become a good father. Fuck, even my own father scared me with how he treated me as a child that I can't help but wonder if I'd turn out the same.

God forbid I have a son one day. Will I treat him like my father treated me? Will I make him a killer like the one I was made into?

What if instead of a son, I have a daughter? What happens then? Will I marry her off, like my father is doing to my sister, just for money and power?

Also, who's supposed to help me make these children?

Is it Serena in this scenario?

God, these are not questions that I'm ready to answer. I have enough to deal with, there is no need to add hypothetical children into the mix.

The rest of the flight to San Pedro is silent, which has been normal for us ever since the shoot-out at the warehouse. We don't really spend these flights talking each other's ears off. It's like we are just going through the motions as two complete strangers, that's it.

We don't even sleep in the same bed, for crying out loud. She sleeps in my bed and I sleep in the bedroom next door.

We are complete strangers that are married. That's what it is.

Once we land, we head straight to the estate. Maybe once we are in our quarters, we can have a conversation or something instead of falling into the same routine of ignoring each other until the morning.

I'm actually about to suggest having dinner and maybe watching a movie together when I hear my name being called.

"Leonardo."

My father's voice rings through the courtyard and by the tone of it, I know I can't ignore him.

I look over to him and he gives me a hard glare before he retreats back inside. I guess I'm supposed to follow.

"I'll meet you in a little bit, okay?" I direct Serena to the outside path to the south wing.

She nods before leaning up and placing a kiss on my

cheek, yet again taking me by surprise. "I'll see you at dinner."

I watch as she turns and walks down the path and once she is out of my sight, with a security guard following her of course, I head to meet with my father.

Given that it's a weekday, I find him getting settled in his study instead of the patio. I knock on the door, and wait for him to invite me in.

Even as his son, I have to wait to be invited in.

Once I have the okay, I walk in and take a seat in one of the chairs I was in all those weeks ago when I came back from Vegas.

"How is everything going with the distribution with Chambers?"

I nod, bringing my leg up to rest against my other knee. "Good. We just sent out the third shipment and the payments are schedule to be received on time. He wants to meet in a few weeks to see if we can up the quantity."

There was a moment that I thought that the Vegas deal with Chambers was going to get fucked up. Thankfully everything has been going according to my plan, not fucking Emilio's. And hopefully, in a few weeks, we will be able to expand.

Ronaldo nods. "Good. When the time comes, take care of it." I nod. He knows I will. "Have you found anything out on the other front?"

The other front.

That's what he's calling the situation with someone being after Serena, a front.

My father couldn't care less about her. If it was one of

his daughters, he would have turned every inch of this planet over. Or maybe he wouldn't. You never know with the king; power is more important than family.

I stiffen up. "Nothing. I can't find anything on the men or who might have hired them. It's as if they came out of nowhere."

I can't help but wonder if the man lied to see if I would spare him his life. If I can't find anything then, there is no way to tell if he was telling the truth or not.

Whatever the case may be, I won't stop until I find out exactly what is going on and Serena is safe.

"You think it was one of our own that called the hit?" I look at my father with a surprised expression.

He is looking at me like he actually cares about the situation.

It's one thing for me to think it was one of our men, it's another for my father to voice it.

"It was a thought, but I couldn't come up with anyone that would have ordered a hit without one of us finding out." *Unless it was you that ordered it*, I don't voice.

He nods. "Work harder on finding out. Whoever it is, is putting not only that *gringa* of yours in danger, but they are also putting Isabella and Camila in the middle. I won't let anyone harm them if I have a say."

I hold in a snort at his show of caring. "I'll make a few calls to see what I can find."

Calling Elliot Lane might be a good idea.

"Anything else you needed from me?" We could have had this conversation outside.

"I need you to coordinate with your sisters. We are

having a celebration and I need you to meet with them so that they can plan it." He says, something in his eyes telling me to tread carefully with my next words

"And what celebration would that be?" I raise an eyebrow.

"Your wedding of course. No son of mine is going to get married in *pinche* Las Vegas. You will have a traditional wedding here, at the estate"

For fuck's sake.

"Serena and I aren't going to stay married. There's no need for a *celebration*." I spit out the words like it has a sour taste on my tongue.

"Then I guess you have from now until the wedding to find another bride then because I will not have you embarrassing this family any more than you already have."

With one final look at me, my father stands up from his chair and walks out of the room.

Leaving me to contemplate what just happened.

My father's reasoning for this celebration, as he is calling it, is flawed. I know it is.

There has to be something deeper as to why he wants us to do this.

I can't pinpoint what that something is just yet.

I guess I will be adding my father's mind games to everything else I have to do.

My top priority right now though is keeping Serena alive.

23

AFTER LEAVING my father's study, I should be heading to Serena and tell her about our "celebration" that my father wants to plan.

Instead, I hold off on finding her and pull out my phone to make a call.

A call to Chicago.

"I hear congratulations are in order." Elliot's cocky tone comes through the line, and I can't help but feel more frustrated.

"And how did you hear about that?" We don't run in the same social circle and I sure as hell didn't tell him.

"I have my ways. Nothing that happens in Vegas, actually stays there."

I'm not even going to question those ways.

"Yeah, that's why I'm calling." I pinch the bridge of my nose, trying to calm myself down.

"What can I help you with, kind sir?" This cheeky motherfucker.

"I need you to find out who leaked the news about my marriage and who put a hit on Serena's head." If I can't get the information, Eli sure as hell can. He has a lot more power than I do and a lot more technology on his side.

"I'm guessing that Serena is the blushing bride, but I have a question. Why do you think that I have the ability to find out anything that has to do with the cartel and who is after your wife?"

I let out a frustrated sigh. "Because don't you have a brother that is like ten years old or something that knows his way through the dark web?"

Like I said the Lane family is a powerful family and it's not just Elliot and his uncle, it's his siblings too.

"He's sixteen, that cocky little shit," He takes after his brother then. "And why should I bring my brother into this?"

"Because you're my friend and you know I would do the same for you if asked."

And I would.

After a long minute, a sigh comes through from the other line.

"I'll give him a call. He's in Texas right now actually, at school. I'll let him know what is going on and send him your info. I just can't guarantee that he will find anything." As he says the words, I hear a different tone in his voice. He sounds like a completely different man than who was speaking a few minutes ago.

I nod even though he can't see it. "As long as he tries."

It wouldn't hurt, right? To at least try to figure out who

is after Serena. Maybe he will even find out what the DEA has on us.

"I'll get a hold of him and have him get in contact." With that the line goes dead. I pocket my phone and head off to find Serena.

And after I find Serena, I have to go and find my sisters. This should be fun.

Hopefully Isabella's claws stay in this time.

To say that Isabella and Serena don't get along is an understatement. From what I know, they have only had one interaction and that was when I introduced them to each other. Other than that, the whole time that Serena has been here, the only one that interacts with her is Camila. She comes to my side of the estate every few days and has dinner with us. But she's nineteen, she likes every person she interacts with.

I head to the study thinking that she might be there working but I find it empty. I'm about to call her name when I hear her talking in my bedroom.

"I don't know, hopefully soon?" she says and when I approach the door, I see that she's talking on the phone.

"I know Aria, I miss you too, but I doubt Leo is going to let me out of his sight if he thinks there is a threat out there."

She's right, I wouldn't.

"Maybe you can come here on a weekend you don't have to work, and we can have a movie night and just hang out." She sounds so happy at the prospect of possibly seeing her friend. Makes me realize that maybe I was wrong bringing her here and taking her away from everything she knows.

"Yeah, I'll talk to Leo. I'm sure it will be fine." I can hear the smile in her voice.

I knock on the door and Serena jumps at the sound, giving me a smile when she sees that it's me.

"Aria, I have to go but I'll see you tomorrow at lunch." There's a pause and her smile grows even more. "I love you too."

"You're meeting up for lunch tomorrow?" I ask as soon as she hangs up the phone.

She nods. "Aria is coming by the school to have lunch, so you don't have to worry. I won't be leaving campus until you pick me up." She gives me an eye roll but her lips twitch fighting a smile.

I should lay her across my knee for being so cheeky. I just give her a nod, trying my hardest to keep my dick in my pants.

"Everything okay with your dad?" Interesting how one simple word can change the feel of the conversation.

Dad.

Ronaldo has never been *dad*.

"Yeah, he just wanted to touch base on a few things." Do I tell her about the *celebration* he wants to throw? Might as well. "And the reception slash wedding he wants to have here at the estate."

Serena's eyes get a cloud of confusion over them. "A wedding? A wedding for who?"

"A wedding for us."

Now instead of confusion, her eyes go wide and look like they might pop out of her head.

"Are you serious?"

I nod. "He has it in his head that we need a proper traditional wedding, one that doesn't embarrass him. His words, not mine."

Her mouth pops open, and then she closes it to only have it open again. "But what if this doesn't work out?"

What if I ask for a divorce? I know the real question she wants to ask.

If I'm being honest with myself, I'm very surprised that she hasn't asked for one already. Especially when I shot three men in cold blood right in front of her.

Instead of staying where I am, I head over to her, placing both my hands on her face, tilting it up so I can look into her eyes. Her beautiful hazel eyes.

"We don't have to go through anything we don't want to. We can placate my father and go through the motions and if at the end of it you want no part of it, we call it. That's it. The man cannot and will not force us into something that we don't want."

I won't force her to stay with me, not even with how badly my body craves hers. Staying married to me has to be her decision and hers alone. My father can't throw a wedding at us and expect us to just slap a smile on our faces and go through with it.

Serena looks up at me with doe eyes and pouty lips.

We haven't been this close in weeks and my body is having an instant reaction. I slide my thumb along her cheekbone and just gaze into her eyes.

In another lifetime, maybe we would have been excited about a wedding.

Maybe in that same lifetime I wouldn't have been afraid to fall for this woman and have the courage to give her everything she wanted.

The marriage.

The hot as sin fucks.

The children.

All of it.

But we live in this fucked up world and none of that is possible.

That doesn't stop me from leaning in and placing my lips to hers, though.

It doesn't stop me from sliding my tongue along her bottom lip and asking for entry.

It doesn't stop me from letting my hands travel down from her face to her ass, gripping her tight and lifting her from the ground.

The second her legs wrap around my waist, I let out a primal growl and turn us, slamming her back to the wall.

Serena lets out a moan when I grind myself against her core.

I take her lower lip between my teeth, before moving my lips down to her jaw and settling on her neck.

"I almost forgot just how good you feel, *princesa*." I tell her before I run my tongue on the length of her neck.

"I've missed you calling me *princesa*," she pants out, her words making my cock harder.

Since the shoot-out, I haven't called Serena *princesa*, for the sole reason that it seemed too intimate. It seemed like it was too much.

In my head, there was no reason to call her that because she was going to leave me soon and take the name with her. So, I stopped for my own sanity.

"Mm what else have you missed?" I thrust into her covered core, wishing she was wearing a skirt instead of pants for easier access.

"Your cock," she moans, making me thrust into her again. "It's been so long."

Since Vegas.

I haven't been inside of her since Vegas.

How the everlasting fuck I went that long without being inside of her is beyond me.

Restraint. It has been all about restraint.

Well restraint just went out the window.

"Let's change that shall we? Because my cock has certainly missed you."

Detaching my lips from her neck, I move us over to the bed, where I throw her like a rag doll in the middle of it.

With her eyes on me, I work at her black dress pants, wasting only a second in pulling them off and throwing them on the ground. Then off come her panties that barely cover anything and then I make my way to her shirt. Pulling it open, scattering the buttons everywhere.

Her giggle fills the room as I do it.

"Such a perfect set of tits," I say when her bra is visible. Lace and see-through and not going to last very long.

My theory is correct when I dig my fingers into the

material and rip it off her. I guess I will add this to the other pieces of clothing I already owe her.

I ravish her chest as soon as it is bare and asking for attention. Digging my fingers into the delicate flesh, marking them as mine.

"This is going to be fast and hard, *princesa*. I will make it up to you, I promise." I say against her skin, wrapping my mouth around her perky nipple, sucking on it hard.

"Leonardo, please." Fuck, I love it when she says my name like that.

Pulling away from her, I get undressed as fast as I possibly can, my cock hitting my stomach when it springs free.

Serena licks her lips at the sight, and I watch as one of her hands travels down her body until it's rubbing at her pussy.

"What do you want, baby?" I pull at my cock, my mouth salivating at the thought of tasting her, of sliding into her tight, hot pussy.

"Fuck me."

With a growl forming in my throat, I climb onto the bed, situating myself between her legs. I slap my dick against her a few times, sliding it against her wet folds, letting her think it's going to be nice and sweet.

Without any warning, I slam into her. Her moans and cries of pleasure fill the room.

We both need this, we both need the release, so I continue to thrust into her over and over again until I feel her tighten around me.

"You ready to come, *princesa*? Are you ready to cover

my cock with all of your cum and milk it until it's fucking dry?" I lean forward, taking one of her tits in my mouth.

"Yes," She moans, arching her body even more, filling my mouth and my hand perfectly.

"You fit perfectly in my hands. It's as if you were made for me. Maybe you were. Maybe you were made for me and you were being punished with small dicked assholes until you crossed my path."

"Yes!"

"This pretty pussy of yours Serena, is mine. All fucking mine." I bite down on her nipple and tighten my grip on her other breast. If it wasn't bruised before, it sure as hell would be now.

And with my mark.

"Yours. I'm yours." Her back arches even more as her core tightens around me, milking me for all that I have.

"Come, Serena. Come," I say against her lips and within seconds she is exploding around me.

Not giving her any time to breathe, I slide out of her, flip her onto her stomach and slam back into her.

I grip her hips and watch her ass move as she takes every single inch of me. Hearing her moans and feeling her body in my hands is enough for me to reach my own release.

With one last hard thrust, I slam into her and release everything that I have in me into her body.

Feeling spent, I fall to her side making sure I don't crush her and bring her close to me.

We lie there in silence, her head on my chest and my

arm around her shoulders, just trying to control our breathing.

That is until there is a loud knock on the door.

Serena shoots up, her eyes automatically going to the wooden door, trying to figure out who it might be.

"Were you expecting someone?"

It's an honest question, since she's been here, we don't really get many visitors.

I sit up, shaking my head. "No, but I can guess who it is."

I start getting dressed as does Serena and she's pulling one of my shirts over her head when another knock rings.

"Who?" Serena asks when we are both situated.

"My sisters. They're here to plan our wedding."

24

SERENA

NEVER IN MY life have I been so happy that I got married in Vegas. Planning a wedding, one that isn't necessary I might add, is stressful.

Very, very stressful.

And it's not the big things that are stressful, no it's the tiny things. It's the minuscule things that make you want to pull your hair out.

I have so much more respect for wedding planners now more than ever before.

I would rather do something completely different than doing anything wedding related right now. Like maybe riding my husband for example, that would be more fun than talking about flowers.

"Are you even listening?" Isabella yells, taking me out of my would-be sex fantasy about my husband.

AKA her brother, oops.

"Sorry, it's just that all this feels a little unnecessary," I tell her.

For the past three days, when I've gotten to the estate from school, I've met with Isabella and Camila to put together Leo and I's wedding. At his father's insistence of course.

My evenings have been filled with choosing tablecloths and colors and even cutlery. Everything that you can think of for a wedding, we have covered it.

Today it's flowers. So many flowers.

I wish Aria was here with me, she would be making this meeting a lot more fun, and I'm sure she would have a field day with Isabella.

"Oh, you're right, this wedding is completely unnecessary, but at least you had a choice as to who you wanted to marry. So, pull up your big girl *chonis* and suck it up and pick a damn flower already."

Isabella's nostrils are flaring and if I didn't know any better, I would say that she was getting ready to slap me across the face.

She's pissed and part of it might be at me for taking her time with this, another part might be on someone else. But who?

"What do you mean, I had a choice? You have a choice too." I give her a confused look. Her expression goes from pissed off to one that I can't really pinpoint.

I look over to Camila for answers, but she just shakes her head, making my gaze land back on her sister.

"Isabella, you have a choice, don't you?" Is that why she is so hostile toward me? Because I got to choose who to marry, and she doesn't?

Isabella squares her shoulders and composes herself to

the point that she looks unbothered by everything around us.

"It doesn't matter. Let's just pick a flower so we can get this over with and give you the perfect wedding you don't want." There is a bite to her words, and instead of just picking a flower, it makes me want to know more.

"No." I sound like a petulant child but if this is the only way for her to tell me what she meant, then so be it.

"What do you mean 'no'? I'm taking time out of my day to help you, and you're telling me 'No'? You're such an entitled bitch, I'm out of here." Isabella pushes her chair back, and with anger in her eyes she starts to walk away.

I reach out and grab her by the elbow, which in retrospect was a bad idea because I get a snarl when my hand touches her.

"I'm not saying no to you helping me, I'm grateful that you're here. I'm saying no because I'm not going to pick a flower until you tell me why you think you don't have a choice." Leo mentioned something about choosing a wife a few weeks back, but I brushed it off as the heat of the moment. Now I really want to know.

"It's not that I think that I don't have a choice. I fucking *know* I don't have a choice. You got to marry a complete stranger in Vegas because you wanted to, I have to marry a complete stranger because my father is forcing me to! I don't have a choice who I marry, because my father already chose him and in a few months' time, I will be married to him."

There are tears running down her face, tears of anger

and sadness and I try my hardest to stay seated and not wrap my arms around her.

Holy shit.

Ronaldo arranged a marriage for Isabella? How can someone do that? I understand that sometimes an arranged marriage is a part of someone's culture, but if they don't want it? Shouldn't the parent put that into consideration and put a stop to it?

I don't have to know Isabella all that well to know that she hates the situation that she is in. Not only does she hate it, but she's in pain over it. Serious pain.

"I'm sorry." I say, my voice so low that I have no idea how she heard it.

She scoffs. "Sorry for what? Making me cry?" She wipes at her tears, rolling her eyes in the process.

"No, I'm sorry that you're going through this. You shouldn't have to marry someone you don't know and don't want to marry; let alone someone you don't love."

My heart hurts for her.

"Did you love my brother?" She throws the question at me, taking me by surprise. Before I can answer she continues. "Better yet, do you love my brother now?"

Do I love Leo?

During our time together in Vegas, I was intrigued by the man. I think I loved the feeling he gave me when we were together during that short period of time. It made me feel wanted and worthy of everything in the world, something that no man has ever shown me before. I felt safe with him and in a way, complete, and because of that, I didn't want our time together to end. That's why we got married, I think, because even when drunk and complete strangers, we felt whole when the other was around.

Ever since then, the more and more time we have spent together, the more I've gotten to know him and see who he was, captivated me even more. We don't know everything about each other, but those types of things take time.

Yes, he describes himself as a killer and a criminal and he is. He is those things, but that isn't who he is at his core. Deep inside, Leonardo Morales is a caring, loving, intellectual person that would kill for those he loves and cares for.

He did it for me and I know he would do it all over again if needed. Leo would do it for any woman sitting in this room right now.

And if he would let me, I would stand by his side through all of it. No matter how many people he has killed, or how many pounds of drugs he has moved, I would be by his side.

Whoa.

Where did that come from? Never in my whole life have I ever thought it would be okay to align myself with the cartel, but now I am. I would align myself with Leo in a heartbeat and never regret a single thing.

Is that love?

"I think at first, it was infatuation, but even in the short amount of time together, it felt bigger than that. It felt as if I was supposed to meet your brother and he was supposed to be a part of my life. I can't really explain it but it felt a lot more than lust, but it wasn't love." She asked, might as well give her the God honest truth. I don't look at either of them as I speak, I just let my words flow. "Now I like the person that I'm getting to know. I like seeing him in his element and seeing how protective he is. How even when we haven't known each other for very long, he would drop everything and come when I needed him to. Do I love your brother? I don't know, but I have a feeling that the more time I spend with him, the more I see the type of person he is, that maybe will turn into a yes. It's just a matter of time for that to happen. No matter how many times he tells me to leave him, that this life isn't for me, and I tell him no, I still care deeply about him, and I won't give him up very easily."

The room is silent as I finish speaking. I realize that I zoned out somewhere and I'm staring at the wall in front of me. Hopefully what I was trying to say made some sense because honestly, I don't remember saying most of it.

I shake the daze out of my mind and turn to look at Isabella and Camila, both looking at me like I have two heads.

"What?" Oh my god, did I say something stupid?

"I wanted to hate you so much, but then you go and let out your internal monologue and I think I might actually like you now." Isabella groans before slamming her head against the small table in front of us.

"Ignore the drama queen over there. Did you really tell my brother no to leaving him?" Camila smiles at me like she's excited about the possibility of me telling her brother no.

"Yes?" I answer more like a question than anything.

"And he took it? He just let you tell him no and he

didn't fight you on it?" Camila slaps her hands against the table, not believing me.

I nod, not knowing what to say. Why is she so excited?

The thumping of Isabella's head against the table takes my attention away from her sister, and I focus on her.

"Why do you keep saying shit that is making me like you?" Thump. "Please." Thump. "Stop." Thump.

"Okay, are you two going to tell me why you are reacting like this? I don't know what scares me more, Isabella when she's angry or when she's telling me she likes me."

But of course, she is starting to like me, I'm a freaking peach to be around.

"Because Leo always gets what he wants. He doesn't know what the word no means. Well, when it comes to us." Camila waves between the two of them.

I believe that. I'm pretty sure that I've seen that side of Leo more than once. He's a scary man when he's like that, but it's not something I'm afraid of. Leo is just a big ass teddy bear.

Well, in front of me at least.

"Okay, enough of this makes-us–like-you shit. Pick a flower, so we can move on and I can go back to thinking that you're a gold-digging bitch."

Isabella pushes herself up and picks up one of the flower catalogs from the middle of the table.

This conversation is taking so many turns it's giving me whiplash.

"Okay, pick one." Isabella places the catalog in front of me, opened to a page full of beautiful flowers.

As a little girl, I never really thought about how my wedding would look like. Nothing was more than a thought. I think the more persistent one was that my father wasn't going to walk me down the aisle because he would be God knows where.

I never thought about the flowers.

"These." I point to some colorful ones that I've seen not only around the estate but around San Pedro whenever we drive to and from the airport.

Marigolds.

Bright oranges and reds fill the page and just by a small picture I know that they would make any white flower pop.

"You want *flor de muertos* at your wedding?" Isabella asks in disbelief.

"They're called the flower of the dead?" I feel my eyebrows raise at the name.

Isabella nods. "The official name is marigolds like you might know them, but here in Mexico they are known as the flower of the dead. Mostly because they are the flowers that are used to make altars during the day of the dead celebration."

"What do they symbolize?" Marigolds have always been something that has stood out to me, more so since spending more time here in San Pedro.

"They can symbolize a lot of things, but mainly legend has it that the vibrant colors are supposed to lure the spirits or souls of the deceased back to the land of the living," Camila answers, getting a nod from her sister.

"Our mother used to love them. That's why they are planted all over the estate. Her favorite time of year was during summer when they would bloom. She said it was like the estate was coming to life." There is a sadness to Isabella's voice and hearing it is enough to make up my mind.

"Do you think that these would go well with white roses? We can use the different colors and with the white, they would pop." I start to point to different white flowers in the catalog, voicing my idea.

If Isabella is this affected just by from talking about a flower, then I think picking the marigolds as a part of our wedding flowers would mean a lot to Leo as well.

"I think that would look very nice." Isabella gives me a smile, an actual smile, all while Camila silently agrees with her.

"Then we have flowers then." I smile back at them, finally glad that we had this meeting today.

It feels that even though we spent the majority of time arguing, we made progress in our non-relationship.

We continue to talk about different aspects of the wedding, this time with a lot less tension.

One big thing that we discuss is the wedding date. Given that the marigolds are the most vibrant during June to November, we have only a short period of time, since it's September, to get this done.

After agreeing to talk to Leo about the date, the girls start packing up all of their things to head out. Camila leaves with a smile and before Isabella leaves, I place my hand on her shoulder, stopping her.

"It's not my place, but there's someone, isn't there?

Someone you wish your father would have chosen for you to marry?"

I got the feeling that there might be when she was talking about love earlier when I saw all her sadness rolling across her face.

She looks at me in silence for a few seconds before she closes her eyes and nods.

Isabella is in love with someone and is set to marry another man.

I give her shoulder a reassuring squeeze. "It will work out. I don't know how, and I don't know when, but it will work out. You will one day find yourself with the man that you love."

"You have no possible way of knowing that." She shakes her head as if what I said was absurd.

"If that man is anything like your brother, then I know for a fact that it will happen."

It may be ill-fated, but I have to have hope that Isabella will be able to live the life she wants to live with who she loves.

"And what type of man is my brother?"

"The type of man that will act like a villain to everyone else but a prince for you and only you. Saving you from every dragon that need be."

25

I FEEL something warm against me.

Reaching for it, I feel that whatever is against me is soft and when I run my hand up and down, I feel curves.

Serena.

Last night, I spent many hours in my study, trying to find any lead that I possibly could. Leads to who sent the men that went after Serena and anything I could find on the men that talked to the feds.

In the last couple of months, things have been quiet on that front, but it being quiet could mean a lot of bad things coming our way.

When I came to bed, Serena was already asleep and the second that I laid down, she got comfortable in my arms.

This has been the routine since we finally had sex again a few days ago. Usually, our evenings are filled with getting home from Austin and sex marathons then I go to work for a few hours before coming to bed.

I like it more than I should, but I would like it more if I could actually spend time with my wife.

Yes, I said it.

I, Leonardo Morales, the second most dangerous man in all of Mexico, have become so pussy-whipped that he would rather spend time with his wife.

Never did I think that day would come.

I bring my wife closer to me and bury my face against her neck, breathing in her scent.

"Good morning." Her voice is raspy and full of sleep and hearing it makes my morning wood harder than it already was.

"Good morning, *princesa*." I lick the length of her neck and she lets out a sweet moan that is like music to my ears.

"I love it when you call me that." She arches her back, needing more attention.

"Because that's what you are. A *princesa*." I place a kiss on her pulse before moving farther down her body. "*Mi princesa*."

Mi reina.

Because that's what she is. My queen, no matter what I do to push her away. No matter how much I want her to sign those papers. Serena Davidson is mine and mine alone.

"Leo," she breathes out as I place an open mouth kiss on her covered mound.

I've learned that Serena likes to sleep in T-shirts and panties. Preferably my T-shirts.

Never understood why men got all giddy with their women wearing their clothes. Now I get it. It's like this animalistic feeling deep inside that makes you want to pound your chest and have the glory of her claiming that she is yours.

I fucking love it.

Pushing the T-shirt up, enough to reveal her panties, I kiss through the lacy fabric, poking my tongue through the holes of the material.

I want to savor her because who knows how much time I have left with her.

"Leo," Serena says my name again in that breathy tone that makes my dick hard, her hand going to my hair, asking for more.

"What do you want, baby?" I continue to kiss her through the lace, but now adding the motion of my fingers moving up and down her slit.

"For you to eat my pussy." She pulls my face closer to her and I can't help but grin at her for what she asks of me.

To the dickhead that told this woman that she was bad in bed, you have no fucking idea how to please a woman.

Serena Davidson is a sex vixen and should get everything that she wants.

"Fucking gladly." I reposition myself so that her legs are lying on my shoulders, and I place my mouth on her again, still not removing the fabric.

"Oh my god." Her hips buck as the friction of the panties meets her bare pussy, and combined with my mouth, it must feel like a good sensation.

I continue to rub at her folds as I bite down on her clit causing her to let out a moan.

Not wanting to torture her anymore, I pull her panties

off and get re-situated between her thighs and do what she asked me to. Eat her pussy.

And what a delicious pussy it is.

Inserting two fingers into her, I take my time savoring every single inch of her cunt. Sucking, nibbling, everything and anything that will get her closer to the edge.

"Come on my face, baby. Cover me with everything that you have." My plea is met with another moan and tightening around my fingers.

I fucking love that this woman is a moaner. There's something about it that gets me going.

To push her where I want her to be, I slide my pinky down to her crack and to her puckered hole. Slowly, I slide my finger into her, instantly feeling her tighten even more.

"Fuck. Oh, fuck." With no other warning, she pulls my hair, holding me to her but also at the same time trying to push me away, and she explodes.

Her sweet and tangy taste fills my mouth and I lick up every single drop that I can as she comes down.

"Holy shit." She's out of breath when I finally pull away from her, placing one last kiss on her mound before dragging my body up until I reach her lips.

Serena doesn't give a shit if I'm giving her a taste of her pussy, she takes everything that my mouth has to give her. Every lip bite, every tongue suck, everything.

"Get in the shower. You're going to suck my cock and then get ready for work."

She lets out a giggle when I slap her ass as she gets out of bed. Soon the water is running, and Serena is on her knees while I fuck her mouth.

I finish faster than I intended to, since this woman has the mouth of a goddess, and we start cleaning up soon after.

Within an hour of me eating her pussy beyond no return, we are on the jet to Austin to start off our day. The whole plane ride and the drive to her school, Serena stays at my side, with my arm around her shoulders and her fingers drawing small circles on my slacks.

When we reach the school, I place a chaste kiss on her lips and once she is out of the car, I watch as her hips sway as she walks into the building. We don't pull away until she is out of sight, behind closed doors.

The only thing keeping my sanity is seeing my men parked in the parking lot, keeping watch for anything suspicious.

Once I'm situated at the warehouse, I think I'm having a good day.

That is, until my phone rings with a Chicago number flashing on the screen.

Not many people have my personal number, and given the area code, this must be Elliot's brother.

"Yeah?" I greet whoever is on the other line.

"Am I supposed to greet you as your royal highness or something? Since you're Mexican royalty and all."

Fuck, this kid sounds just as cocky, if not more than, his brother.

"Elliot's brother, I presume?"

"Yes sir, Mr. Morales, sir. Drake Lane at your service." I'm sure if we were in person, he would have saluted me or some shit.

"Do you have something for me, Drake?" Who in their right fucking mind names a kid Drake?

"I do." There is a shift in his tone, as if the kid that was just joking around is gone.

"What is it?"

"So to start, the hit on Serena Davidson," —of course he knows her name—"nothing concrete came up. There has been some speculation about you being married on a few boards but there is no mention of her name or any plans to go after her."

Fuck.

That means...

"My guess is that whoever went after her, is someone in your inner circle. Someone who has seen you with her," Drake finishes my thought process.

Someone that has seen her with me.

That list isn't very long, and I can't count anyone out. Adolfo already betrayed me, who else is on that list?

The only people that I can think of are those that are in and out of the estate on a daily basis.

Not something I want to think of right now.

"And the FBI and DEA?"

"That's where things get tricky. Both agencies are working together to bring down one man and one man only, Ronaldo Morales. The file that they have on him is so thick that it can take someone years to go through. They have him for drug trafficking, human trafficking, any crime against the United States that you can think of, they want to pin on him. I have no idea how they have gone this long without capturing him."

I do.

My father is anything but a stupid man.

Out of everything that he owns, nothing is in his name. When my mother was alive, everything was under her name, nothing of value was under the name Ronaldo Morales. When she died, all the things that she owned went to my sisters. The two individuals that would never be tied to the cartel, unlike me.

The estate, the jet, everything that isn't a warehouse, is under their names.

Another thing that my father wasn't stupid about was that he knew that he had to stay hidden. Never show his face, never do anything suspicious, never give the *federales* any reason to know what he looked like.

Ronaldo Morales hasn't stepped foot onto US soil in decades, because he knew that his actions would come and bite him in the ass if he ever did.

The only way that the FBI or DEA will ever get their hands on my father is if they come knocking on our door. And I highly doubt that they even know where said door is located, but they may have an idea.

"I can ask you the same question regarding your hacker skills," I state, trying to think of something other than what he just told me.

Drake chuckles. "Touché, but when you have a family like mine, you learn to do a few things without the government knowing." What it's like to be a Lane, I will never know.

"Is that all you found out?"

"I got a name. There is one agent that from the looks of

things has a vendetta against your father. He's leading the DEA charge and working very closely with the FBI."

I hold in a chuckle. My father has made a lot of enemies in his lifetime. I'm not even a little surprised that one of them is a federal agent.

"What's the name?"

"Nathaniel Madden."

Fucking hell.

Out of the thousands upon thousands of agents in the DEA, my father had to make enemies with one of the most cold-hearted bastards there is.

"Send me all the information that you were able to find. I'll take care of it from here." I need to do my own research.

"I really shouldn't be asking this, but how exactly are you going to be taking care of a DEA agent?"

I let out a chuckle. "You're right, you shouldn't be asking that. Send me the information."

Without another word, I hang up the call and pocket my phone.

All this shit with the DEA just got a lot more complicated. Before I figure out a plan to find the assholes that are after my wife, I need to have a conversation with my father.

I need to know exactly why DEA Special Agent Nathaniel Madden has a vendetta against him.

And just how deadly it is.

26

SERENA

IT'S DONE.

All the wedding planning is done.

I cannot tell you how happy I am to not look through book after book of wedding themes and decorations anymore.

After choosing the flowers, the date was finally settled, after Leo asked Ronaldo for permission of course.

The third Saturday in November.

It was a day I chose at random that got a few eyebrow raises from Camila and Isabella. When I told Leo the date I had chosen, I got the same reaction from him.

When I asked him if there was anything wrong with that date, he shook his head. He was silent for a few minutes after that until he finally told me the meaning behind the date that I had chosen.

His mother's birthday.

I had randomly chosen his mother's birthday to have the wedding that his father requested.

That's why I had asked Leo to ask his father for permission. I didn't want to overstep and take over a day of remembrance. That day should be about Leo's mother, not about a wedding I don't even want.

I expected Ronaldo to say no, but the man surprised me and said yes. So, I made it my mission to make it a day to honor Rosa Maria Morales. She will be a part of the wedding in one way or another.

Something that made Leo happy, even if he didn't voice it.

Now we have three weeks until the wedding, something that Leo keeps reminding me of. Every day, at least two times a day, he asks me if I am ready to walk away.

There are days where I do hesitate, but my answer is always the same. No.

The moments of hesitation come more from wanting to make him happy and keeping him safe, than it being something I want. If I were to walk away, Leo wouldn't have to worry about me and whoever is after me. He would just be able to be Leo.

But I'm not ready to ask for a divorce yet, and the more time I spend with the man, I don't think I ever will.

I put the idea of even asking for a divorce on the back burner for now. At this moment I have more important things to concentrate on. Like building this altar.

"Is this okay?" I ask Isabella as I place the last flower on the table's edge.

She comes over, of course in all her perfection, and inspects my handiwork.

In the last month or so since we decided on the

flowers for the wedding, our relationship has gotten some-what better. Definitely not the cold shoulder and bitchy attitude that it was before, but I'm still not her favorite person.

Which, hey, I will take.

"It looks good. I think once everything is lit up and the food is in place, it will all look perfect."

I smile at her statement.

Before this year, I only thought of the day of the dead as an extension of Halloween. Growing up in California and then later moving to Texas, I heard of the celebration but never really did any research on it.

There is a lot more to the tradition than kids dressing up as their favorite superheroes. It's a celebration of the lives that have passed and a way of honoring them. It turns out that it's a big event in this part of Mexico. The whole town puts on a celebration.

It may be to honor those that Ronaldo and the cartel have killed but it's a celebration, nonetheless.

About a week ago, Camila came to me and asked if I wanted to take part in putting together the altar for their mother and grandparents. I jumped at the chance.

I wanted to know more about their mother and hear the stories from when she was alive.

No idea why I feel compelled to know about a woman I never met, but I am.

I think it may have to do with the distance that I have with my own mother.

The three siblings talk about theirs like she was the greatest person in the world. When I'm asked about mine, all I say is that she's just a mom. That isn't a good response, but I have nothing much to say.

My parents were a part of my life, but work and travel were more important. I was always a second thought and it showed in their parenting.

I also think that's the reason that I'm so fascinated by Rosa Maria is because I want to know how she died.

It's never mentioned. There aren't any pictures around the estate of her either. It seems odd to me, for a woman that is so loved.

"When will you put out the food?" I ask Isabella.

"On the night of the thirty- first. That way it stays fresh through the second." She gives me a small smile before going back to what she was doing.

For the remainder of the afternoon, we work in silence only saying a few words here and there. She mentions the town festival and how we are expected to attend.

Which makes my ears perk up. "Attend? Like go out into the town square?"

Leo has been extra protective these last few weeks and I have no idea why; he won't tell me. Going into the town square may be a bad idea.

Isabella nods. "It will be safe, and nobody will know who you are. I promise."

Her eyes are filled with sincerity, and I can't help but believe her, so I give her a nod.

"Isabella." I turn at the name being called and I see Santos standing at the entryway of the living room we took over.

"Yes?" She answers without even looking at the man.

"Your father wants to see you," he says, a look of impatience crossing his face.

Isabella doesn't answer him still, she just continues to do what she was doing when he walked in. Santos looks at her for a minute then two, and as more time passes, he gets more agitated.

"Isabella," he says again, in a more authoritative tone than before but yet she still doesn't turn.

Interesting.

In the time that I have been here, I have always seen Isabella give every single person she talks to her full and undivided attention. What makes Santos different?

"Bella!"

Beya? I've heard everyone call her Bella or her full name but never that.

Weirdly enough is at that name that she finally turns to face him, shoulders back, face blank of any expression.

"¿Qué quieres Santiago?" She may look like Santos being here doesn't affect her but the way her voice sounds you would think otherwise.

"Your father wants to see you. Now."

Isabella doesn't move, she just continues to stand there staring at the man in front of her as if he doesn't matter.

But strangely enough, I get the feeling that he does. Santos means a lot more to Isabella than what she wants to let on.

Finally, she nods and walks out of the room with Santos following close behind her.

I should ask Leo about those two.

"*Dime!*" Tell me.

"*No sé nada!*" I don't know anything.

Cries fill the room. Cries of desperation, cries for help. They fill the room, but that doesn't mean that anyone on the other side of the door will hear them.

The place is locked up tight. The only people hearing the screams and cries are the ones within the four walls.

"*Si sabes. Nomas no quieres decir porqué tienes miedo qué te voy a matar.*"

Fear of death always keeps someone from talking, but this fucker should be fearful. He knows something and I'm holding death over his head.

"I don't know anything," he cries, the ties around his wrist pulling slightly as he tries to free himself.

"Yes, you do, and you aren't getting out of the chair until you tell me everything." I crouch down at his level, grabbing him by the hair to make him look at me.

Otro desgraciado.

You would think with me killing Adolfo, one of my most trusted men, these fuckers would have learned to not cross me. I guess I was wrong.

After my conversation with Drake Lane a few weeks ago, I went into a black hole trying to find information.

My first stop was my father.

I asked him question after question about Nathaniel Madden and not one of them was answered. Every time a question left my mouth, he would just shrug and change the subject, even telling me to go back to my whore wife.

After what felt like the fiftieth shrug, I gave up and went on to find the answers on my own.

Countless hours were spent looking through the files that Drake had sent over, and yet I still came up empty on anything that has to do with Madden.

There's no connection. At least not one that I could see right away.

It wasn't until one night around two in the morning when I should have been with my wife, that I finally found a small glimmer of information.

It was a picture.

To Drake it would have had no meaning, nothing that would have stood out to him. Frankly, it didn't stand out to me until I went back to it for the third time. They say that a picture is worth a thousand words and the one I found is worth millions.

A picture of my parents, looking happy and all smiles, standing next to a man. A man that looked a lot like an older Nathaniel Madden, one that could be very much his father.

How I missed that connection the first two times is beyond me.

To anyone else, it would look like a picture of a group of friends enjoying a night out, and that's how I saw it the first couple of times. But the more I looked at the picture, the more I saw.

The money at the edge of the picture.

The cigars in the men's hands.

The smiles.

The camaraderie.

The relaxation.

The individuals in that picture were friends, maybe even more than that. This picture gave out a story but not a complete one.

A lot more questions sprung into my head after my little discovery. I couldn't go to my father, because he wouldn't answer anything. He would just brush it off.

So I decided to go back to what started all of this.

Adolfo.

He was talking to the DEA, most likely Madden, so someone in his close circle had to have come in contact with him. Had to have seen him orchestrating something against the Muertos.

One by one I went through the men that were closest to him. Adolfo might have been one of my main soldiers, but he had men under him doing his biddings when he didn't want to get his hands dirty.

The first two men I went looking for weren't any help. They broke, pointing all the blame at Adolfo and Adolfo only, before they screamed for me to take their life. Which I gladly took for wasting my time.

Now I'm on the third man.

He knows something, I know he does, he's just too afraid to speak.

"Tell me. Tell me what you know, and I will let you walk away." It may be a broken promise, one he knows isn't going to go in his favor. But if it's the only way to get him to talk, so be it.

A whimper leaves his mouth, followed by a shaking breath before he speaks. "I don't know everything."

About fucking time.

"What do you know?" I cross my arms across my chest and lean against the wall, making myself comfortable.

"An agent approached Adolfo at the start of the year. I didn't know the guy was an agent until I saw him the second time and got a glimpse of his badge." Manuel, the fucker tied to the chair in front of me, lets out another shaky breath. It's either from the pain he is in or the fear running through his veins. "I didn't see him much; he was only around a few times and all he and Adolfo did was talk."

Highly unlikely that all they did was talk.

The DEA knows about drug routes and who is set to run certain ones, they were supposed to intercept Adolfo's last run, after all.

They have important information, but I want to know if Madden was holding something over Adolfo's head, or if this really was all for power.

Adolfo was not a stupid man, so if he thought that the only way to get power was to get rid of my father and me, he would do anything. Including becoming an informant.

"Did you ever hear their conversations?"

Adolfo was the type of man who lived and breathed the Muertos. In all the years that Adolfo had been a member of this family, he never gave the indication that he was unhappy being a soldier. Most men are loyal to the cartel until their last breath. Any individual in the cartel already has power and it had to take a seriously sick man to want more.

To want more power and control the whole organization.

Adolfo was one of those men.

Manuel starts breathing heavily. "Adolfo wanted to be in charge, and he thought that if he spoke, that would mean that you and Ronaldo would be put away and he would take over. The DEA wouldn't come looking at the cartel if they trusted him."

I can't help but roll my eyes.

I guess these men don't know that it would be easier to get power by putting a bullet through my skull. It would have saved everyone a lot more trouble.

"What else?" I need him to tell me more, I need him to tell me that if Adolfo mentioned anything about someone else within the cartel working with him.

Manuel shakes his head. "That's all I know. They talked a few times and then Adolfo was dead. That's all."

That only leaves one question then.

"Has the agent approached you?" I don't take my eyes off of him as I ask the question. He doesn't have to speak for me to know the answer. I can see it in the way his body tenses up even more from where he is tied up.

The DEA won't stop once one man is dead. They will find out anything from anyone willing to cooperate.

And Manuel cooperated.

Without any hesitation, I pull the Glock from my waist-band, firing one single shot.

The body in front of me, going limp, just like the body that was sitting in that very position weeks ago.

These fuckers will never learn not to cross me or this family. The body count will only keep rising at this point.

I put the gun back in its place and leave the room, having more pressing things to deal with instead of the dead body of yet another soldier.

Before making my way through the estate, I check myself for any blood splatters or anything that might give Serena something to investigate.

Her seeing blood on me can spook her.

Isn't that what you want?

Is it?

In the last few weeks, Serena and I have spent count-less days and nights together. Our time together has been incredible, and I don't know if I have it in me to give her up.

I will if I have to, but it will have to come from her. She has to make that decision, all because I can't force myself to walk away from her. I don't think I will be able to.

Shaking my head, I inspect my clothing one more time, not seeing any blood, and make my way through the property.

All I want to do is get to my side of the estate, find my wife and get lost in the taste of her pussy on my tongue.

My mouth is watering at the thought, when I feel something, or better yet, someone slam into me.

Looking down, I see Isabella with her head down and I try to steady her as much as I can.

"Whoa there." I place my hands on her shoulders, keeping her upright.

My sister looks up at me with eyes that remind me so much of our mother's. They are red and tears are pulling along the lash line and there is so much sadness coating her face.

"Isabella? What's wrong?" I look her up and down, trying to find if she is hurt or something but there is nothing that I can see.

Isabella sniffles and tries to take a shaky breath before she answers me. "I just got engaged to Emilio."

As soon as she lets out Emilio's name, my sister bursts into tears, a sob filled with pain escapes her throat and she burrows into my chest.

I hold her to me and all I can think of was that I should have tried harder.

I should have tried harder to leave this life and bring my sisters with me.

I should have tried everything in my power to at least get them out of this life, but I didn't.

They shouldn't have to be put in arranged marriages because our father wants to gain more power.

But they are.

There also shouldn't be a body down in the basement with a bullet from my gun.

But there is.

27

SERENA

THERE'S BEEN a change in the atmosphere, and it has nothing to do with a new month starting or the change between fall and winter.

This change is different, it's more with the moods and attitudes than anything physical you can see.

I'll give my husband as an example. In the last couple of weeks, he has been more distant, more inside his head and never fully here. He has even gone back to sleeping in a separate room again and having Santos take me up to Austin.

He's trying his hardest to push me away and I have no idea why.

But he's not the only one that has been acting slightly strange. Santos, Isabella and even Camila have all been acting weird. Santos has resorted to only talking to me in grunts and Isabella has gone back to hating me. Camila still speaks to me and tries to act like nothing's wrong but even in the short time I've known her, I know she's lying.

It's frustrating not knowing what is going on with everyone. I'm at a point where if I don't get an answer, I'm asking Leo to take me back to Austin.

It may be a drastic move, but I don't like not knowing what is going on and being in the dark. If things keep going this way, it may be best for me to distance myself. Married to Leo or not, it may be something that I have to do.

Right now, though, I'm not thinking about how everyone around me is acting, I'm concentrating on not messing up the face paint that Camila spent hours on.

The day of the dead celebration is finally here, and if it weren't for everything going on with everyone around me, I would be more excited.

I look at myself in the mirror and look at the intricate pattern that Camila was able to come up with. All the different colors and lines bring out the sugar skull design making me look like a completely different person.

Camila even went as far as making me a flower crown and dressing me up in a traditional dress that took my breath away when I first saw it.

When I saw the finished product, I had to ask if it was okay for me to wear such traditional and cultural aspects. I didn't want to offend anyone.

After reassuring me a good five times that I was fine, she gave me a bright smile, one that didn't reach her eyes and left the room.

A knock on the door takes my concentration off my reflection and I turn to see who's there.

I had a small smile on my face thinking that it was Leo

who was knocking. I feel the smile disappear when I see who is standing in the doorway.

Ronaldo.

My body goes completely still when he walks into the room without an invitation.

In the time that I have been here at the estate, my interactions with Ronaldo have been limited. Very limited.

Leo has made sure of that.

If I think about it, the last time I was within ten feet of the man, was when we arrived back at the estate one day after Leo picked me up from school.

Now here he is.

"I see Camila already got her artistic hands on you." He looks unimpressed as he walks closer to me.

All I can do is swallow down the knot forming in my throat and nod at him.

"It looks like I have to also worry about one of my daughters, on top of my son, getting attached to you."

Getting attached?

There must be confusion coating my face because Ronaldo lets out a chuckle, one that sounds dark and puts a few inches of fear in me.

He steps even closer and when I take a step back to put space between us, he still closes in.

"Do you really think that I'm going to let you stay here longer than needed? The only reason that you are here is because Leonardo has his head so far up his ass that he doesn't see what I see."

I open my mouth to ask a question but all I'm able to do is feel my jaw tremble and my mouth close again.

Ronaldo steps a few inches closer, his fingers raising, tracing the lines of my face makeup. I feel bile rising up my stomach at the feel of his fingertips on me. Nothing compared to what the touch of his son makes me feel.

"Ask whatever you want to ask, Serena." His eyes are dark and terrifying, and I have to work up the courage to let the words escape my mouth.

"Then why have us plan a wedding?" My voice is barely a whisper, but going by his sadistic smile, Ronaldo heard me.

"Thought it would give Leonardo the realization that he doesn't want to stay married to someone of your background. That maybe he would find someone more *suitable* for this lifestyle."

Suitable.

He means someone who isn't a *gringa* like me.

In the eyes of Ronaldo Morales, the white girl would never be suitable to be married to his son.

Not now, not ever.

The question that I have is, why go through the trouble of telling Leo that he wanted us to get married the traditional way? Why not just kill me and be done with it?

Unless...

"You sent those men, didn't you?" The question just leaves my mouth without a second thought.

It makes sense.

The fact that Leo hasn't been able to find anything about there being a hit on me.

Neither Leo nor Arturo recognized the men.

Someone powerful had to call the hit, why not Ronaldo?

He has the means to do something without anything pointing back to him.

And when his plan to kill me off didn't go the way he wanted, he thought that going the wedding route would work.

He probably thought that as the wedding planning progressed, Leo would get tired of dealing with me, that he would just leave and find someone else. Someone more *suitable*.

A shiver crawls down my spine when he moves his finger down from my face to my neck. He drags small circles with his fingernail before he wraps his hand around my neck, a gasp leaving my mouth.

"I can see why my son is so enamored with you. You are a very smart woman, and beautiful, even I would go for a *gringa* like you."

His grip tightens and I can feel his fingers dig into my skin.

"Ronaldo," I begin, but he starts cutting off my air supply.

"I should just kill you right now, it would make my life easier. But where is the fun in that? I'd rather watch someone else drain all the blood out of your body than do it myself."

I didn't need him to say anything more. As his hand tightens around my neck, I know that Ronaldo was the one that called for my kidnapping. He may not have gone after me himself, but he did hire someone. At least that's what I'm getting from this whole altercation.

"Serena?" I hear my name being called somewhere in the distance.

Leo.

He had gone somewhere earlier today and said he would be back before the festivities started.

His voice sounds too far away, and if Ronaldo tries anything he won't get here in time.

"Break his heart." Ronaldo's voice has me turning my eyes back to him, away from the door that his son is about to walk through. "Leave him. Leave him before he gets killed instead of you. You and I both know that you are not made for this world, that you're not made for him. Leave him now and maybe then I can guarantee that whoever is after you will stop. Or maybe instead of you, they will go after him."

I feel his fingernails going into my skin. There will probably be little crescent moon marks on my neck, marks that nobody will ever know are there because he was strategic with his hand placement.

There is no oxygen moving through my lungs as I stare into dark orbs that are filled with evil.

"Serena?" At the sounds of Leo's voice, this time a lot closer than it was a few seconds ago, Ronaldo finally drops his hand, letting me be able to take in a deep breath.

At the sound of footsteps approaching the entryway, Ronaldo puts a good twenty feet between us. I can feel my throat burning and tears forming in my eyes, but I try to compose myself as best I can before Leo even walks in.

His dark eyes, nothing like his father's, find me right away. I definitely didn't succeed in calming myself all the way because as soon as he lays eyes on me, his facial expression goes from relaxed to one of high alert.

He looks me up and down, trying to figure out what is wrong, but with the makeup, he won't be able to see anything. After looking at me, he scans the room, and he finds his father standing by the door with his arms crossed.

"What is going on?" There is an edginess to Leo's voice. He's on high alert and he has every right to be.

"Nothing," Ronaldo says, giving his son a smile. "I was just walking by when I heard your wife coughing, and I came in to check on her."

I can't believe how effortlessly the lie falls from his lips.

Leo doesn't take his stare off his father as he makes his way over to me. It's not until his hand meets my waist that he finally breaks my trance and looks me over once again.

"Are you okay?" Leo asks, giving my hip a reassuring squeeze before moving his hand up to cup my cheek, not worried at all about the makeup adorning my face.

I nod, giving him a small smile, not being able to speak just yet. If I do my voice will probably break and for sure tell him something is wrong.

Ronaldo leaves the room without saying another word. Both Leo and I turn in the direction of the sound of footsteps, following them out.

"What was he really doing here?" The question leaves Leo's mouth as soon as his father is out of sight.

I look up at my husband, trying to figure out what to say.

What do I tell him?

That his father caught me when no one was around and basically told me that he was the one that ordered a hit on me?

I can't do that.

Not if his life would be at risk if I do.

So I give him another small smile, "He was checking to see if I was okay, then he started complimenting me on the work that Camila did with the face paint."

I hate lying to him but in this case, I have to.

Leo continues to look at me like he doesn't believe a word that just came out of my mouth, but after a few seconds, he nods, accepting it.

"Camila did do an amazing job," he says, running his fingertips along the lines drawn on my face, like his father did earlier. The only difference between Leo's and Ronaldo's touch is that Leo's doesn't repulse me, it makes me lean into it and wanting more.

"Your sister is an artist." That isn't a lie. At nineteen, Camila holds more talent in her hands than I will ever hold in one finger.

She's a true artist.

Leo nods before he leans in and places a kiss on my lips.

"Are you ready to go?" he asks when he pulls back and holds a handout for me to take.

I shouldn't take it.

I keep thinking about what Ronaldo told me a few minutes ago. That I should leave Leo and break his heart because eventually, I will get him killed.

He's right.

I'm already a weakness for Leo. I have been since the second we met in Vegas.

I should walk away, but I'm not ready to do that just yet.

So, I take his calloused hand in mine and hold it tightly.

"Yeah, I'm ready."

One more night.

Just one more night with this man and then I will walk away.

One more night, before I break everything in me and leave him.

28

SEEING my father so close to Serena made my blood boil. For weeks I've been trying to keep them as far away from each other as possible and so far, it's worked.

Until tonight.

Something happened between Serena and my father but of course being the headstrong woman, that Serena is, she isn't going to tell me.

For tonight I will let it slide but come tomorrow, I'm going after answers.

Tonight, I'm going to try and give Serena a good night.

Ever since the night that my father forced Isabella's engagement, I've been trying to push her away even more than before.

Seeing the pain in my sister's eyes and hearing her sob in my arms over something that our father was forcing her to do, was the catalyst for me.

I may not be able to walk away from this life fully, but I

can change it. I can change it so that my sisters could live the lives that they want.

I can change it for them, because for me it's far too late.

The one thing that I can do for my own life is let Serena go. She deserves better than a killer that climbs into her bed at night. She deserves better than me.

So, I have to give her the life that she deserves.

I'm starting with tonight and then tomorrow, I will have the divorce papers drafted and hand them to her.

She will fight me, but it's for her own good. It will hurt less for me to watch her walk away on her own than it will to have her die in my arms.

"Isabella told me what to expect but never did I think it would be like this," Serena says from next to me as we walk the town square.

Every year, San Pedro puts on an amazing celebration to honor our dead, and this year is no different.

Flowers everywhere. Post selling treats and music playing in the distance. It's a true celebration to honor those that we have lost.

"It's a true celebration." I give her a real smile, one only meant for her, and she gives me one in return.

We continue to walk through the town square arm in arm as people sing and laugh all around us. When we finally reach the cemetery, I direct her to the grave that holds someone near and dear to me.

My mother.

Like the altar back at my father's estate, her gravesite is surrounded by her favorite flowers and small pieces of her favorite foods.

"Rosa Maria Morales. A beautiful soul," Serena says out loud as she crouches down and places yet another bouquet of flowers on top of my mother's grave.

"She would have loved you." It's not a lie.

My mother would have been mad at me for getting married in Vegas, but she would have accepted Serena with open arms. That was just the type of woman she was.

Her only flaw was just how much she loved my father.

That woman died for him.

"Tell me about her." Serena's smile is bright and inviting and has me wanting to tell her everything she wants to know.

"She did different activities with all three of us. With me, she would have me helping her out in the garden. Every time she had a new tree to plant, she would come to my room and tell me that I needed to help her out. I never needed to. I just wanted to. Any time I could spend with her, I would take it. With Isabella, it was always making clothes or anything to do with sewing or cooking. And Camila, well, she had to get her artistic side from somewhere. The two of them would sit out in the courtyard for hours just drawing and coming up with these intricate designs that would just leave you in awe."

I still have a few of their drawings in my office that I look at from time to time. Just a little something that makes the memories not feel like memories.

"Would it be okay if I asked how she died? You don't have to answer." I look down at Serena and see that she's fidgeting with her dress, not looking up at me.

"I'll answer," I say, taking her attention away from her

dress. "She married the wrong man, one that she loved with all her heart and ultimately, that's what killed her."

There is no need to give her all the gory details on exactly how it happened.

Serena seems to understand what I mean by my words because soon, she is nodding, giving me yet another sad smile.

"She sounds like she was an amazing woman." I give her a smile, dropping the conversation about my mother altogether.

Serena gives me a few minutes alone with my mother's grave and soon we are back to walking the square, enjoying the night.

We spend the next few hours taking in all the traditions that the night has to offer and by the end of it, I'm glad that I was able to partake in something my mother loved.

Sometime around eleven at night, Serena and I head back to the estate. As soon as we are in our quarters. Serena heads to the bathroom to wash off her makeup and comes back a few minutes later in one of my T-shirts and a freshly washed face.

"Thank you for tonight. It was really nice getting to know more about your mom and this celebration that she loved." She stands on her tiptoes and she places a kiss on my lips.

It's sweet and short, and being the feral man that I am, I want more.

I let my hands travel down her body until they are

cupping her ass and I'm lifting her off the floor. The second her legs are around my waist; I walk us over to the bed where I can better devour her body.

"Leo," she moans out when I grind my hips against her.

"You sound needy, *princesa*." I move my lips down her neck and suck on the skin of her collarbone, enjoying the way that her nails dig into my shoulders.

"I am needy, for you." Her words sound like a plea and no way I'm able to deny her.

"You have me," I say against her skin.

I'm hers, and I don't give a shit what the rest of the world thinks, this woman is fucking mine.

Mine and mine alone.

I make my way down her body, sliding up the shirt as I crawl down, exposing inch after inch of skin.

Skin that feels so smooth against my calloused palms. Skin that I want to mark every inch of.

As soon as I have her panties off, ones that I bought her to replace the ones that were destroyed in Vegas, my mouth lands on her bare pussy.

I lick every inch of her, from her clit to the outer rim of her hole. I leave no inch or crevice untouched.

Serena's moans fill the room as I get a fill of everything her pussy has to offer. Once I have her where I need her to be, I pull away, placing a few kisses on the edge of her thigh.

"What are you doing?" There is a slight annoyance to her tone that I can't help but chuckle at.

"Patience, *princesa*." I place one last kiss on her thigh

before sitting up and flipping her over onto her stomach, slapping her ass in the process.

"You're wearing too many pieces of clothing." Her ass bucks back as I straddle her thighs, the material of my slacks rubbing against her skin.

I slap her ass again, running a gentle hand against the skin afterward. "What did I say about patience?"

She lets out a whimper when I start moving the shirt back up her body. I make it seem as if I'm going to pull the shirt right off, but instead of stripping her of it, I tie her hands together with it.

Serena looks back at me with confusion at what I just did. I lean forward and kiss her pouty lips before I tie the t-shirt to the headboard.

Once I release her lips, I move off her and before she can say anything, I turn her around.

I take a second to marvel at the beauty that is lying completely naked in front of me.

Every inch of her body is mouthwatering.

Every curve needs to be cherished.

If I were a lesser man, I would keep her tied up for me to have my way with her whenever I want.

Keeping my eyes on hers, I start unbuttoning my shirt. There shouldn't be anything sensual about removing a shirt but there is, especially when the person you are undressing for has lust-filled eyes.

Her tongue darts out when the shirt is fully unbuttoned, and I push it off my shoulders.

She starts rubbing her legs together when I unbutton my slacks and push them down with my boxers.

She lets out a moan when she sees my hard cock pointing right at her.

Done with my striptease, I grab her legs and open them wide, licking my own lips when I see her pussy glistening back at me.

"Have I told you how beautiful you are?" I rub a finger along her lips, causing her to throw her head back.

"Stop teasing me."

I chuckle. "I'm not teasing you, *princesa*." I insert a finger into her pussy. "I'm just simply stating a fact. You're the most beautiful woman I have ever laid eyes on."

I slide my finger in and out of her, giving her a small taste of what she really craves.

"Leonardo!" Fuck. Something about the way she says my full name makes me want to go primal.

I've teased her enough.

Positioning myself between her thighs, I take my finger out, coat my cock with her arousal, and slide into her without any warning.

"Fuck. I love how big you are." Her legs go around my waist, holding me to her.

I fuck her like this is the last time that I would be able to slide into her. It's primal and not even close to quenching my thirst for this woman.

Every single thrust feels better than the last. Everything feels more heightened.

Fucking her tonight feels different than every other time, it's as if more is at stake this time around.

Love.

That's what's different.

I fucking love this woman.

I love my wife.

But I don't tell her.

I continue getting lost as I thrust into her and her moans as they fill my ears.

Soon enough, I feel her tighten around my cock, so I move my hand between us and stimulate her clit.

"Cover my cock, baby. Come all over it. Mark it as yours," I growl out and when I pinch her clit between my fingers, she explodes.

"Oh. My. God!"

I grab her by the hips and flip her onto her stomach and slam back into her.

Her pussy feels like a vise, and I can't take it anymore and release my seed deep into her.

"Fucking hell," I grunt out before falling to her side. After taking a few minutes to catch our breath, I finally let Serena's arms loose from the shirt.

She settles in my arms once her hands are free of the T-shirt. I fall asleep surrounded by Serena's scent embedding itself in my brain for the millionth time.

In the morning, I'm reminded that I completely forgot to close the blinds before we went to sleep last night.

There is something about the sun in this part of the world that is vicious in the morning.

With a grunt, I roll over, trying to bring Serena's body back to mine. Maybe we can get a quick fuck session in before heading to the airport.

I feel around but come up empty.

Opening my eyes, I see that I'm the only one in bed.

Strange, but not atypical.

Sitting up, I call out her name. "Serena?"

No answer.

Throwing the sheets off my body, I get out of bed and head to the bathroom, hoping that she is there, but it's empty and the shower is dry.

"Serena?" I call out again as I walk out of the bedroom and into the main portion of the wing.

Nothing.

Not even a peep.

What in the actual hell? Where is she?

I head back to the bedroom to grab my phone so that I can check the time. Did I oversleep and miss her going to work?

No, she would have woken me up if that were the case.

I go to grab my phone from the nightstand when I see a note with my name on it. I don't have to open it to know what it says, but I do it anyway.

I couldn't tell you to your face. You've been telling me since the day we got married that you wanted me to walk away, and I didn't want to do it. I just couldn't. I still can't but I have to. Me leaving might be the only way to keep you alive. So, that's what I'm doing. I'm finally going to ask what you wanted me to ask from the very beginning.

I want a divorce, Leo.

I'm so sorry.

I love you.

Your Princesa.

SHE WANTS A DIVORCE.

And because I love her, I'm going to give it to her.

29

SERENA

Do you ever do something that you instantly regret?

You would figure that getting married in Vegas was the only time that I would feel that way but that doesn't even come close to the regret I'm feeling right now.

Leaving Leo, has to be the hardest thing that I have ever done. I knew I was making a mistake the second I detangled myself from his arms and left the room. You know when tears threaten to escape the whole time you are packing that you are doing the wrong thing.

But it needed to be done. I needed to walk away from Leo, or Ronaldo would keep sending people after me, and possibly hurting Leo in the crossfire.

That can't happen.

Leaving was the only option I had, even if it's fucking destroying me.

I woke up close to six in the morning. Leo was still sleeping and after I looked at the gorgeous man next to me, I made up my mind that I had to leave. This would be my only chance, because if he were awake, I wouldn't be able to walk away. It would be ten times worse than not saying a word.

So, I left.

I packed my stuff up in record time and I left.

Somehow, I was able to get a cab to pick me up in the town square and drive me to the United States border.

Getting to the border was the easy part, crossing it was a different story. I completely forgot that I needed a passport to cross over to the other side, something that I wasn't using since the Morales have a private plane that passes over that small little detail. All I had on me was my driver's license.

The agent must have felt sorry for me. The tears running down my face might have helped with that, because she let me pass after ten minutes of groveling.

After thanking her profusely, I was able to cross and find a car rental company down the street and was able to make the three-hour drive to Austin.

Now, I'm five minutes away from my apartment building and all I want to do is turn around and go back to lying in Leo's arms.

This is for the best.

Fuck you brain, nobody asked you.

Okay, I need to calm down or I'm going to give myself a headache by arguing with myself.

It is for the best, but what if Leo changed his mind and now doesn't want a divorce?

What am I going to do if he comes knocking at my door, asking me to come back?

Do I go back and just throw caution at the wind and act like the perfect cartel wife?

That is if Ronaldo lets me live for that long.

I'm sure he is spending his morning looking for a new bride for his son to marry in two weeks.

God, Leo's reaction to me leaving and what is going to happen to that wedding is not something that I can think about right now.

I need to collect myself. Maybe seeing Aria will help with that.

After driving around the block, I am able to find a parking spot a street over from the apartment building. I get out of the car and walk toward home in a haze.

"Serena Davidson?" a male voice calls out my name, and instantly the haze is gone. A shiver climbs up my spine.

I turn and find a man dressed in running shorts, a crewneck and a baseball cap covering half of his face, standing a few feet away from me.

He doesn't look familiar, and how does he know my name?

"Yes?"

Is he one of Ronaldo's men? Is that how he knows my name?

I inch closer to the building where I know there are cameras that will catch anything that could happen.

The man gives me a tentative smile. I know it's supposed to be a reassuring gesture, but I still take a step back. I have no idea who this man is and what he is capable of.

"I'm not here to hurt you," he says after seeing how guarded my stance is. "I'm just here to ask you some questions if I can."

"Who are you?"

He shifts and pulls out something from his pocket. For a quick second I think it's a weapon but when I see it's a wallet, I relax slightly.

"My name is Nathaniel Madden. I'm a federal agent with the Drug Enforcement Administration. I was wondering if I could ask you a few questions regarding your husband."

Drug enforcement?

I remember vaguely, a conversation I overheard a few weeks ago between Leo and Santos where they were talking about the DEA. Does this have to do with the cartel?

Of course, it does, but how does the agent know who I am?

I don't know, but I need to get out of here.

"I'm sorry, I think you must be mistaken. I'm not married." I turn toward the building, but I'm stopped when the agent speaks his next words.

"Serena Davidson married Leonardo Morales in Las Vegas on August eighth of this year. The same Serena Davidson that is a schoolteacher at the school a few blocks away and shares an apartment lease with Aria Winters. You're that Serena Davidson, correct?"

How does he know all this information about me?

I turn back to him in a slow manner, my eyebrows

raised almost to my hairline, throwing silent questions at the agent.

"The thing about getting married in Clark County is that everything is public. The second that the paperwork was filed with Mr. Morales' name, we got wind of it."

Of course, they did.

If the DEA has been keeping a close tab on Leo, I'm a little surprised that it took them this long to get in contact with me.

"Sorry to be the bearer of bad news, Agent Madden, but that marriage is over. I cut ties with Leo Morales."

It may have been just a few hours ago, but he doesn't know that. He doesn't know that I spent last night wrapped up in my husband's arms, falling more in love with him than I already am.

"I would say that your daily trips to Austin with him tell a different story." There is a smugness to his face that I just want to punch off.

"You don't know what you're talking about. Now if you'll excuse me, I have things to do."

I turn, and this time I make my way to the building without hesitation.

"The Muertos Cartel are bad people, Ms. Davidson. Leonardo Morales being one of the most dangerous. You've spent time with them. You must know something that happens inside those walls. You can help me take them down," Agent Madden yells behind me.

I stop in my tracks. There is no reason to turn back, I should just square my shoulders and walk into my building and be done with this whole thing. Yet, I don't do what I should.

"I don't know who you think I am, or what I know, but you're wrong. I don't know anything about the cartel or about what Leonardo Morales does. Now I suggest you leave me alone before I call the police."

Without another glance in his direction, I walk into the building and make my way up to the apartment.

I just lied to a federal agent to protect my husband.

And I would do it again if it meant that I was protecting Leo. His father, I couldn't care less about. He can go to hell for all I care, but Leonardo is a whole different story.

Instead of taking the elevator up to my floor, I opt for the stairs, gives me more time to get my mind straight before I see Aria and cry in her arms.

Because after the morning I'm having, a good cry fest is needed, believe me.

Maybe a good bath too would help with all the emotions.

That's what I will do, cry on Aria's shoulder and then wallow in a nice hot bath.

My mind is set as I approach my apartment door. I'm about to reach for my keys when I see that the door is slightly ajar.

That's weird.

Did Aria get an emergency call this morning and forgot to close the door all the way when she ran out?

She never leaves the door open, she's very methodical about locking it, especially with everything that has been going on with me.

I push the door open a little bit more, just enough to poke my head inside.

"Aria?" I call out but don't hear anything from where I'm standing.

Maybe she did just run out and forgot to close the door.

"Aria? I'm home," I call out once again, this time stepping into the apartment and closing the door behind me.

Still nothing.

She must have gone to work.

Great. I guess my crying fest will have to be a party of one.

I put the one bag that I was able to pack down on the couch and then head to the kitchen to make myself a cup of coffee. It's when I'm pouring the dark liquid when I hear a crash.

Where did it come from?

I look around the kitchen and living room and nothing is astray.

Was it just my mind playing tricks on me?

I close my eyes and listen closely.

Thump.

Thump.

My eyes spring open. The noise is coming from down the hall.

Someone's here.

I put the coffee down and slowly start making my way to the hallway, where the thumping noise is more prominent.

"Aria?"

The thumping noise gets louder the closer I get to her room.

There are so many scenarios running through my head. None that I'm going to let settle. None that I'm ready to face.

"Aria?" There's a lump in my throat, and I try my hardest to keep myself calm as I approach her bedroom door.

My hand is shaking as I turn the knob as slowly as humanly possible. Once it's free of the latch, and I push it forward, the tears finally escape followed by a sob.

Aria is lying in the middle of the bed, blood not only on her face but on her chest and her legs. Her arms tied with rope to the headboard, a piece of cloth around her mouth, keeping her from screaming.

I stand still as I take her in, and when I finally meet her bloodshot eyes and hear her sob, I'm finally able to unfreeze and rush to her.

"Who did this?" I ask in a frenzy as I try to untie the knot that is holding the cloth around her mouth.

As soon as the knot comes loose, Aria lets out a blood-curdling scream. One that makes me want to scream right next to her.

I try to move quickly to untie her from the headboard, and once she is free, I wrap my arms around her as tightly as I can. At this moment, her pain is mine and I would do anything to take it away.

"Aria, please tell me what happened." I sob into her hair, trying to be strong but I don't know if I can. Not when the person that is the closest thing I have to a sister, is in such distress.

"I thought it was the building manager with the new showerhead. So, I opened the door without checking and there were two guys I've never seen before on the other side." Another sob escapes and I hold her as her body shakes in fear.

"It's okay. Everything is going to be okay." My words probably have no power behind them but in the moment, this is all I can think of doing.

Call Leo.

I need to call Leo. Even if I left a few hours ago, he will be here in less than an hour and take care of things.

"Serena." She takes a deep breath, before speaking again. "They..." Swallow. "They tried to..." She doesn't have to finish the sentence. Her sobs are enough for me to put it all together.

That's why she's covered in blood. The bastards tried to rape her.

Aria continues to sob in my arms, and I sob with her. The men came here, they weren't looking for my friend, no, they were here for me. I know they were.

And since I wasn't here, they went after Aria. Most likely to send me a message.

"We need to call Leo." He will know what to do and keep me and Aria safe in San Pedro.

I reach for my phone and before I can press my finger on Leo's contact, there is a loud crash coming from the living room.

Someone is here.

The men must have left and must have seen me outside.

I freeze, my finger hovering over the number, a scream begging to be let out, then two men burst into the room.

That's when the screams are finally able to escape.

Guns get pointed at me and Aria.

Then a darkness that comes out of nowhere.

Then there's nothing. Absolutely nothing.

It's only been three hours since Serena left, and I'm already in the worst fucking mood.

I have to keep reminding myself that this is what needs to happen in order to keep Serena alive. Just because it needed to happen, doesn't mean I fucking like it though.

This might make me a pussy, but Serena leaving feels like something was ripped out of my chest and there's a void left in its place.

Not something that you would expect to come out of the mouth of a cartel second-in-command, is it?

This is what I get for marrying a strange woman in Vegas. I fall in love with her and then get my heart fucking ripped out when she finally takes my offer of a divorce.

"What the fuck is up with you? Why are you all broody and shit?" Santos asks from his spot in the chair stationed in front of my desk.

I just give him a grunt in response.

The bastard chuckles. "What, did Serena tell you to sleep on the couch last night? Is that why you're grumpy?"

If I could punch the smirk off his face without having to reach over the desk, I would.

Might as well tell him. "Serena left this morning."

My friends' eyebrows bunch up in confusion. "Left as in, she went to Austin for the day?"

"Left as in, she asked for a divorce." I rub at my temples. Just thinking about it is making my head hurt.

"Sorry to hear that." There is sincerity in Santos' voice, something that I'm sure I wouldn't get from my father.

"Yeah, me too." I pinch the bridge of my nose.

"Did something happen?" That's the question, isn't it? The same one that I have been asking all morning.

Yes, ever since Isabella told me about her engagement, I have been pushing Serena more and more for the divorce. She doesn't belong in this world. She needed to get out.

But I can't help but to think that maybe something happened that made her decide to finally pull the trigger.

The only thing that I can think of is my distance over the last few weeks.

That and my father speaking to her yesterday.

Did he say something to drive her away?

I'm convinced that he did, I just don't know what.

"Ronaldo was in our bedroom last night. Something tells me he told her something that spooked her, so she ran."

It's a theory of course but at the very least, a strong one.

"And that doesn't make you angry?"

"It pisses me the fuck off," I say through gritted teeth. I don't give a shit what my father's intentions were when talking to Serena. He had no right.

"Then do something about it." Always the voice of reason.

What exactly do I do? Serena left, she asked for a divorce, something I wanted her to do from the very beginning, and now she finally did. Whatever my father told her shouldn't matter.

As long as she is out of this life, and she is safe, then there isn't much that I can do.

"She made the decision. I need to respect it."

"You're an honorable man." He nods, condemning my decision.

"Yeah, well, if I was a better man, I would be in Austin right now talking to her. Not here canceling anything that has to do with the wedding."

That stupid wedding.

Why I even went with my father's idea for a wedding is beyond me. It's the most ridiculous thing in the world.

"You can always leave everything and let your sister take over." There's a bite to his tone as if he were angry about Isabella's engagement. If I were in his position, I would feel the same.

"I wouldn't do that to my sister, especially with the bastard that she's marrying." What I don't say is that if it was a different man, I would make it happen.

"Still can't believe that Ronaldo would do that to his own daughter."

I agree. It takes a certain kind of man to give his

daughter away to a spineless bastard in exchange for money and power.

I'm about to make a comment about how Ronaldo Morales would do anything for more power when my cell phone starts to ring.

Not the phone that I use for cartel purposes, but my personal.

The number only a select few have.

I take the phone out of my pocket and see Serena's name glowing over a picture I took of her while she was sleeping.

She's calling.

Is she calling because she got to Austin and realized she made a mistake?

Or maybe she's calling because she forgot something here and wants me to take it to her.

I continue watching the screen as it rings, but don't make a move to answer it. I should, but something deep in me is telling me that we should keep communications to a minimum. Things would be less difficult that way.

So, I let it ring until she hangs up.

"You're really not going to talk to her? You wanted her to leave."

Have I mentioned that I hate my friend sometimes?

I nod. "I did. She probably forgot something; I'll call her later." Fuck, even to myself I sound defeated. Something like this shouldn't affect me so much, but I guess that's what love is right? It affects you to the core.

My phone dings, notifying me that there is a new voice mail.

"I'll let you listen to that." Santos stands up from the chair and leaves my office.

I stare at my phone for way too long, contemplating if I should listen to the voice mail she left or just ignore it.

Talking to her will have to happen eventually, might as well do it now rather than prolong the whole ordeal.

I swipe the screen open and put the voicemail on speaker.

The blood in my body drains when I hear the gut wrenching screams.

Instantly I'm on my feet, grabbing my gun from the drawer and running out of the room.

The voice mail is still playing.

"Serena!" Aria cries on the other side, her screams followed by the sound of broken glass and grunts of pain.

Then there's silence.

"Say something. SAY SOMETHING!" I yell into the phone, bringing it up to my ear to hear more clearly.

I'm able to make out male voices in the background but their voices are muffled by something. The only thing I can make out is that they are speaking Spanish.

The voice mail ends.

I listen to the message again as I run through the wing, catching up to Santos.

"What's going on?" He turns to me when he hears my footsteps approaching.

Instead of answering, I pull my phone away from my ear and let him listen for himself.

Without me having to say a word, we both start running.

We need to get to Austin.

"Leonardo." I hear my father's voice, but I ignore it and continuing my way to the car.

"Leonardo!" he yells down the corridor. I stop abruptly and face my father. I don't know how it's possible, but he looks indifferent and pissed off at the same time.

"Whatever it is, it can wait. I have to go," I say through my teeth and start moving again.

"*La familia es más importante.*"

My ears are fucking bleeding hearing my father say that family is more important. At this moment all I care about is getting to Serena and finding her alive.

I grind my teeth together as I turn toward my father. "Serena is in trouble. I don't have time for your shit. Whatever you want to talk about can wait."

The man has the audacity to roll his eyes, which angers me even more. "That *gringa* has made you weak, *hijo*. Just let whoever has her take her and do what they want with her. Kill her for all I care. She's not your problem."

My hands ball up into fists as I go through what he just said in my head again.

I never told him that she was taken.

"I never said what kind of trouble she was in." My jaw is locked as I take a step closer to my father.

He doesn't say a word as I approach him, he just keeps his stance there, looking at me as if I'm a piece of scum and not his son.

"You sent them, didn't you?" I stand toe to toe with him, the few inches I have on him giving me some leverage. "You're the one that ordered the hit on Serena. The one that sent the men after her all those weeks ago. Let me guess, you saw that she left this morning and ordered another hit. You sent someone to kill her this morning, didn't you?"

How could I have been so fucking blind? I should have seen that he was the one that has been calling all the shots from the very beginning.

And the reason he was in our room last night? He probably said something to her that spooked her, that's probably why she ran and asked for a divorce.

It's all because of him.

Ronaldo shrugs. "It might have been Emilio's idea. I was just the one that had the means to execute it."

Without even thinking about it, I swing my arm back and strike him right in the jaw. I don't stop after one hit. I continue to strike my father's face until we are both on the ground and men are pulling me off him.

"You're dead to me. You hear me? *Muerto.*" I spit at him as soon as Santos pulls me away from him.

Without a final look at the man bleeding on the ground, I turn around and head to the nearest available vehicle.

Santos has the right mind when he gets into the driver's seat and directs us to the airport. While he calls our pilot to get everything ready, I make a call to a certain teenager.

"You know, I was hoping you would call again." Drake answers the phone, and if it was any other day I would go along with pleasantries.

Today, I don't have time for bullshit.

"I need you to pull up security footage for an apartment building in Austin."

"Do you have the address?" he asks, not even stopping to ask why.

I rattle out Serena's address.

"I guess you want to know if there is anything suspicious on the footage?"

I grunt out my response.

"Okay, I will send everything I find to your phone right now."

Without another word, I hang up the call and wait for the notification that the files were sent over.

A few seconds later, my phone beeps and a few videos come through.

The first is a video of three men suspiciously waiting by the lobby door and then walking in. They disappear inside the building for a good half hour before they come out again.

Then it's a video of Serena, not even ten minutes later approaching the building but she gets stopped. From the way that the camera is angled, I can't see who she's talking to but the conversation doesn't last long.

The third video is of the three men, five minutes after Serena walks into the building. Right away they walk in, without hesitation, and from the angle of the camera, I can see that they are armed.

The last video to come through is the one that has me seeing blood. The three men come back into view, but this time they aren't alone. This time as they come out, two of them are carrying women that look as if they are in deep slumber.

Serena and Aria.

Fuck.

I look at the time on my phone.

That last video was taken no more than ten minutes ago. Right around the time my phone rang.

I should have answered it, and maybe then I would have been able to find out more about the situation.

Maybe if I had answered the call, I would have been able to hear where they were being taken.

Now I'm going to be running around Austin with my head cut off hoping that we find the two women alive.

My phone dings one more time as we approach the airport.

This time instead of a video, it's a picture with a message attached to it.

DRAKE: *You may want to see who she was talking to.*

I open the picture and have to look at it twice just to make sure that my eyes aren't playing tricks on me.

Nathaniel Madden.

DEA Agent Nathaniel Madden was the man talking to Serena outside of her building.

As if this whole situation can get any fucking worse.

But maybe...

Before I can think about it further, I'm shooting off a text to Drake.

· · ·

LEO: Get me a number.

FORTY-FIVE MINUTES.

I have forty-five minutes to fly into Austin and figure out where the fuckers my father hired took my wife and hope to whatever god will hear me, that I find her alive.

Otherwise, everyone in the crosshairs will die a painful death.

No one will stand between me and what is mine.

Not even my father.

31

SERENA

I FEEL SO disoriented right now. I don't even know what way is up or down.

I can't even remember where I am.

My eyes feel like they are being held down by something and my whole body feels as if I was run over by a dump truck.

Even trying to move an inch, hurts.

"Serena." I hear a voice that sounds oddly like Aria's, but it sounds far away, like she's calling me from the living room or something.

Are we in our apartment?

Did I get home yesterday morning and just drink myself to a stupor? Am I hungover right now, is that why I feel like this?

I try to open my eyes again, but they still feel so heavy. Maybe I will just lay here for a few more minutes and I will feel better.

"Serena." Aria's voice sounds a lot closer but still far away.

I groan as I try to move, instantly feeling a dizzy spell even with my eyes closed.

A hand lands on my shoulder, shaking me. Whatever I'm lying on is hard and cold and feels nothing like my bed or the bed back at the San Pedro estate I shared with Leo, for that matter.

"Serena, please. Please wake up." My friend's voice sounds as if she were in pain just like me.

Something's wrong. I can tell by the way her voice is sounding. My friend is a happy-go-lucky person, and she wouldn't sound so scared unless she really was.

Is this a dream? Is my dream trying to tell me something?

My shoulder gets shaken again and this time I try my hardest to open my eyes, to remove the heaviness from them and force them open.

I groan when a blinding light comes through the slit of my eyes.

It takes a few seconds to adjust but when I do I see Aria's covered in cuts, bruises, and blood looking down at me with worry. The blinding light is coming from the window above her.

It wasn't a dream. What I walked into back at the apartment really happened. Aria was really tied up to a bed in only a t-shirt and men really took us.

I groan as I sit up, my whole body aching. "What happened?" I try to remember what happened after the men came crashing back into the room, but my mind is drawing a blank.

"The last thing I remember was that they put us in an SUV and drove away. I woke up a few minutes ago." I can hear it in her voice that she is trying her hardest to keep calm, but it's damn near impossible in a situation like this.

"Are you okay? I heard a gunshot, but it could be something that I imagined."

Aria nods. "One of the men pulled a gun out and pulled the trigger. It just grazed your shoulder." I try to move my arm and sure enough, I feel the pain.

"But are you okay?" I forget about my shoulder for a second and concentrate on my friend.

She nods again. "Just cuts and bruises." Tears spring in the corner of her eyes and I move toward her to console her. It's a good thing these men didn't tie us up.

"We'll get out of here," I say through my own tears.

"How do you know that? They can come back and kill us." Her shoulders shake on the last two words. I'm shaking right next to her.

The three men can come back and do heinous things to us.

I try to swallow down the fear brewing inside of me. "I just know. We will get through this. Alive. I promise, and if I break that promise, you can kick me in the ass as many times as you want."

A small chuckle leaves her, fear forgotten for just a few seconds. "I will hold you to that."

We hold each other tightly, trying to get through this

and I can't speak for Aria but I'm trying to convey as much positive energy as I can so we can make it out of this alive.

I can't help but let my mind wander as to how I got here.

How did a drunk day by the pool lead me to this? Still married to the man whose arms I stumbled into and ultimately here?

I don't know what led me from being drunk and stumbling to being here, but I don't regret anything about it.

That pool day in Vegas brought me Leo, and I will have to die before I can give him up.

The only regret that I have is that I didn't force Aria to come with me to San Pedro, then maybe she wouldn't be in this cold room with me.

Footsteps sound in the hallway outside, causing both Aria and me to look in the direction of the door. Voices accompany the footsteps as they come closer to the door.

We cower closer to the wall as the locks start to unlock and someone turns the knob.

The only thing separating us from these men right now is a wooden door and, in a few seconds, it will be gone.

"*Abre la pinche puerta.*" I've been around Leo enough to have picked up some Spanish. Open the damn door.

The wooden rectangle swings open and in walks the three men from earlier with another man, dressed in a red button down and cowboy boots behind them.

There is something about the man that seems familiar to me, but I can't pinpoint it. I've seen him before, but where?

"I thought that I told you to tie them up. What's so hard

about that?" The man in the red shirt growls at the other men before looking at the two of us like we disgust him.

I don't take my eyes off the red shirt as he moves deeper into the room, inspecting us. It's like he's planning the best way to kill us.

Where have I seen this man?

"You are a hard woman to get hands on, Serena," Red Shirt says with a slight Mexican accent to his voice. "Do you know how long I waited for you to be alone?"

It's a rhetorical question, but I still shake my head in response.

"Since I figured out that Leo cared about you, that's when I figured out that you were his weakness. The one thing that would destroy him, next to his sisters, of course. But fuck, that man doesn't let you out of his sight. Even when you think he doesn't have an eye on you, he does."

The man crouches down in front of me, taking my chin between his fingers. His grip is tight and gets tighter the more I move.

"I told Ronaldo that you made his son weak, and the old man believed me. So, when I suggested he let me take care of it, he took it like candy. I just waited for the right moment, and that was this morning when you left."

This morning?

That means that he had to have seen me leave the estate. If that were the case, then this man was there.

His grip on me grows tighter and I try to think how I know this man as I stare into his black eyes.

The dinner.

It was the dinner that Leo took me to, the one where he introduced me as his wife to his family.

This man was there, standing in the shadows with a drink in his hand, a sinister smirk on his face as he watched me with Leo.

I've seen him a few other times on the estate, always with Ronaldo, but never said a word to him.

"You are part of the cartel," I mumble through his grip, the smirk on his face growing even more.

"*Princesa*." The way he says the word turns my stomach. "I run my own motherfucking cartel. The only reason I'm doing business with Ronaldo is because it makes me more money and gives me power. It also isn't a bad deal when the man is willing to give me his daughter in order to achieve that."

Isabella.

This is the man she's marrying.

"You're just as evil as he is." I spit, but it only makes him laugh.

"I can see why Leo has kept you this long, you have fire in you. Makes me wonder if that fire also comes out when he fucks you." He's so close that I can smell the alcohol and nicotine on his breath. It's repulsive. *He's* repulsive.

When he doesn't get the reaction he wants out of me, he lets go of my chin and stands at full height.

"Tie them up. I will deal with them later." With one last look of disgust in our direction, the man leaves, leaving the three other men in the room with us.

They tie us up and once are hands and legs are secured, the men leave.

Aria releases a sob as soon as the door closes behind them. Seconds later it's followed by my own.

I'm going to break my promise to Aria.

We are going to die here.

All I can do is pray to God that someway, somehow, someone rescues us.

If someone is on their way to us, I hope they make it in time.

Or we will just be another set of bodies added to the cartel body count.

32

THE CAR DOOR SLAMS.

Any other time in this type of situation, I would have my gun drawn, or at least already reaching for it.

For as long as I can remember, my father ingrained into me to never go into a meeting with a *federal* without a gun drawn. No gun would make it easier for them to take you down.

Right now, I'm throwing all of that out the window as Agent Nathaniel Madden approaches us.

"Give me one good reason why I shouldn't arrest you, right now?"

"Because it's not me you're after and if I remember correctly, I was the one that called you here. That has to serve as some sort of truce, right?" I feel a smirk playing on my lips. I can make a career out of taunting a federal agent.

Madden narrows his eyes at me, and for the briefest moment I think he's going to be the one to draw his gun and point it at my head as he arrests me.

Then he nods. "How'd you know I would follow them?"

"I didn't. I just hoped that you were at least a decent enough man that wouldn't think twice about helping women when they needed it."

It was a long shot, but after seeing that the photo of Madden talking to Serena was only eight or so minutes from when the men took the girls, I had to guess that Madden must have seen it happen. He must have been waiting outside the apartment to be able to corner Serena again.

He could have done a number of things. Just watching it happen and not moving from his spot could have been one of them, but he didn't. He followed the men and was sitting stakeout when I called him on the number that Drake found.

To say he was surprised when he answered the call and heard who was on the other side of it, was an understatement. He was even more surprised when I told him I needed his help finding my wife.

Reluctantly, he gave me his location and well, here we are. Standing across the street from an abandoned house.

"I guess it doesn't matter if the woman is tied to the cartel or not, I would try to save their lives in any way I can." There is no malice in his tone, just God's honest truth.

I can see why this man is a federal agent and why some of my men were giving intel.

"Who's in the house?" I nod, trying to make sure to stay out of view of the windows.

"From what I was able to grasp, six men and the two women."

Six?

"Who are the other three men?" Santos asks as he surveys the house.

"Emilio Castro and two of his men."

Motherfucker. Ronaldo was right. Emilio is involved in this, but not for long. I'm going to end the bastard.

"Any movement inside?"

I look at the house and try to picture where they would put Aria and Serena. If I were them, I would put them somewhere on the top floor if there wasn't a basement. It would be the corner back room, away from where anyone would hear them or see them peeking through a window.

Looking at the front of the house, it looks like it has at least four bedrooms on the top floor. They could be anywhere, and we don't have much time.

"Mostly downstairs. My guess is they have two women somewhere on the second floor. The second that Castro arrived, the light at the center window turned on."

I nod.

Like I said, upstairs back bedroom.

"Any ideas on how to approach this?" Madden asks as I do my assessment.

"Kick the door open. Kill every fucker in sight and get my woman out of there."

Madden actually snorts at my suggestion. "Solid plan, and when they have more weapons than you do, what are you going to do?"

"Who the fuck said that we weren't prepared?" Santos

growls at the agent before popping the trunk and showing off our artillery.

"For fuck's sake. I can arrest you right here and now just for the amount of ammo you have in this car." Madden shakes his head.

"We're in Texas. It's legal."

"Yeah, they are but I'm guessing that each of one those weapons were purchased under someone else's name, on top of the fact that these weapons are being used to cause bodily harm."

Remind me to never work with a cop or a federal agent again, all they care about is the stupid law.

"You don't have to go in there. We'll handle things from here." I grab a semi-automatic with a silencer attached and then a couple magazines to keep me loaded.

Madden stays silent as he watches both Santos and I get ready to go into the house. I can see that he's debating between leaving and pretending he was never here or going into that house and saving Serena and Aria.

Santos goes to close the trunk, but he gets stopped by Madden. He looks at the two of us before looking back to the house and finally shaking his head. He reaches for his gun that is hidden by his sweatshirt and places it in the trunk before grabbing another semi-automatic.

The man just chose the cartel over his badge.

"I get to take in five of the men, Emilio is yours. You walk free. This time."

Fine by fucking me.

Without any further discussion, the three of us start heading to the front of the house.

Whoever owned this house did a good job with adding bushes all around, giving us a perfect shield from the windows.

Given the shit that is happening behind the walls of the house, I'm a little surprised that Emilio doesn't have men guarding the house in some way. I guess the bastard is just as stupid as I thought he was.

When we reach the door, Madden looks through the window that sits at the side of it, nodding that it's clear.

I listen for a few moments. There is the sound of a TV playing somewhere, but they aren't able to mask the voices on the other side of the door. I can clearly hear someone talking, giving orders.

Emilio.

I can hear his voice loud and clear. He's telling his men to keep the women locked up until they get a call from him.

He's leaving.

Not on my watch.

I don't think twice when I kick the door open and fire the first shot straight into the skull of the man that was standing closest to the door. Blood splatters everywhere.

"*Chingada madré,*" one of the men is able to say before more shots start ringing out.

Within a few seconds, two more of Emilio's men fall to the ground while their faithful leader runs out of the room.

I fire one more shot before following him and up the stairs. He runs down the hall and into a room at the end.

The second he steps into the room; the sounds of

women's screams fill the hallways. It's gut-wrenching as I speed up and run into the room, gun still drawn.

Emilio has Serena pulled up by her hair, a gun pointed at her temple.

"Leo," Serena cries out the second that she sees me, tears are running down her cheeks and her face is covered in cuts and bruises.

I look at my wife and then I look around the room and see Aria in the fetal position in the corner, holding her stomach.

They are both still alive.

"Let her go," I say through my teeth, directing my gun to Emilio.

He presses the gun tighter into Serena's temple and gives me a sinister grin. "Never thought I would see the day when Leonardo Morales would come running after a woman. The Leo I always heard of wouldn't have cared about who his father went after, he would just turn a blind eye."

"You don't know anything about who I was or who I am." My grip on the gun grows tighter.

Serena lets out a whimper, and I try my best to reassure her with my eyes that everything will be okay.

"For years, I thought of you as this unstable force, then you married this bitch and I found out that you are weak and stupid. A man so undeserving of the title that he has."

"A title you want, I'm guessing." I move deeper into the room, but it just makes Emilio to tighten his hold on Serena and move toward the window.

If this fucker jumps out, I swear...

"A title I fucking deserve. It should have been my family with all the power, not yours. I should be the one that Ronaldo calls his right-hand man, not you. Not someone that can get so easily distracted by a piece of ass."

If he wants whatever my father gave me, he can fucking take it, just as long as he lets go of Serena.

"I don't give a shit what you want. Let. Her. Go."

He lets out a laugh. "You will have to kill me then if you want me to let her go, but you're not going to get that far."

I'm getting tired of these games. "And why is that?"

"Because if you kill me, my men will kill your sister."

If the blood hadn't drained from my body when I saw a gun pointed at Serena's head, it's sure as hell drained now.

"What does Isabella have to do with this?" I feel my jaw tightening and my teeth grinding at the thought of anything happening to her.

I already lost my mother; I could lose Serena. I can't lose her too.

"Not only did your father promise mine more money and more pull, but he also promised your sister to me. If I can't have her, then no one will, it's that simple."

"Over my dead body." I hate my father even more now. I place my finger on the trigger, angling the gun down away from his head.

"You don't know unless you kill me." His sinister grin is back. I should just point my gun at his face and shoot it off.

He may be bluffing, but I'm not going to risk my sister's life. This fucker already went after my wife to prove that I have a weakness that could bring me down. I don't want to think about what he would do with Isabella involved.

I hear footsteps behind me. By the look on Emilio's face, it's Madden and Santos.

Their appearance is enough of a distraction that Emilio drops the position of the gun from Serena's temple to her shoulder.

"Let her go," I growl out once again.

I look at Serena and see the fear in her eyes. Her tear-filled eyes move to where Aria is lying, eyes also filled with fear.

This shouldn't have gone this far.

I should kill Emilio right now without a second thought, but if I do, I'm risking Isabella's life too.

"Look at you. You can't even kill me. That's how weak this bitch has made you. You are a disgrace to your own family."

I've had enough of his bullshit manifesto and pull the trigger, which creates a domino effect, and he pulls his. A bullet going straight through the fucker's leg as one goes into Serena's shoulder.

Serena and Aria both release a scream and as soon as Emilio releases my wife and before she falls to the floor, I have her in my arms.

"I got you. I got you," I say into her hair as Serena sobs into my chest and I put pressure on her shoulder.

Emilio is groaning on the floor. Fuck him.

Turning, I check on Aria and see Santos is consoling her, checking on her for any injuries.

"I'm calling 911." Madden calls out.

"No." I say through clenched teeth, trying to keep my concentration on Serena.

"What do you mean, no? She has to go to the hospital." He points at Serena on the ground.

"I will take her. The cops coming here raises too many questions." I tear at Serena's shirt and place it over the bullet wound. "Can you keep your hand here?" She nods, but I can see that she is losing consciousness.

I lift her up, and once I have her in my arms, I turn to Santos. "Clean up and get the asshole back to the estate, I don't give a shit if he bleeds out. Grab her and follow me," I say to Madden, nodding toward Aria, before walking out of the room.

Ignoring the dead bodies on the first floor, I rush Serena to the car with Madden on my tail with Aria.

"You're going to be okay, baby. I promise. You're going to be okay," I say to Serena over and over again as I get her into the car.

Once she's settled, with her hand still on her wound, I push her hair back and place a small kiss on her lips.

"I got you, baby. Just hold on, okay? Hold on."

She closes her eyes and takes a deep breath. "Leo?"

"Yeah, baby?"

"I love you."

I stand there waiting for her eyes to open back up again, but they don't. Slamming the door, I rush over to the driver's side and speed off to the hospital.

When I look in the rearview mirror, I see that her hand has fallen limp and her bullet wound is gushing with blood.

Fuck.

I need to make it to the hospital before I lose her forever.

I love you.

I love you too Serena.

I love you too.

33

SERENA

THERE IS A BLINDING light overhead again that needs to be turned off. Even with my eyes closed, it's so bright that it hurts.

Everything hurts. My head, my face, my arms. Everything has an aching feeling to it, and it's definitely not like when I woke up earlier.

That type of pain I could handle, this though, I cannot.

I let out a groan when I open my eyes and the blinding light becomes even more unbearable.

"Hey, baby."

I hear his voice and then I feel his hand on my forehead, pushing my hair back, soothing me.

I push through the light until Leo's face comes into view. There are worry lines forming around his eyes and his hair is all over the place as if he was running his fingers through it all day.

"Hi." My voice is raspy and in desperate need of water.

Leo hears it and reaches over to the stand next to the

bed, grabbing a cup with a straw in it and brings it to my lips.

"Drink," he orders. I don't put up a fight and take a sip. The ice-cold water feels refreshing as it goes down my scratchy throat and settles in my stomach.

"Thank you."

He nods and puts the cup back on the table. I watch as he looks down at my hand and hesitates for the briefest moments before taking it, like he was thinking he shouldn't.

"How are you feeling?" His eyes are filled with concern, and it breaks my heart to know that I'm the one that is the cause of it.

I give his hand a reassuring squeeze. "I'm okay. In pain, but I'm okay. Where's Aria?"

Leo gives me a tight smile. "She's in the room next door. They had her checked and are keeping her overnight for internal bleeding. She says that Emilio kicked her?"

I nod. "When he came running into the room. She was trying to keep me away from him, but he pushed her down and kicked her in the stomach."

I can still hear her moans of pain when his boot hit her. I wanted to crawl next to her and take her pain away. She was already going through enough.

"I should have gotten there sooner or had followed you to Austin when I realized you had left." He places his forehead on my chest and I can't help but run my fingers through his hair.

"You did everything you could, and I understand why

you didn't follow me. I asked for a divorce, I would have done the same."

I had thought that writing that note was the hardest thing that I had to do but lying in a hospital bed with a bullet hole in my shoulder is up there.

"Still doesn't make up for the fact that I should have done something a lot sooner so that you wouldn't be in here."

His grip on my hands gets tighter, and I can't help but sigh. "We aren't going to get anywhere with us blaming ourselves for what happened."

Leo lifts his head, and his beautiful brown eyes grasp my gaze and suck me in. "I know." He lets out a sigh and lifts his hand to my face. I lean into his touch; it is as if I haven't felt it in ages. "I have to ask you something."

"What is it?"

He continues to stroke my cheek and I close my eyes to bask in the warmth of his touch. "Do you really want the divorce?"

My eyes spring open.

Do I?

I'm already shaking my head. "I didn't want a divorce in the first place. The only reason I left and asked for one was because your father told me that it would be better; before you were the one that got killed instead of me."

Saying the words has tears forming in my eyes and even though I fight extremely hard to push them back, they still slip out.

Leo wipes away the tears. "You were protecting me," he states, and I nod.

"You were pushing me away anyway, I thought it was for the best."

Leo is shaking his head before I even finish. "I was pushing away for the same reason that you left, to protect you. Isabella had just come to me in tears about her engagement to Emilio. I was trying to figure out a way to get you out, so that you wouldn't have to live the same life my sisters were, or the life that my mother lived. I guess, I succeeded."

"I'm still here though. I don't want the divorce; I just want my princely villain and all that he has to give."

He lets out a low chuckle at my nickname for him. "I guess if I were to be someone's prince, I would want to be yours."

Who is this man? "Now he gets it. The villain is only a prince for me."

He starts to laugh again and then he turns serious. "Is that what you really want? To stay married to me when there can be a dangerous unknown around every corner? Because I can tell you right now that bullet that went through your shoulder, won't be the last one that either one of us will receive, give, or see."

He's right. There might be other bullets that will be directed at us, with some possibly being catastrophic. But is that enough to convince me to walk away for good?

Finding out that he was the son of a drug lord didn't make me want to run away. Why would this?

I pick up his hand and bring it to my lips. "I want you. Yes, this life scares me, and it will continue to scare me, but I will stand by your side every step of the way. Even when you go from being a prince to being king. I will be there."

Because it will happen eventually. Something will happen to Ronaldo and Leo will have to step into his father's shoes. One day he will be the boss, the kingpin and the most feared man in all of Mexico, no longer the second. He will have people that will be after him and people that will use me to get to him. It's not if it will happen, but more of a when.

"I will get us as far away as possible before that happens." We both know that it won't, but neither one of us voices it.

"What happens now? With Emilio and your dad?" After everything that Emilio did, will Isabella still have to marry him?

Leo shakes his head. "I don't know. I have to talk to my father. There is no way in hell I will ever let my sister marry that asshole. I need to come up with something to end whatever arrangement my father has with the Castro's before it's too late."

"What if it is? Too late I mean." I don't want to think about what could possibly happen to Isabella if she does marry that evil man. It makes my stomach churn. We need to get her out of this arrangement.

"Then I will kill Emilio with my bare hands and anyone else that dares to go after my family. My father included."

And he means every word.

Leonardo Morales would do anything for the people that he loves and when it comes to me and his sisters, he would stop at nothing until we are protected. Even if that means pushing someone away for their own good.

"You undoubtedly have my support," I say to him. Whether I like it or not, I'm part of the cartel now. I'm married to Leo and that sure as hell isn't going to change.

Leo just nods and leans in and plants a kiss on my forehead. "Get some sleep. You've had a long two days. We will handle everything when you wake up."

"Can I see Aria?" I need to see with my own eyes that she is okay. Physically she might be, mentally it might take her a while to where she was before.

"I will make sure she is in here the second you open your eyes." I give him a smile to show my gratitude.

I try to scoot to the edge of the bed to make room for him to come lie with me, but the pain in my shoulder stops me from even moving an inch.

Leo chuckles and scoots his chair closer to the bed, taking my hand in his and stroking my knuckles.

We lay like that for a few minutes, my eyes getting heavier and heavier from the pain medicine.

"Leonardo?" I call his name before sleep takes over.

"*Si, mi princesa.*"

"*Te amó.*"

My eyes close seconds before I feel a set of lips against my own.

"I love you too, Serena."

The stranger I married in Las Vegas loves me.

The villain loves the princess.

And I love him.

34

AGAINST MY BETTER JUDGMENT, I left Austin and Serena, and came to San Pedro.

It's been a week since Serena left and Emilio took her and Aria against their own will. In that time both Serena and Aria had been released from the hospital and I was able to get them set up in a place where no one can find them. Especially not my father.

While I spent the week in Austin taking care of my wife and her friend, Santos has been in San Pedro taking care of Emilio. That is after he and Madden took care of the bodies from the shoot-out.

You heard that right, DEA Agent Nathaniel Madden helped the Muertos Cartel in disposing of bodies. Who would have thought that would have happened. Not me.

After the bodies were disposed of and the house caught fire due to an aerial firework, my idea, Madden decided to catch a flight back to Brooklyn. It won't be the last that we see of Agent Madden, but at least for right now, he's off the cartel's back. He didn't make any promises though, so I'm not holding my breath.

Once the bodies and the house were taken care of, Santos concentrated on Emilio.

There wasn't much that he could have done to the bastard since he was protected by my father the second that he got him back to the estate. Yet Emilio's injuries were far more extensive than just a bullet to the thigh. I heard that he also had a broken nose, a few broken ribs and possibly a stab wound or two.

Wonder how that happened.

Now, a week later, I'm back in San Pedro to meet with my father and finally put an end to this vendetta he has against me and my wife.

I'm tired of his bullshit and I don't give a shit if he's my father or the head of the cartel. He will pay for his actions.

The car pulls up to the front of the house and I half expected to have half of the cartel meeting me outside. I did hit the kingpin after all but arriving at the house without any fanfare is slightly disappointing.

I walk through the house like I own the damn place and head straight to my father's office.

After speaking to my father, my sisters are my next priority.

The door is slightly ajar as I approach it, so I just walk in without knocking.

Sitting at his desk, with his glass of scotch at his side, is my father looking down at a map trying to find a new route that will secure a load to the United States.

"*Hijo mio*, to what do I owe the pleasure of you coming to see me?"

When he looks up from the map, I see the slight discoloration from where I hit him last week.

I should have hit him harder.

"I wanted to tell you how things are going to be going forward." I don't take a seat in the chair in front of his desk, instead, I stay standing, looking down at the man.

"You wanted to tell me? It sounds like you are forgetting who runs things around here, son." His face changes from nonchalant to pissed off.

"And I think you're forgetting who's going to run this shit show once you're dead." My jaw feels stiff, and I have to control myself before I end up punching him again.

"Who says I'm going to die? I may just live forever." He leans back and gives me a smirk that is so much like my own.

"We both know that's not going to happen. You piss off too many people, you will either spend the rest of your life behind bars or in a box six feet under." I can see his jaw tic with my words. He knows I'm right; he just doesn't want to admit it.

"Tell me, son, what are things going to look like going forward."

I guess that's enough of our father-son bonding time.

I give him a smirk of my own. "From now on, I will be operating everything from the warehouse in Austin. I won't step foot on this estate unless absolutely necessary. I will do things my own way and you will not get a say. Not in how I run my routes or who I do business with. You definitely will not have a say in anything that has to do with my wife, because yes, the *gringa,* as you like to call her, is still my wife and she isn't going anywhere. You will get a cut, but that's it. I want nothing to do with you, you're dead to me, and once you really are six feet under, this cartel will change and will be nothing like what you built. I can fucking guarantee that."

Ronaldo grabs the glass of scotch and takes a drink. "Is that all, or is there more?"

"Get Isabella out of whatever deal that you have with the Castros'. She won't be marrying Emilio." If I was in my father's shoes, that arrangement would have been over by now.

But of course, I'm talking about the man that went after his son's wife because she wasn't "suitable" for him. The exact words he told Serena.

"That is something that I can't do, Leonardo."

"Can't or won't?"

The way his smirk grows tells me exactly which one it is.

Sick bastard.

"The Castro Cartel coming together with us will be very beneficial to me. If giving Emilio my daughter is what makes me unstoppable, so be it. They will get married, and our families will unite."

He's talking about this like Isabella is some kind of dog and not his daughter.

Before the trip to Vegas, I saw things the way my father did. I saw the need for more power and how bringing the two families together could be beneficial. Yet seeing the type of man Emilio really is and how terrified my sister is of him; it's changed my perspective. It also helps that I have had Serena with me since then.

"He tried to kill my wife," I say through my teeth, but my father doesn't even flinch.

Ronaldo shrugs. "You've killed more men than I can count. What makes you any different?"

Un-fucking-believable.

"I will stop that wedding. Isabella is not going to marry that asshole. I don't give a shit what you have to lose from it. It's not happening." I will protect the women in my life unlike he failed to do with my mother.

"I would like to see you try."

I'm fucking done with this.

Without another word or look at my father, I leave his study and head to find my sisters.

I get lucky and I'm able to find the two of them in Isabella's part of the estate, cuddled together on the couch.

They both turn in my direction the second I walk in. Camila is the first to rush to me, closely followed by Isabella.

In the week since I've seen them, they have been texting me and calling, trying to get any update they can on Serena.

"Is Serena with you?" Camila asks as soon as I let her go and hug Isabella.

I shake my head. "It was best for her to stay in Austin. No way in hell am I bringing her here."

What I don't say is that I shouldn't have brought her here in the first place but keeping her here under my watch was what was keeping her safe from Emilio and my father.

I catch Isabella cringe slightly at my words. She is able to compose herself though, just enough to ask me a question.

"How's her shoulder?"

"The doctors say that it's healing up fine, but it will be a few weeks before she has full motion. She wants to go back to work next week."

God. that was a long discussion. That woman is stubborn beyond belief. It's annoying.

But you love her.

I do.

"And you're letting her?" Camila's eyebrows lift in surprise.

I sigh. "Not much I wouldn't do for that woman." Both of my sisters' jaws drop at my statement. "What?"

"I need her to teach me her ways. Imagine what I can get you to say yes to?" I narrow my eyes at the grin that is taking over Camila's face. Is she serious?

I already have a pain-in-the-ass wife at home. She wants to be another? No, thank you.

I shake my head at my youngest sister and turn to Isabella. There are tears forming in her eyes and I have no idea why.

"Bella?" I ask, placing a hand on her shoulder.

"Even with everything that happened last week, you look happy." She releases a shaky breath. "I want to be happy." There is no holding back when I take her in my arms and console her as best I can.

"I will get you out of this. I will do everything in my damn power to make sure that you do not marry Emilio."

"How? How will you do that?" She sobs into my chest and pulls me even tighter to her. My strong sister that never lets anything get to her, is breaking in front of me and it's all my father's fault.

"I don't know, but I will. You won't be walking down that aisle. I don't give a shit if I have to kill the bastard myself, I will put a stop to this. You will be happy." I pull back slightly from Isabella to see that Camila is standing next to us, also with tears in her eyes. I reach for her and wrap my arms around both of them. "You both will, or I will die trying."

I will do everything in my power to give my sisters the life that they deserve, a normal one. One that doesn't have dead bodies falling out of the sky and drugs to haunt their past. Not the life that Ronaldo is giving them.

After spending a few more minutes with my sisters, I leave the estate and head to the airport to fly back to Austin.

Within the hour, I'm back in Austin and heading back to where Serena is. Only a total of three hours away from her and I'm uneasy.

Before arriving back at the building, I pull to the side and pull out my phone, instantly going to my contacts.

My thumb hovers over the number.

I shouldn't do this, but I have no other choice.

Pressing the number, I bring the phone to my ear. The phone rings about five times before the person on the other side answers.

"Madden."

"I'll help you bring him down," I say into the phone. This might be the worst decision of my life, but if I want to protect the women I care about, it's the only way.

"Bring who down?"

"You know exactly who I'm talking about. I'll help you."

"What's the catch?"

Why the fuck is talking to a federal agent so damn frustrating?

"You get him and only him. I don't give a shit what crimes you pin him for, you only get him. And if you are a nice little pig, I might throw you a bone and give a few more men, but that's it. You stay away from me and my men and any other cartel business. Do you want my help or not?"

This is going against every ounce of my being, but Ronaldo needs to be taken off the throne. I wasn't lying when I said that his time as king would end, I'm just moving things along.

"You are comfortable testifying against your own father?"

"That's not going to happen. You're a smart man and you will figure out how to handle this." It doesn't escape my attention that I killed men in the last few months for doing exactly what I'm offering Agent Madden. For giving him intel.

Unlike Adolfo and the men that followed, I have the power that they wanted, and I won't be stupid in my actions. Not like they were.

"Fine. I will take what I can get, but I can't guarantee

everything will be in your favor. Let me move some things around and I will get back to you." With that, Madden hangs up the phone.

I've become a narc on my own family.

Whatever it takes, right?

I start the car again and make my way to my wife.

As soon as I get to where we have been staying for the last week, I shut the car off and head to our floor. The second that the alarm is off, Serena appears.

Her long brown hair is down, flowing down her back. Her hazel eyes are looking straight at me, and a smile is playing on her lips.

Even with her arm in a sling and wearing sweatpants, she looks just as beautiful as she did the day she stumbled into my arms in the hallway in Vegas.

"How did it go?" Serena comes over to me and wraps her good arm around my waist. I can't help but to dig my fingers into her hips and bring her closer to me.

Even being apart for three hours makes me miss her.

"As bad as I expected. Didn't really get anywhere with him, but I will continue to work on it. Soon we will be out of his grasp." As soon as Madden gets to work to take him down.

"I'm sorry you feel like you have to do this. To take a step back from your father. You shouldn't have to do that." She takes her bottom lip between her teeth, and I release it before she is able to make it bleed.

"You're right, I shouldn't. I want to. I *need* to. It's the only way to keep you safe. If my father was a better man, he would make life easier for us, not what he's been doing.

Not go after you because he has the insane thought that you make me weak."

"But I do make you weak." Her hand that's around my waist starts to loosen, but I grip her tighter, trying to get my point across.

"You make me stronger. Never think that you make me weak. You make me want to be a better man, not only for you but for my sisters. You make me want to tear this world apart and put it back together at the same time. Never, and I mean never, think that you make me weak."

I lean forward and place a kiss on her delectable lips. They're soft and full and I can spend hours nibbling on them, tasting her.

"Do you regret it?" she asks when I pull away.

"Regret pulling away from my father?"

Serena shakes her head. "Regret meeting in Vegas and getting married after only three days of knowing each other?"

I can say that I have done a lot of regretful things in my life. Some include pulling the trigger while aiming at the wrong person. Or even regret that I wasn't able to save my mother.

But never anything that led me to Serena.

I let go of her hips and place my hands on either side of her face.

"Not for a second." Tears spring up in the corner of her eyes, as I continue. "Meeting you has given my world a light that wasn't there before. I used to go through my days as if they were my last, there wasn't a care in the world. You changed that. In just a short time you changed that, you made me see everything from a different perspective. I will never regret marrying you, and I will tell you that for the rest of my life if I have to."

A tear escapes and I wipe them away with my lips. I kiss away each and every tear that escapes to show this woman that she is meant to be with me and I with her.

Her good hand travels from my waist to my face, bringing my lips to hers, giving me every inch of her mouth for me to taste.

"I love you, Leo." She pants when my lips travel down to her collarbone.

"*Princesa*, I will love you until the day I die and beyond."

I slide my hands down the body of my wife, conscious of her shoulder, palm her ass and show her over and over again just how much I love her.

Never in my wildest dreams did I think a wedding in Vegas would result in something like this. In a love that would become embedded so deep in you, you forget how to function. A love that you would literally kill for.

The way we met and how this marriage started is unconventional at best, but now that I have a hold on this woman, I'm not letting her go.

You would have to shoot me between the eyes to let her go.

The princess fell in love with the killer, the drug dealer, the fucking villain.

Such a sadistic love story.

EPILOGUE

SERENA

I CLOSE my eyes and let the wind blow around me. It's calm today, and there is a touch of coldness to it that feels refreshing against my skin.

This is the type of wind that I wish could coat my skin back in Austin. As it blows, it allows me to forget about what's going on in the world around me and think about what's to come.

At the sound of the bells ringing, my eyes spring open and I can't help but smile at the sight in front of me.

Leo, my husband, crouched down taking flowers from one of the little girls that have been running down the street in hopes of getting a glimpse of today's princess.

Even with the dark cloud looming over the events of today, I can't help but marvel at the man before me. The smile he has on his face as he takes the flowers from the little girl is bright and not one that is forced. It makes me proud to be able to call him my husband and father to our future children.

My hand inadvertently slides to my stomach at the thought of future children. They aren't so hypothetical, given that the future is only seven months away.

It's been ten months since we got married in Vegas, seven since Emilio took me, and one since we found out that I was pregnant.

When I took the test, I was terrified of how Leo would react. With everything that has happened with his father and in the world that we were a part of, having a child would be a bad decision. Not only would I need protection, so would they.

I debated for days on how to tell him. Eventually Aria told me to rip the Band-Aid off and just do it.

So, I did.

He was silent for the longest time. He just looked at me like I had three heads. Finally, after what felt like hours, he spoke.

"Do you think I will be a good father?"

His question broke me. I went straight to him and wrapped my arms around him and kept repeating over and over again that he will, in fact, be a great father.

The way he treated his sisters, the way he treated me, was proof of that.

We have yet to figure out how we will handle bringing a baby into the cartel world or how to even tell his family.

His sisters will be accepting.

His father might put another hit on me for ruining his bloodline.

Everything is up in the air, but eventually, we will have to figure it out.

The bells ring again, signaling that it's almost time.

Leo looks over at me from where he is and gives me a sad smile.

He tried.

He tried his damn hardest to not let this day happen, but in the end, there was nothing that could be done.

Now we are forced to partake in it, to witness it and hope that this day doesn't bring a deadly outcome.

I hold out my hand for Leo to take, and when he does, he holds on to it so tightly that he could break a bone.

"Are you ready?" It's a stupid question to ask, but I ask it anyway.

"No," he says through his teeth, a completely different man than he was with the little girl. "If he hurts her, I will kill him with my bare hands."

A very logical response.

"If that happens, you have my full support. That is if Santos doesn't beat you to it." I'm trying to make light of a dark situation.

Santos has been in a dark place since the date was announced. I wonder just how well he has composed himself today.

"I wouldn't put it past him," Leo grumbles as we approach the church.

Before we walk in, he pulls me to the side and takes my face between his hands.

"I don't deserve you."

"Yeah, you do. You deserve me and everything the world has to offer." I place a kiss against his jaw to drive my point.

This is what getting married in Vegas got me, and I'm not giving it up without a fight. Not even death can stand in the way.

"*Te amó.*"

"I love you too."

EXTENDED EPILOGUE

ISABELLA

The church bells ring throughout the whole town, signaling that there's an important event happening.

Usually, the bells ring when there is a funeral or a wedding. Or, in my case a wedding that should very much be a funeral.

A bride's wedding day should be the happiest day of her life. She should be looking forward to starting a new chapter with her groom and thinking about all the adventures they will go on when the day is over.

This day shouldn't be filled with the bride crying tears of fear as she prepares to walk down the aisle.

Tears of fear, not because she's afraid of tripping on her way to the altar, but fear because she's afraid of her future husband and what he is capable of.

Tears of anger geared toward her father for forcing her to go through this marriage, for the good of the family.

Tears for herself because the second she says the words "I do," she will never be the same person that she was before all this began. The person that loved everything about her life, the person that wanted to travel the world with her one true love.

The second I leave this room; I will lose everything that makes me *me* and hand myself to an evil man that would rather see me dead and gain power than love me.

I don't want to do this.

Please, God. Please don't make me do this.

If my mother were here, she would have been able to talk my father out of this hideous idea. Would have been able to talk some sense into him and let me marry who I wanted to marry.

But she's not here.

She's dead.

There's a knock on the door of the room I'm currently occupying.

I look at myself in the mirror and try to cover up the tears and compose myself so that to the outside world, I will look like the perfect bride. The bride that is ready to marry Emilio Castro and be called his wife.

"Come in."

I close my eyes and take a deep breath.

"Are you ready?"

Never in a million years will I be ready to do this, yet I open my eyes and plaster a fake smile on my face and nod.

"I'm ready."

The end.

Until the next one...

PLAYLIST

Devil - Cash Cash
Señorita - Kurt Hugo Schneider
I want to - Rosenfeld
All Mine - PLAZA
Pray - XANA
I Found - Amber Run
I Fell In Love With The Devil - Avril Lavigne
Do It For Me - Rosenfeld
Crazy in Love - Eden Project
Bad - Royal Deluxe
Black Sea - Natasha Blume
Play With Fire - Sam Tinnesz
Born For This - The Score

ACKNOWLEDGMENTS

I know what you may be asking... Jocelyne, is that pizza place real? Yes reader, yes, it is. There really is a secret pizza place in the Cosmopolitan Hotel in Las Vegas. The pizza is awesome!

Now that, that, is taken care of, let's talk Serena and Leonardo, shall we?

I got the idea to write this book back in February of this year. There I was driving to work when it hit me, why not write a cartel romance? Within a fifteen-minute car ride I had it figured out. Now going from idea to execution of that idea was a different story.

Serena and Leo's story was a hard one to write, not because their story was complicated but because I couldn't figure out the right words to have them say. Their story brought a lot of writing blocks but I'm grateful for them. This story needed time to write and I'm so in love with how it came out.

I'm so happy that I was able to write this story and these characters.

There will be more of Serena and Leo, I promise.

Now before this gets out of hand, let's get into the thank yous!

Ellie at My brother's Editor - Ellie thank you for all

your work! I don't know how you do it but you catch things that I wasn't able to see after four time (facepalm) You are awesome!

Shauna and Wildfire Marketing - Promo scares me. I tend to clam up when it comes to promoting anything. Thank you, Shauna and Wildfire, for being awesome and helping me with all things promotions and ARC because I will for sure be lost!

Book and Moods PR - Ladies! Thank you so much for the awesome cover! I love it and it's everything that I had hope it would be and more. Thank you.

Readers - I can never thank you enough, and with every new book I get to write I will thank you all over again.

Guy I match with on bumble - Yes, I'm adding you to this lol. Thank you for the encouragement! You have no idea how helpful it was to hear your encouragement when I didn't want to write anymore. Also thank you for your opinion on a few scenes.

Thank you all for the support.

Now onto the next on!

BOOKS BY JOCELYNE SOTO

ABOUT THE AUTHOR

Jocelyne Soto is a writer born and raised in California. She started her writing journey in 2015 and in 2019 she published her first book. She is an independent author who loves discovering new authors on Goodreads and Amazon. She comes from a big Mexican family, and with it comes a love for all things family and food.

Jocelyne has a love for her mom's coffee and writing. In her free time, she can be found reading a romance novel off her iPad or somewhere in the black hole of YouTube.

Follow her website and on social media!
www.jocelynesoto.com

facebook.com/authorjocelynesoto

twitter.com/AuthorJocelyneS

instagram.com/authorjocelynesoto

pinterest.com/authorjocelynesoto

tiktok.com/@authorjocelynesoto

goodreads.com/jocelynesotobooks

bookbub.com/profile/jocelyne-soto

JOIN MY READER GROUP

Join my ever-growing Facebook Group.

https://www.facebook.com/groups/jocelynesotobooks

NEWSLETTER

Sign up for my newsletter!
You will get notified when there are new
releases to look out for, giveaways and more!

https://www.subscribepage.com/
authorjocelynesotonewsletter

Made in the USA
Coppell, TX
23 September 2023